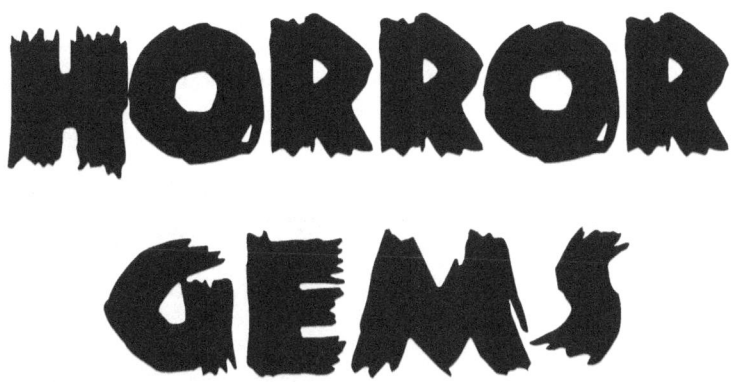

HORROR GEMS

Volume 8
Algernon Blackwood
and others

Compiled and Edited by
GREGORY LUCE

I0616936

ARMCHAIR FICTION
PO Box 4369, Medford, Oregon 97504

For more information about Armchair Books and products, visit our website at…

www.armchairfiction.com

Or email us at…

armchairfiction@yahoo.com

WHAT EVILS LAY BEYOND THE DOOR OF DARKNESS?

While you're happily reading "The House in the Valley" or "A Guest of Ganymede," try to remember that it couldn't happen to you…it just couldn't…or could it?

What kind of monstrosities are lurking just outside our doors? "Emissary," and "Hand of Death," might give a clue. Let's hope you don't find out…the hard way!

It's been said, "If something exists, somebody somewhere collects it." With "Something in the Wind," or perhaps "Father's Vampire," you may think twice about your own obscure collections…

We've got the hauntings, the fear of the unknown, the dark recesses of human nature, and other shadowy evils that will give you goose-bumps in this great new collection of Horror Gems!

TABLE OF CONTENTS

THE SOFTLY SILKEN WALLET

By David Wright O'Brien

The wallet was soft and silky, but there was something very horrible about it, like death…

THE thin, sharp-featured little man standing at the rear of the Elevated platform in the swirling snow that chilling March afternoon, was pleased. His pleasure was evident in the smirk on his thin lips and the glitter in his gimlet eyes as they moved restlessly, appraisingly over the crowds that jammed the station.

Marty Merkin was thinking that, despite the cold and the snow and the crushing jam of passengers waiting on the platform for trains, this was a hell of a good day for business.

On a day like this, he reflected, people were conscious only of their own weariness, discomfort and the immediate problem of forcing their ways through the elevated doors to find seats for the homeward trip.

On days like this, consequently, sharp-eyed pickpockets like little Marty Merkin were in clover.

An Evanston Special rolled up to a stop, and Marty grinned as he watched the people on the platform surge forward, fighting each other to be first inside the opening doors.

But he didn't move forward to mingle with them and press closely against them. Instead he stood there watching and smiling and taking his time. There was plenty of time, just like there was plenty offish, he told himself. It was just a matter of standing back and casing the crowd until a really ripe customer happened along.

That big fat guy, Merkin observed, arms full of bundles, was well dressed and obviously in the chips. Yet Marty's long practiced analysis told him unfailingly that the fat guy wouldn't be the sort to carry his dough around in big wads. There'd be maybe ten, maybe fifteen, in the fat guy's wallet. Not enough to bother with on a day like this.

"Day like this," Marty told himself, "I don't settle fer no small stuff."

So he continued to watch the crowd, smirking happily at the prospects he knew to be ahead, taking his time and watching for the right one.

The right one came along less than ten minutes later. He was a tall guy and thin as a beanpole. Marty watched him come out onto the platform, noting that he had musician-length gray hair that came almost to the collar of his thin gabardine topcoat. This right one was middle-aged, Marty saw, with a long, lean, horse-like face and deep, sunken gray eyes.

He was carrying a large instrument case, which Marty judged to contain a cello or some stringed instrument similar in size and shape. That was, of course, the absolute confirmation of Marty's judgment that the guy was a musician.

The thin, beanpole-ish guy stood there on the platform, the wind and swirling snow flapping his topcoat grotesquely against his thin shanks and gaunt frame.

Marty couldn't restrain a grin, as a gust of wind caught the man from the rear and outlined, momentarily, the bulky block of a wallet in his right hip pocket.

That was double confirmation for Marty. Confirmation that these musician guys were the type to carry most of their wad with them, and to be very careless about it. He wet his thin lips in anticipation; and moved forward until he was less than four feet behind the musician.

A RAVENSWOOD Express rolled into the station at that moment, and the tall, gaunt, horse-faced musician began to move forward to push with the crowds toward the door.

Marty stepped up directly behind the fellow, pressing hard against him, as if he too were trying to push for a seat on the Ravenswood Express. Several other passengers pushed in behind Marty, which increased the surging pressure and pleased Marty additionally.

The beanpole-ish musician was having a time of it with his big cello case. He had to hang onto it with both hands, and turn it from side to side to keep the crowds from damaging it. This was an additional boon to Marty, though he scarcely needed it.

Marty stared: SLAYINGS HAVE OFFICIALS AROUSED. Another: DRAGNET FOR ALL CRIMINALS SEEN AS POLICE SEEK SOLUTION OF FOURTH RIPPER MURDER IN WEEK.

"Well, I'm damned," Marty confessed. "The net, huh?"

"That means they might be bothering us," Leo said. "That means that maybe we'd be smart to lay low for awhile and knock off work until it all blows over."

"Ahhhhh," said Marty, "g'wan. That don't mean nothing."

Leo shook his head. "Maybe you think it don't. Maybe I think it does. Anyway, I'm taking it easy. That's always the way, this so-called Jack the Ripper who's committed them four murders this last week, he's an amatoor if I ever seen one. Them nut killers is all amatoors. But what happens, we professional heist operators has gotta suffer onaccounta an amatoor's blunders."

Marty picked up the contagion of Leo's indignation.

"Yeah," he said. "The rat!"

MARTY placed his bets, bid the time of day to Leo, and left the cigar store. His recent conversation, however, left him no peace of mind as he strolled slowly down State Street in the direction of his favorite tavern.

That dragnet business was no good. Even if they didn't nab you for what they wanted, they always found something else. Marty had been the victim of general dragnets several times before. They weren't pleasant. Maybe Leo had something. Maybe it would be smart to stop operating for a few days, maybe a week, until this thing blew over. Hell, he had enough dough. Almost three hundred, bucks—well, about two-fifty anyway. That was enough to see him through a couple of weeks, provided that he didn't go on any benders.

Marty stroked his weasel chin. "Yeah," he muttered. "Maybe Leo ain't so dumb. Maybe it's smart I should take myself a vacation of a coupla weeks."

It was a source of annoyance to Marty that he felt ill at ease passing the uniformed copper on the corner a moment later. Hell, his nerves were getting bad, he told himself.

"A little layoff," he decided, "don't hurt nobody."

Marty hurried onward, suddenly anxious to get to his hotel room. The nervousness the sight of the copper had brought on was now increasing.

He stopped at a liquor store several blocks from his hotel, and ten minutes later was safely closeted with a bottle in his room.

After a snort or two, Marty pulled forth his lucky wallet and examined once again its smooth, fine leather texture. It was almost as soft as satin, almost as smooth as human skin.

He moved from his pleasurable examination to the even more satisfying examination of the billfold's contents.

Flick-counting the bills with his thumb, Marty stopped short, stared popeyed at the roll, then counted again, carefully and slowly.

His voice was hoarse as he spoke aloud.

"Geeeeze, four hundred and twenty smackers!"

There should, of course, have been something less than two hundred and fifty dollars. There should not, under any circumstances, have been such an appreciable increase.

Marty counted the money again, this time swiftly. There was no doubt about it. Absolutely no doubt. Somewhere, somehow, the contents of his wallet had increased.

Marty tore the bills from the billfold, spread them out on his bed, counted them feverishly. He licked his lips, swallowed uncertainly. He felt a feverishly greedy elation at his discovery but was somehow uncertain in his joy.

"But how?" he muttered. "How did I pick up this extra moola?"

It occurred to him that he might have miscounted earlier in the day when he had first discovered the billfold. But he knew that such an error would have been in direct contradiction to his habits of a double dozen years. No, that could not possibly serve as an explanation.

Marty put the money carefully back into the sleek wallet, put the wallet in his shirt pocket, and had a drink on his discovery. Then he had another. The succession that followed was inevitable.

IN THE room adjoining his own, someone had turned on his radio more loudly than necessary. A newscast was in progress, and Marty found himself unwillingly listening to the announcer's voice.

14

"Police Commissioner Eaker has promised that the general criminal dragnet he forecast earlier today will be started without further delay," the announcer was saying. "This declaration comes as a result of two more 'Jack the Ripper' killings which were discovered today. The badly mutilated body of an unidentified man, discovered early this morning in an alley in the Ravenswood district, and the similarly mutilated body found late this afternoon on a south side beach, brings the number of such murders to six, all perpetrated within the last ten days."

Marty had no way of shutting off his neighbor's radio. But he was able to walk into his bathroom and turn both washbowl spigots on full. Their noise drowned out the announcer's voice.

His hand was not too steady as he poured himself a long hooker a moment later. The announcer had reminded him all too forcefully of the dragnet he feared, and had added positive prediction to his fear by stating that the dragnet was no longer in the planned stages, but was starting immediately.

"Hell," Marty said, disgusted with himself. "Supposing they pinch me. I kin get sprang inna hour. Besides, I got this dough. I ain't no vag. I kin stand my own bail."

He had succeeded only in half reassuring himself, however. In the back of his mind was the memory of more than one occasion when—picked up in a dragnet—he had been unable to spring himself with any such ease. On those occasions, however, he told himself, it had been different. He had not had the money he now possessed. Nor had he had the cockiness his present affluence gave him.

He had another drink, while considering this. He was now reaching a condition of bolstered ego. A devil-may-care sort of recklessness was taking hold of him, pushing aside the inborn caution of criminal experience.

He took the wallet from his pocket again, opened it, removed the money, rifled it speculatively, put it back in the wallet.

"Hell," he muttered a trifle thickly, "they ain't got nothing on me."

He put the wallet back in his pocket, looked about for his coat, donned it, struggled into his topcoat, found his hat and started for the door.

Once outside his hotel, Marty hesitated a moment, then decided to find a saloon which was not so likely to be subject to a police raid.

A taxi was passing, and Marty hailed it. He gave the driver the address of a downtown bistro which, to Marty's mind, was a most respectable place.

Hell, he thought, settling back against the cushions, if he was going to have a time of it, he might as well enjoy himself among the elite, and in surroundings which were the best.

Marty magnanimously told the driver to keep the change when he paid him off with a dollar bill in front of the semi-swank bar he'd selected.

Marty was already going through the doors of the place when the driver, staring at the bill, called out:

"Hey! What the—"

The driver's jaws suddenly clamped shut, he folded the bill neatly, put it in his pocket, stared hard at the door through which Marty had vanished, then, grim-faced, threw the cab into gear and roared away from the curb.

INSIDE the plush surroundings of the bistro, Marty found a place at the bar, ordered a double Scotch and soda, and sat back on his stool to drink in the higher-priced atmosphere which was the hallmark of the place.

This wasn't the sort of joint to be raided. He'd be perfectly safe here from any dragnet stuff. It occurred to him that he might even be smart to register at the hotel of which this bar was a part. He'd be safer in its confines than he would in his own cheap dollar-a-day hideout.

The bartender returned with Marty's double Scotch. Marty found the sleek-soft wallet, removed a twenty-dollar bill from it casually and flipped it across the bar.

The bartender picked it up, to Marty's disgust, without a second glance or any indication that he was impressed by the bulging wallet from which it came.

Marty watched him carry it to the cash register, ring up the sale and begin to shove it in the drawer of the till. The bartender's back was to Marty, so he didn't see the sudden whitening of the man's face, the swift horrified alarm that came into his eyes.

But Marty did see the man swing around toward him, twenty-dollar bill in his hand, and fix him with a shocked stare.

The bartender's reaction was not at all what the little pickpocket had expected. It caught Marty quite by surprise and nettled him considerably.

Suddenly the bartender had returned to where Marty sat, the bill still in his hand, and was standing there before him, white-faced and distraught.

"Say, mister—" the barkeep began.

Marty cut him off.

"Whatsa matta? What's eating you?"

"This," the bartender said, shoving the bill toward him. "How did you come by this bill?"

Marty stared down at the bill, bewildered.

"Whatsa matter with it?" he demanded.

"Good God, man, didn't you notice?"

Marty squinted at the bill through eyes clouded by alcohol. And then he saw the inch-wide smudge in the corner of the twenty. It was a red smudge, a sticky smudge. A red, sticky smudge to which a strand of unmistakably human hair was stuck.

Marty almost broke his glass in the sudden horrified impulse that made his fists squeeze together hard. He felt suddenly out of breath, panic-stricken. His gimlet eyes bugged.

"Blood and hair," the bartender whispered huskily. "How do you explain it, mister?"

Marty's mental gears were grinding furiously in an effort to set his nimble wits into motion. They took hold, but his effort to keep a straight face didn't match the quick alibi that popped from his lips.

"I—I hadda accident," Marty heard himself saying. "Cut myself a little while back onna window."

Marty glanced at the mirror behind the bar, then, and his reflection told him all too clearly that his effort to keep a poker face to match the alibi had failed. And, from the expression on the bartender's face, so had the alibi itself.

"Where," he demanded suspiciously, "did you cut yourself?"

"Gimme the bill if you don't want it," Marty croaked hoarsely. He pulled out his wallet, dug desperately in it until he found a dollar bill. He shoved this across the counter, grabbed for the twenty.

"Just a minute!" the bartender exclaimed, grabbing the twenty just as Marty's fingers touched it.

They both pulled at the bill simultaneously. It ripped apart.

MARTY was badly frightened now. He looked around, saw that the scene was being watched by the other customers in the place. His panic increased. He could think only of flight.

He pushed himself back from the stool. It tipped sideways, crashing to the floor. He turned, bolted for the door.

"Hey!" the bartender shouted. "Stop that—"

The rest of the cry was lost to Marty's ears. He was in the street, running, moving south along Wabash Avenue as though pursued by a million demons.

His breath was coming hard now, searing his lungs, and the blurred vision he had of pedestrians' faces as he passed them on the run told him that he was drawing too much attention to himself. He turned down the first alley he came to, slowed to a gasping walk. He had to walk; his legs could run no further.

Wildly, Marty looked back over his shoulder. He could see no signs of pursuit. His gasping sob was one of relief. He stopped, leaning against the rusty lower braces of a fire escape foundation.

Though it was cold, perspiration ran in rivulets down Marty's forehead, soaked his shirt to his back. The ache was leaving his lungs, strength was returning to his legs, and his dazed brain was trying to comprehend what had happened.

THAT bill...bloody money. What the hell? How? Why? Marty found the wallet, opened it with trembling fingers. It was fatter than it had been before, considerably fatter.

He forced himself to count it. Five, twenty, a hundred, a hundred and fifty, two hundred, three hundred, four hundred, four-fifty, sixty, five hundred dollars! More had been added!

It was while he counted them dazedly the second time that he realized that many of the bills were sticky, bloodstained. Marty's sob was terrified. It was not the money, not the bloodstains, that made him sickly frightened. It was the implication, overwhelmingly, horribly insinuating, that filled his soul with terror.

Suddenly he became aware of the soft, silken texture of the wallet in his hand. Not as he had been aware of it before, however, not with the pleasure of knowing that it was fine and expensive. This new awareness was different, frightening. There was something hideously familiar in the softness of the leather, something he could not bring himself to name, something that stuck in the passages of his mind and sent all other thoughts tumbling one upon the other in a jumble of panic.

He became once more aware of where he was, of the sounds of traffic, the noise of the Loop everywhere about him. It crashed in on his ears thunderously as if the gates of his hearing had suddenly been opened to its flood.

In a daze that was half-terror, half-drunkenness, he crouched there, shrinking up against the side of the building, staring down in horror at the wallet in his hands.

He shrieked, trying to throw the thing from him. But it seemed adhesively a part of his hands. He shook his hands wildly, wringing them together hysterically in an effort to wash the wallet from them. He could not rid himself of it.

ACROSS the alley there was a door. It was the fear of pursuit that moved him toward it, made him hurl himself against it. The door was unlocked, and Marty tumbled through it as it gave before his slight weight.

He landed on his shoulder and side, jarringly. And as he climbed wildly to his feet, he saw that he was in some kind of a storage room, musty and dimly lighted by a single bulb hanging from a cobwebbed cord above a pile of packing cases in a corner.

The door through which he'd hurled himself had closed as it rebounded from his impact.

He stood there, staring wildly at the emptiness of the room, his body shaking in convulsions of terror. He didn't dare look down at his hands. The wallet was still in them, his fingers closed tightly around the silken smooth leather, powerless to release their grasp on it.

And it was then that he realized there was someone else in the room. Even though he could neither see nor hear the other person, Marty knew he was not alone. He could feel the presence of the other, and he knew, without having to look, that his companion in the room lurked behind those packing cases in the corner.

He found himself moving toward that corner of the room in spite of the screaming fear that told him not to. His face was bathed in sweat, his balding hair plastered flat against his rat-like skull. His steps were slow, deliberate, like the mechanical motions of a powerless puppet.

They drew him irresistibly toward the corner of the room.

Saliva drooled from the corners of the pickpocket's mouth, his stare was idiotic, his mechanical steps grew shuffling.

And then the other person stepped out from behind the packing cases.

Marty had known instinctively who that other person was. But his appearance brought a dull moan from Marty's sweat-caked lips.

He was tall, cadaverously thin. His face was long, horse-like, and his eyes were dark, sunken sockets from which a pair of yellow-gray sparks flickered mockingly. His hair was long, its bristly gray strands coming to his collar. He wore a gabardine coat which hung shroud-like over his bony frame.

It was the musician from whom Marty had stolen the wallet on the elevated platform.

"No," Marty gurgled. "No. Damn you—" His throat constricted and he could say nothing more.

The tall, cadaverous, sunken-eyed man in the flapping gabardine coat spoke expressionlessly.

"You have brought it back to me."

His eyes didn't move from Marty's face, but the pickpocket knew what he meant.

The sunken-eyed man stepped back as Marty shuffled forward. He matched his steps to the pickpocket's, retreating as Marty advanced, until they were behind the packing cases.

Then the cadaverous fellow spoke again.

"Hand it to me," he said tonelessly.

He had stopped, his back against the packing cases, his thin, claw-like right hand extended toward the pickpocket. But Marty didn't notice the outstretched hand. He was staring in awful fascination at the open cello case which lay beside the other's feet. The inside edges of the case were stained a brownish red, a freshly sticky red.

And the contents of the case sent Marty reeling backward as screaming insanity shred the remaining fibers of his reason.

The gaunt, gray-coated figure grinned ghoulishly.

"Yes, human skin. I will make a wallet even softer than the one you have brought back to me."

Something burst in Merkins' brain then, and he began to giggle.

Then his laughter rose shrilly to a higher, louder pitch. He screamed harshly, insanely, and laughed again, saliva sliding down the corners of his mouth, tears pouring from his eyes. He was screaming and laughing and sobbing all at once, and the wallet was clutched in his hands...the soft, satin-like wallet...the wallet as smooth as silk...smooth as human skin, which it was...

THEY found Marty Merkins beside the ghastly cello case some hours later. The wallet was still in his hands, and he was crumpled inertly over it, laughing and sobbing and gibbering idiotically.

There was no one in that storage room, of course, save the utterly insane little pickpocket, the gruesome evidence in the bloodstained case, and the horribly damning wallet of human flesh.

Perhaps the judgment of the court might have been more fair had Marty been committed to a mad house, as the attorney for his defense pleaded. But public indignation toward the ripper-killer—and the evidence that he was the killer was undeniable—insisted on the supreme penalty.

He was babbling idiotically about the man in the gabardine coat even to the moment they turned on the current of the electric chair. Which was ridiculous, of course. For had there been a man such as the one he droolingly insisted existed, the ripper-killings would not have ceased with Marty Merkins' death.

Yet they did cease then. At least around that section of the world. There might have been others. Somewhere else...

THE END

A GUEST OF GANYMEDE

By C. C. MacApp

The boundary between horror and science fiction is often a vague one. This excellent novelette by C. C. MacApp starts out as a pure science fiction-intrigue tale, before veering sharply into what can only be described as pure, inescapable horror as it races to its terrifying conclusion.

CHAPTER ONE

His employer had paid enormously to have the small ship camouflaged as a chunk of asteroid-belt rock, and Gil Murdoch had successfully maneuvered it past the quarantine. Now it lay snugly melted into the ice; and if above them enough water had boiled into space to leave a scar, that was nothing unique on Ganymede's battered surface. In any case, the Terran patrols weren't likely to come in close.

Murdoch applied heat forward and moved the ship gingerly ahead.

"What are you doing now?" Waverill demanded.

Murdock glanced at the blind man. "Trying to find a clear spot, sir, so I can see into the place."

"What for? Why don't you just contact them?"

"Just being careful, sir. After all, we don't know much about them," Murdoch kept the annoyance out of his voice. He had his own reasons for wanting a preliminary look at the place, though the aliens had undoubtedly picked them up thousands of miles out and knew exactly where they were now.

Something solid, possibly a rock imbedded in the ice, bumped along the hull. Murdoch stopped the ship, then moved on more slowly.

The view screens brightened. He stopped the drive, then turned off the heat forward. Water, milky with vapor bubbles, swirled around them, gradually clearing. In a few minutes it froze solid again and he could see.

They were not more than ten feet from the clear area carved out of the ice. Murdoch had the viewpoint of a fish in murky water, looking into an immersed glass jar. The place was apparently a perfect cylinder, walled by a force-field or whatever held back the ice. He could see the dark translucency of the opposite wall, about fifty yards away and extending down eighty or ninety feet from the surface. He'd only lowered the ship a third that far, so that from here he looked down upon the plain one-story building and the neat lawns and hedges around it.

The building and greenery occupied only one-half of the area, the half near Murdoch being paved entirely with gravel and unplanted. That, he presumed, was where they'd land. The building was fitted to the shape of its half-circle, and occupied most of it, like a half cake set in a round box with a little space around it. A gravel walkway, bordered by grass, ran along the straight front of the building and around the back curve of it. The hedges surrounded the half-circle at the outside.

There was an inconspicuous closed door in the middle of the building. There were no windows in the flat gray wall.

The plants looked Terran, and apparently were rooted in soil, though there must be miles of ice beneath. Artificial sunlight poured on the whole area from the top. Murdoch had heard, and now was sure, that something held an atmosphere in the place.

"What are we waiting for?" Waverill wanted to know.

Murdoch reached for a switch and said, simply, "Hello."

The voice that answered was precise and uninflected. "Who are you?"

"My employer is Frederick Waverill. He has an appointment."

"And you."

"Gilbert Murdoch."

There was a pause, then, "Gilbert Andrew Murdoch. Age thirty-four. Born in the state called Illinois."

Murdoch, startled, hesitated, then realized he'd probably been asked a question. "Er—that's right."

"There is a price on your head Murdoch."

Murdoch hesitated again, then said, "There'd be a price on your own if Earth dared to put it there."

Waverill gripped the arms of his seat and stood up, too vigorously for the light gravity. "Never mind all that. I hired this man because he could make the contact and get me here. Can you give me back my eyes?"

"We can but first of all I must warn both of you against trying to steal anything from us or prying into our methods. Several Terrans have tried but none have escaped alive."

Waverill made an impatient gesture. "I've already got more money than I can count. I've spent a lot of it, a very great lot, on the metal you wanted, and I have it here in the ship."

"We have already perceived it and we do not care what it has cost you. We are not altruists."

That, thought Murdoch, could be believed. He felt clammy. If they knew so much about him, they might also be aware of the years he'd spent sifting and assessing the rumors about them that circulated around the tenuous outlaw community of space. Still, he'd been as discreet as was humanly possible.

He wondered if Waverill knew more than he pretended. He thought not; Murdoch's own knowledge was largely meticulous deduction. This much Murdoch knew with enough certainty to gamble his life on it: the treatments here involved a strange virus-like thing which multiplied in one's veins and, for presumably selfish or instinctive reasons, helped the body to repair and maintain itself. He knew for dead certain that the aliens always carefully destroyed the virus in a patient's veins before letting him go.

He thought he knew why.

The problem was to smuggle out any viable amount of the virus. Even a few cells, he thought, would be enough if he could get away from here and get them into his own blood. For it would multiply; and what would be the going price for a drop of one's blood—for a thousandth of a drop—if it carried virtual immortality?

A man could very nearly buy Earth.

The voice was speaking again. "Move straight ahead. The field will be opened for you."

Murdoch got the ship moving. He was blanked out again by the melting ice until they popped free into air, with an odd hesitation and then a rush. The ship was borne clear on some sort of a beam. He could hear water cascading outside the hull for a second, then it was quiet. He glanced at the aft viewer and could see the tunnel where they'd come out, with a little water still in the bottom, confined by the force-field again. The water that had escaped was running off along a ditch that circled the clearing.

They were lowered slowly to the graveled area. "Leave the ship," the voice directed, "and walk to the doorway you see."

Murdoch helped Waverill through the inner and outer hatches and led him toward the building. His information was that a force barrier sliced off this half of the circle from the other, and he could see that the hedges along the diameter pressed against some invisible plane surface. He hesitated as they came to it, and the voice said, "Walk straight ahead to the door. The field will be opened for you."

He guided Waverill in the right direction. As they passed the midpoint he felt an odd reluctance, a tingle and a slight resistance. Waverill grunted at it, but said nothing.

The door slid open and they were in a plain room with doors at the left and right. The outer door closed behind them. The door on the right opened and Murdoch took Waverill through it. They were in a second room of the same size, bare except for a bench along one wall.

The voice said, "Remove your clothing and pile it on the floor."

Waverill complied without protest, and after a second Murdoch did too. "Step back," the voice said. They did.

The clothing dropped through the floor, sluggishly in the light gravity. Murdoch grunted. There were weapons built into his clothes, and he felt uneasy without them.

At the end of the room away from the middle of the building was another door like the one they'd come through. It opened and a robot walked in.

It was humanoid in shape, flesh-colored but without animal details. The head had several features other than the eyes, but none of them was nose, mouth or ears. It stood looking at them for a minute, then said in the familiar voice, "Do not be alarmed if you feel something now."

There was a tingling, then a warmth, then a vibration, and some other sensations not easy to classify. Murdoch couldn't tell whether they came from the robot or not. It was obvious, though, that the robot was scanning them. He resisted an urge to move his hands more behind him. He'd been well satisfied with the delicate surgery, but now he imagined it awkward and obvious.

The robot didn't seem to notice anything.

After a minute the robot said, "Through the door where I entered you will find a bedroom and a bath and a place to cook. It is best you retire now and rest."

Murdoch offered his arm to Waverill, who grumbled a little but came along.

The voice went on, seeming now to come from the ceiling, "Treatment will begin tomorrow. During convalescence Murdoch will care for Waverill. Sight will be restored within four days and you will be here one day after that then you may return to your ship. You will be protected from each other while you are here. If you keep your bargain you will be of no concern to us after you leave."

Murdoch watched Waverill's face but it showed nothing. He was sure the billionaire already had arrangements to shut him up permanently as soon as he was no longer needed, and he didn't intend, of course, to let those arrangements work out.

CHAPTER TWO

It developed that when the robot spoke of days, it meant a twenty-four-hour cycle of light and dark, with temperatures to suit. Under other circumstances, the place would have been comfortable.

The pantry was stocked with Earthside food that didn't help Murdoch's confidence any, since it was further evidence of the aliens' contacts with men. He cooked eggs and bacon, helped Waverill eat, then washed up the dishes.

He felt uneasy without his clothes; the more because the weapons in them, through years of habit, were almost part of himself. He thought. I'm getting too jumpy too soon. My nerves have to last a long time yet.

While he was putting the dishes to drain, the robot walked into the room and watched him for a moment. Then it said to Waverill, "Keep your hand on my shoulder and walk behind me." It reached for Waverill's right hand and placed it on its own right shoulder, revealing in the process that its arm was double-jointed. Then it simply walked through the wall. The blind man, without flinching and perhaps without being aware, passed through the seemingly firm substance.

When they were gone, Murdoch went quickly to the wall and passed his hands over it. Solid.

The voice came from the ceiling. "You cannot penetrate the walls except when told to. Any place you can reach in this half of the grounds is open to you. The half where your ship is will remain cut off. You may amuse yourself as you wish so long as you do not willfully damage anything. We have gone to great effort to make this place comfortable for Terrans. Do not impair it for those who may come later."

Murdoch smiled inwardly. He'd known the walls would be solid; he'd only wanted to check the alien's watchfulness. Now he knew that there was more to it than just the robot, and that the voice was standard wherever it came from.

Not that the information helped any.

He walked back to the middle of the building and went through the door across the lobby. In that half of the building were a library, a gymnasium and what was evidently a Solar System museum. There was nothing new to him in the museum. Though there were useful tables and data in the library, he was too tense to study. The gymnasium he'd use later.

He went outside, walking gingerly on the gravel. The rear of the building was a featureless semicircle, the lawns and hedges unvaried. He took deep breaths of the air perfumed by flowers.

He jumped at a sudden buzz near his elbow. A bee circled up from a blossom and headed for the top of the building to disappear over the edge. Murdoch considered jumping for a hold and hauling himself up to the top of the building to see if there were hives there, but decided not to risk the aliens' displeasure. He realized now that he'd been hearing the bees all the time without recognizing it, and was annoyed at himself for not being more alert.

He paid more attention now, and saw that there were other insects too; ants and a variety of beetles. There were no birds, mammals, or reptiles that he could see.

He parted the hedge and leaned close to the clear wall, shading the surface with his hands to see into the ice. There were a few rocks in sight. He found one neatly sliced in two by the force-field, or whatever it was, showing a trail of striations in the ice above it where it had slowly settled. On Ganymede, the rate of sink of a cool rock would be very slow in the ice.

Far back in the dimness he could see a few vague objects that might have been large rocks or ships. There were some other things with vaguely suggestive shapes, like long-eroded artifacts. Nothing that couldn't have been the normal fall-in from space.

He went to the front of the building again and stood for a while, looking at the graveled other half of the place. He couldn't see any insects there, and not a blade of grass. He approached the barrier and leaned against it, to see how it felt. It was rigid, but didn't feel glass-hard. Rather it had a very slight surface softness, so he could press a fingernail in a fraction of a millimeter.

He remembered that on Earth bees would blunder into a glass pane, and looked around to see if they hit the barrier. They didn't. An inch or so from it, they turned in the air and avoided it. Neither could he see any insects crawling on the invisible surface. He pressed his face closer, and noticed again the odd reluctance he'd felt when crossing on the way in.

At ground level, a dark line not more than a quarter of an inch thick marked where the barrier split the soil. Gravel heaped up against it on both sides.

He looked again toward the ship. If things went according to plan, the ship's proximity alarm would go off sometime within the next two days. He didn't think the aliens would let him go to the ship, but he expected the diversion to help him check out something he'd heard about the barrier.

He flexed his thumbs, feeling the small lumps implanted in the web of flesh between thumb and finger on each hand. He'd practiced getting the tiny instruments in and out until he could do it without thinking. But now the whole project seemed ridiculously optimistic.

He felt annoyed at himself again. It's the aliens, he thought, that are getting my nerves. I've pulled plenty of jobs as intricate as this without fretting this way.

He began another circuit around the building, and was at the rear when the voice said, almost at his shoulder, "Murdoch, Waverill wants you."

His employer lay on his cot, looking drowsy. He scowled at Murdoch's footsteps. "Where you been? I want a drink."

Murdoch involuntarily glanced around. "Will they let you have it, sir?"

The voice came from the ceiling this time. "One ounce of hundred-proof liquor every four hours."

"Is there any here?" Murdoch asked.

"Tell us where to find it and we will get it from your ship."

Murdoch told them where the ship's supply of beverages was stowed, and headed for the front of the building. The robot was already in the lobby. It allowed him to follow outside, but said, "Stand back from the barrier."

Murdoch leaned against the building, trying not to show his eagerness. This was an unexpected break. He watched the ground level as the robot passed through the barrier. The dark line in the ground didn't change. The gravel stayed in place on both sides. Neither did the plants to the sides move. Evidently the barrier only opened at one spot to let things through.

The robot had no trouble with the hatches, and came out quickly with a bottle in one hand. Murdoch worried again whether it had discovered that the ship's alarm was set. If so, it didn't say anything as it drew near. It handed Murdoch the bottle and disappeared into the building.

After a few moments Murdoch followed. He found Waverill asleep, but at his footsteps the older man stirred. "Murdoch? Where's that drink?"

"Right away, sir." Murdoch got ice from the alien's pantry, put it in a glass with a little water and poured in about a jigger of rye. He handed it to Waverill, then poured himself a straight shot. Rye wasn't his favorite, but it might ease his nerves a little.

"Mm," said Waverill, " 'S better."

Murdoch couldn't see any marks on him. "Did they stick any needles into you, sir?"

"I'm not paying you to be nosey."

"Of course not, sir. I only wanted to know so I wouldn't touch you in a sore spot."

"There are no sore spots," Waverill said. "I want to sleep a couple of hours, so go away. Then I'll want a steak and a baked potato."

"Surely, sir."

Murdoch went outside again and toured the grounds without seeing anything new. He went to the barrier and stared at the ship for a while. Then, to work off tension, he went into the gymnasium and took a workout. He had a shower, looked in on Waverill and found him still asleep, then went back to the library. The books and tapes were all Terran, with no clues about the aliens. The museum was no more helpful. It was a relief when he heard Waverill calling.

There were steaks in the larder, and potatoes. Waverill grumbled at the wait while Murdoch cooked. The older man still acted a little drowsy, but had a good appetite. After eating he wanted to rest again.

Murdoch wandered some more, then forced himself to sit down in the library and pretend to study. He went over his plans again and again.

They were tenuous enough. He had to get a drop of Waverill's blood sometime within the next day or two and get it past the barrier. Then he had to get it into the ship and, once away from Ganymede, inoculate himself. The problem of Waverill didn't worry him. The drowsiness would have to be coped with, but based on the timetable Waverill's symptoms would give him, he should be able to set up a flight plan which would allow him to nap.

The time dragged agonizingly. He had two more drinks during the "afternoon," took another workout and a couple of turns around the building, and finally saw the sunlamps dimming. After that there was a time of lying on his bunk trying to force himself to relax. Finally he did sleep.

He was awake again with the first light; got up and wandered restlessly into the pantry. In a few minutes he heard Waverill stirring. "Murdoch!" came the older man's voice.

Murdoch went to him. "Yes, sir. I was just going to get breakfast."

"I can see the light!"

"You—that's wonderful, sir!"

"I can see the light! Dammit, where are you? Take me outside!"

"It's no brighter out there, Sir." Murdoch was dismayed. He'd counted on another day before Waverill's sight began to return; with a chance to arrange a broken drinking glass, a knife in Waverill's way, something to bring blood in an apparent accident. Now.

"Take me outside!"

"Yes, sir." Murdoch, his mind spinning, guided the older man.

The door slid open for them and Waverill crowded through. As he stepped on the gravel with his bare feet, he said, "Ouch! Damn it!"

"Step lightly, sir, and it won't hurt." Murdoch had a sudden wild hope that Waverill would cut his feet on a sharp pebble. But there were no sharp pebbles; they were all rounded; and the light gravity made it even more unlikely.

Waverill raised his head and swung it to the side. "I can see spots of light up there."

"The sunlamps, sir. They're getting brighter."

"I can see where they are." The older man's voice was shaky. He looked toward Murdoch. "I can't see you, though."

"It'll come back gradually, sir. Why don't you have breakfast now?"

Waverill told him what to do with breakfast. "I want to stay out here. How bright is it now? Is it like full daylight yet?"

"No, sir. It'll be a while yet. You'll be able to feel it on your skin," Murdoch was clammy with the fear that the other's sight would improve too fast. He looked around for some sharp corner, some twig he could maneuver the man into. He didn't see anything.

"What's that sweet smell?" Waverill wanted to know.

"Flowers, sir. There's a blossoming hedge around the walkways."

"I'll be able to see flowers again. I'll..." The older man caught himself as if ashamed. "Tell me what this place looks like."

Murdoch described the grounds, meanwhile guiding Waverill slowly around the curved path. Somewhere, he thought, there'll be something sharp I can bump him into. He had a wild thought of running the man into a wall; but a bloody nose would be too obvious.

"I can feel the warmth now," Waverill said, "and I can tell that they're brighter." He was swiveling his head and squinting, experimenting with his new traces of vision.

Murdoch carried on a conversation with half his attention, while his mind churned. He thought, I'll have to resist the feeling that it's safer here in back of the building. They'll be watching everywhere. He wished he could get the man inside; under the cover of serving breakfast he could improvise something. I'm sweating, he thought. I can just begin to feel the lamps, but I'm wet all over. I've got to—

He drew in his breath sharply. From somewhere he heard the buzz of a bee. His mind leaped upon the sound. He stopped walking, and Waverill said, "What's wrong with you?"

"Nothing. I—stepped on a big pebble."

"They all feel big to me. Damned outrage; taking away a man's..." Waverill's voice trailed off as he started experimenting with his eyes again.

There were more bees now, and presently Murdoch saw one loop over the edge of the building and search along the hedge. The first of them, he thought. There'll be more. He looked along the hedge. Most of the blossoms hadn't really closed for the night, though the petals were drawn together. He walked as slow as he dared. The buzzing moved, tantalizingly closer, then away.

A second buzz added itself. He heard the insect move past them, then caught it in the corner of his eye.

Waverill stopped. "Is that a bee? Here?"

"I guess they keep them to fertilize the plants, sir."

"They bother me. I can't tell where they are."

"I'll watch out for them, sir."

He could see the insect plainly now, and thought, I have an excuse to watch it. The buzz changed pitch as the bee started to settle, then changed again as it moved on a few feet. Murdoch clamped his teeth in frustration. He tried to wipe his free hand where trousers should have been, and discovered that his thigh was sweaty too. He thought, surely Waverill must feel how sweaty my arm is.

The bee flirted with another flower, then settled on a petal. Tense. Murdoch subtly moved Waverill toward the spot. He could see every move of the insect's legs as it crawled into the bell of the flower.

"You can smell the blossoms more now, sir," he said. His throat felt dry, and he thought his voice sounded odd. "It's warming up and bringing out the smell, I guess." He halted, and tried not to let his arm tense or tremble. "This is a light blue blossom. Can you see it?"

"I—I'm not sure. I can see a bright spot a little above my head and right in front of me."

"That's a reflection off the ice, sir. The flower's down here." Holding his breath, he took Waverill's hand and moved it toward the flower. He found himself gritting his teeth and wincing as Waverill's fingers explored delicately around the flower.

The bee crawled out, apparently not aware of anything unusual, and moved away a few inches. It settled on a leaf and began working its legs together.

Murdoch felt like screaming.

Waverill's fingers stopped their exploration, then, as the bee was silent, began again, Waverill bent over to bring his eyes closer to his hand.

Shaking with anxiety now. Murdoch executed the small movements of his right hand that forced the tiny instrument out from between his thumb and forefinger He felt a panicky desire to hurry and forced himself to move slowly. He transferred the tiny syringe to his left hand, which was nearer Waverill. Waverill was about to pluck the blossom. Murdoch moved his right hand forward, trying—in case the aliens could see, though he had his body in the way—to make the move casual. He flicked a finger near the bee.

The bee leaped into the air, its buzz high-pitched and loud. Waverill tensed.

Murdoch cried, "Look out, sir!" and grabbed at Waverill's hand. He jabbed the miniature syringe into the fleshy part of the hand, at the outside, just below the wrist.

"Damn you!" Waverill bellowed, slapping at his right hand with his left. He jerked away from Murdoch.

"Here, sir! Let me help you!"

"Get away from me, you clumsy fool!"

"Please, sir, let me get the stinger out. You'll squeeze more poison into your skin."

Waverill faced him, a hand raised as if to strike. Then he lowered it. "All right, damn you; and be careful about it."

Shakily, Murdoch took Waverill's hand. The syringe, dangling from the skin, held a trace of red in its minute plastic bulb. Murdoch gasped for breath and fought to make his fingers behave. He got hold of the syringe and drew it out. Pretending to drop it, he hid it in the junction of the third and fourth fingers of his left hand. He kept his body between them and the building, and tried to make his actions convincing. "There. It's out, sir."

Waverill was still cursing in a low voice. Presently he stopped, but his face was still hard with anger. "Take me inside."

"Yes, sir." Murdoch was weak with reaction. He drew a painful breath, gave the older man his left arm and led him back.

The tiny thing between his fingers felt as large and as conspicuous as a handgun.

CHAPTER FOUR

Murdoch felt as if the entire place was lined with eyes all focused on his left hand. The act of theft clearly begun, his life in the balance, he felt now the icy nausea of fear; a feeling familiar enough, and which he knew how to control, but which he still didn't like. Fear. It's a strange thing, he thought. A peculiar thing.

If you analyzed it, you could resolve it into the physical sick feeling and the wish in your mind, a very fervent wish, that you were somewhere else. Sometimes, if it caught you tightly enough, it was almost paralyzing so that your limbs and even your lungs seemed to be on strike. When fear gripped him he always remembered back to that turning point, that act that had made him an outlaw and an exile from Earth.

He'd been a pilot in the Space Force, young, just out of the Academy, and the bribe had seemed very large and the treason very small. It seemed incredibly naive, now, that he should not have understood that a double-cross was necessarily a part of the arrangement.

It was in escaping at all, against odds beyond calculating, that he had learned that he thought faster and deeper than other men, and that he had guts. Having guts turned out to be a different thing than he had imagined. It didn't mean that you stood grinning and calm while others went mad with fear. It meant you suffered all the panic, all the actual physical agony they did, but that you somehow stuck to the gun, took the buffeting and still had in a corner of your being enough wit to throw the counterpunch or think through to the way out. And that's what he had to do now. Endure the fear and keep his wits.

The robot had responded to Waverill's loud demand. It barely glanced at Waverill's hand, said, "It will heal quickly" and left. So far as Murdoch could tell, it didn't look at him.

As soon as he dared, he went and took a shower. In the process of lathering he inserted the syringe into the slit between thumb and forefinger of his left hand. In that hiding-place was a small plastic sphere holding a substance which ought to be nutrient to the virus. It was delicate work, but he'd practiced well and his fingers were under control now; and he got the point of the syringe into the sphere and squeezed. He relaxed the squeeze, felt the bulb return slowly to shape as it drew out some of the gummy stuff. He squeezed it back in, let the shower rinse the syringe and got that back into the pouch in his right hand.

He didn't dare discard it. There was always the possibility of failure and a second try, though the timing made it very remote. If the surgery was right, the pouches in his hand were lined with something impervious, so that none of the virus would get into his blood too soon. He lathered very thoroughly and rinsed off, then let a blast of warm air dry him. He felt neither fear nor elation now. Rather there was a let-down, and a weary apprehension at the trials ahead. The next big step was to get the small sphere past the barrier ahead of the time of leaving. He was pretty sure that he couldn't smuggle it out on his person. The alien's final examination and sterilization would prevent that.

Now there came the agony of waiting for the next step. He hadn't been able to rig things tightly enough to predict within several hours when it would come. It might be in one hour or in ten. A derelict was drifting in. He'd arranged that, but it might be late or it might be intercepted. He prepared a meal for Waverill and himself, sweated out the interval and cooked another. He wandered from library to gymnasium to out-of-doors, and fought endlessly the desire to stand at the barrier and stare at the ship.

The robot examined Waverill and revealed only that things were going well. Waverill spent most of his time bringing objects before his eyes, squinting and twisting his face, swallowed up in the ecstasy of his slowly returning vision. When darkness came the older man slept. Murdoch lay twisting on his own couch or dozed fitfully, beset with twisted dreams.

When the ship's alarm went off he didn't know at first whether it was real or another of the dreams.

His mind was sluggish in clearing, and when he sat up he could hear sounds at the front of the building. Suddenly in a fright that he would be too late, he jumped up and ran that way. The robot was already out of the building. It turned toward him with a suggestion of haste, "What is this?"

Murdoch tried to act startled. "The ship's alarm! There's something headed in! Maybe Earth Patrol!"

"Why did you leave the alarm on?"

"We—I guess I forgot in the excitement."

"That was dangerous stupidity. How is the alarm powered?"

"It's self-powered. Rechargeable batteries."

"You are fortunate that it is only a dead hull drifting by, otherwise we would have to dispose of you at once. Stay here. I will shut it off."

Murdoch pretended to protest mildly, then stood watching the robot go. His hands were moving in what he hoped looked like a gesture of futility. He got the plastic sphere out of its hiding-place and thumbed it like a marble. He held his breath. The robot crossed the barrier. Murdoch flipped the sphere after it. He saw it arc across the line and bound once, then he lost it in the gravel. In the dim light from Jupiter, low on the horizon, he could not find it again. Desperately, he memorized the place in relation to the hedge. When he and Waverill left, there would be scant time to look for it.

The robot didn't take long to solve the ship's hatches, go in through the lock, and locate the alarm. The siren chopped off in mid-scream. The robot came back out and started toward him. Involuntarily, he backed up against the building, wondering what the robot (or its masters) right deduce with alien senses, and whether swift punishment might strike him the next instant. But the robot passed him silently and disappeared indoors.

After a while he followed it inside, lay down on his couch, and resumed the fitful wait.

The next morning Waverill's eyes followed him as he fixed breakfast. There was life in them now, and purpose. The man looked younger, more vigorous, too.

Murdoch, trying not to sound nervous, asked, "Can you see more now, sir?"

"A little. Sit me so the light falls on my plate."

Murdoch watched the other's attempts to eat by sight rather than feel, adding mentally to his own time-table of the older man's recovery. Apparently Waverill could see his plate, but no details of the food on it. There was no more drowsiness, though. The movements were deft except that they didn't yet correlate with the eyes. The eyes seemed to have a little trouble matching up too, sometimes. No doubt it would take a while to restore the reflexes lost over the years.

Waverill walked the grounds alone in mid-morning. Murdoch, following far enough behind not to draw a rebuff, took the opportunity to spot his small treasure in the gravel beyond the barrier. Once found, it was dismayingly visible. But there was nothing he could do now. He was sweating again, and hoped with a sort of half-prayer to Fortune that his nerves wouldn't start to shatter once more.

He made lunch, then set himself the job of waiting out the afternoon. Ages later he cooked dinner. He managed to eat most of his steak, envying Waverill the wolfish appetite that made quick work of the meal.

The long night somehow wore through, and he embraced eagerly the small respite of breakfast.

He felt unreal when the alien voice said, "Do not bother to wash the dishes. Lie down on your bunks for your final examination. When you awake you may leave."

The fear spread through him again as he moved slowly to his couch. He thought, if they've caught me, this is when they'll kill me. He was afraid, no doubt of that; all the old symptoms were there. But, oddly, there was a trace of perverse comfort in the thought.

Maybe I've lost. Maybe I'll just never wake up. Then dizziness hit him. He was aware of a brief, feeble effort to resist it, then he slid into darkness.

He came awake still dizzy, and with a drugged feeling. His mouth was dry. Breath came hard at first. He tried to open his eyes, but his lids were too stiff. He spent a few minutes just getting his breath to working, then he was able to open his eyes a little. When he sat up there was a wash of nausea. He sat on the edge of the bunk, head hung, until it lessened. Gradually he felt stronger.

Waverill was sitting up too, looking no better than Murdoch felt. He seemed to recover faster, though, Murdoch thought. He's actually healthier than I am now. I hope he hasn't become a superman.

The voice from the ceiling said, "Your clothes are in the next room. Dress and leave at once. The barriers will be opened for you."

Murdoch got to his feet and headed for the other room. He paused to let Waverill go ahead, and noticed that Waverill had no trouble finding the door. The older man wasn't talking this morning, and the jubilation he must feel at seeing again was confined, outwardly, to a tight grin.

They dressed quickly. Murdoch noting in the process that his clothes had been gone over carefully and all weapons removed. It didn't matter. But it did matter that he had to collect his prize on the way to the ship, and the sweaty anxiety was with him.

As they went out the door, Waverill stopped and let his eyes sweep about the grounds. What a cool character he is, Murdoch thought. Not a word. Not a sign of emotion.

Waverill turned and started toward the ship. Murdoch let him get a step ahead. His own eyes were searching the gravel. For a moment he had the panicky notion that it was gone; then he spotted it. He wouldn't have to alter his course to reach it. He saw Waverill flinch a little as they crossed the barrier, then he too felt the odd sensation. He kept going, trying to bring his left foot down on the capsule. He managed to do it.

Taut with anxiety, he paused and half-turned as if for a last look back at the place. He could feel the sphere give a little; or maybe it was a pebble sinking into the ground. He twisted his foot. He thought he could feel something crush. He hesitated, in the agony of trying to decide whether to go on or to make more sure by dropping something and pretending to pick it up. He didn't have anything to drop. He thought, I've got to go on or they'll suspect. He turned. Waverill had stopped and was looking back at him keenly. Murdoch gripped himself, kept his face straight, and went on.

Waverill had to grope a little getting into the ship, as though his hands still didn't correlate with his eyes, but it was clear that he could see all right, even in the ship's dim interior. Murdoch said, "Your eyes seem to be completely well, sir."

Waverill was playing it cool too. "They don't match up very well yet, and I have to experiment to focus. It'll come back, though." He went casually to his seat and lowered himself into it.

Murdoch got into the pilot's seat. "Better strap in, sir."

He didn't have long to wonder how they'd be sent off; the ship lifted and simply passed through whatever served as a ceiling.

There was no restraint when Murdoch turned on the gravs and took over. He moved off toward Ganymede's north pole, gaining altitude slowly, watching his screens, listening to the various hums and whines as the ship came alive. The radar would have to stay off until they were away from Ganymede, but the optical system showed nothing threatening. He moved farther from the satellite, keeping it between him and Jupiter.

"Hold it here," Waverill said.

Letting the ship move ahead on automatic, Murdoch turned in pretended surprise. "What..."

Waverill had a heat gun trained steadily on him. "I'll give you the course."

Murdoch casually reached down beside the pilot's chair. A compartment opened under his fingers, and he lifted a gun of his own.

Waverill's mouth went tight as he squeezed the trigger. Nothing happened. Waverill glanced at the weapon. Rage moved across his face. He hoisted the gun as if to throw it, then stopped as Murdoch lifted his own gun a little higher.

"You got to them," Waverill said flatly.

"The ones that did the remodeling job on this crate and hid that gun for you? Of course. Did you think you were playing with an idiot?"

"I could have sworn they were beyond reach."

"I reached them," Murdoch got unstrapped and stood up. He had the ship's acceleration just as he wanted it. "And naturally I went over the ship while you were blind. Get into your suit now, Waverill."

"Why?"

"I'm giving you a better break than you were going to give me. I'm putting you where the Patrol will pick you up."

"You won't make it, you son of a bitch. I've got some cards left."

"I know where you planned to rendezvous. By the time you buy your way out of jail, I'll be out of your reach."

"You *never* will."

"Talk hard enough and I may decide to kill you right now."

Waverill studied his face for a moment, then slowly got to his feet. He went to the suit locker, got out his suit, and squirmed into it. Murdoch grinned as he saw the disappointment on the other's face. The weapons were gone from the suit, too.

He said, "Zip up and get the helmet on, and get into the lock."

Waverill, face contorted with hate, complied slowly. Murdoch secured the inner hatch behind the man, then got on the ship's intercom. "Now, Waverill, you'll notice it's too far for a jump back to Ganymede. I'm going to spend about forty minutes getting into an orbit that'll give you a good chance. When I say shove off, you can either do it or stay where you are. If you stay, we'll be headed a different direction and I'll have to kill you for my own safety." He left the circuit open, and activated a spy cell so he could see into the lock. Waverill was leaning against the inner hatch, conserving what heat he could.

CHAPTER FIVE

Murdoch set up a quick flight program, waited a minute to get farther from Ganymede and the aliens, then turned on a radar search and set the alarm. He unzipped his left shoe, got it off and stood staring at it for a moment, almost afraid to turn it over.

Then he turned it slowly. There was a sticky spot on the sole.

The muscles around his middle got so taut they ached. He hurried to the ship's med cabinet, chose a certain package of bandages and tore it open with unsteady fingers. There was a small vial hidden there. He unstoppered it and poured the contents onto the shoe sole.

He let it soak while he checked the pilot panel, then hurried back. With a probe, he mulled the liquid around on the shoe sole and waited a minute longer. Then he scraped all he could back into the vial and looked at it. There were a few bits of shoe sole in it, but none big enough to worry him. He got out a hypodermic and drew some of the fluid into it. The needle plugged. He swore, ejected a little to clear it and drew in some more.

When he had his left sleeve pushed up, he looked at the vein in the bend of his elbow for a little while, then he took a deep breath and plunged the needle in. He hit it the first time. He was very careful not to get any air into the vein.

He sighed, put the rest of the fluid back in the vial and stoppered it, and cleaned out the needle. Then he put a small bandage on his arm and went back to the pilot's seat. He felt tired now that it was done.

The scan showed nothing dangerous. Waverill hadn't moved. Murdoch opened his mouth to speak to him, then decided not to. He flexed his arm and found it barely sore, then went over his flight program again. He made a small adjustment. The acceleration was just over one G, and it made him a little dizzy. He wondered if he could risk a drink. It hadn't hurt Waverill. He went to the small sink and cabinet that served as a galley, poured out a stiff shot into a glass, and mixed it with condensed milk. He took it back to the pilot's seat, not bothering with the free-fall cap, and drank it slowly.

It was nearly time to unload Waverill.

He checked course again, then thumbed the mike. "All right, Waverill. Get going. You should be picked up within nine or ten hours."

Waverill didn't answer, but the panel lights showed the outer hatch activated. Through the spy cell Murdoch could see the stars as the hatch slowly opened, Waverill jumped off without hesitating. Murdoch liked the tough old man's guts, and hoped he'd make it all right.

He closed the hatch and fed new data into the autopilot. He sagged into the seat as the ship strained into a new course, then it eased off to a steady forward acceleration. He was ready to loop around another of Jupiter's moons, then around the giant planet itself, on a course that should defy pursuit unless it was previously known.

He flexed his arm. It was a little sorer now. He wondered when the drowsiness would hit him. He didn't want to trust the autopilot until he was safely past Jupiter; if a meteor or a derelict got in the way, it might take human wits to set up a new course safely.

He had all the radar units on now. The conic sweep forward showed the great bulge of Jupiter at one side; no blips in space. The three Plan Position screens, revolving through cross-sections of the sphere of space around him, winked and faded with blips but none near the center. He thought, *I've made it. I've gotten away with it, and I ought to feel excited.* Instead, he was only tired. He thought, *I'll get up and fill a thermos with coffee, then I can sit here.*

He unstrapped and began to rise. Then his eyes returned to one of the scopes.

This particular one was seldom used in space; it was for planet landings. It scanned ahead in a narrow horizontal band, like a sea vessel's surface sweep. He'd planned only to use it as he transited Jupiter, to cut his course in near to the atmosphere, and it was only habit that had made him glance at it. The bright green line showed no peaks, but at the middle, and for a little way to each side, it was very slightly uneven.

He thought, *It's just something in the system, out of adjustment.* He looked at the forward sweep. There were no blips dead ahead. He moved the adjustments of the horizontal sweep, blurred the line, then brought it back to sharpness. Except in the middle. The blurriness there remained.

He opened a panel and punched automatic cross-checks, got a report that the instrument was in perfect order. He looked at the scope again. The blurred length had grown to either side. Clammy sweat began to form on his skin. He punched at the computers, set up a program that would curve the ship off its path, punched for safety verification, and activated the autopilot. He heard the drive's whine move higher, but felt no answering lateral acceleration. He punched for three G deceleration, working frantically to get strapped in. The drive shrieked but there was no tug at his body.

The blurred part of the green line was spreading.

He realized he was pressing against the side of his seat. That meant the ship was finally swerving. But he'd erased that program. And now, abruptly, deceleration hit him. He sagged forward against his straps, gasping for air. He heard a new whine as his seat automatically began to turn, pulling in the straps on one side, as it maneuvered to face him away from the deceleration. He was crushed sideways for a while, then the seat locked and he pressed hard against the back of it. This he could take, though he judged it was five or six G's. He labored for breath.

The deceleration cut off and he was in free fall. His screens and scopes were dark. The drive no longer whined. He thought, something's got me. Something that can hide from radar, and control a ship from a distance like a fish on the end of a spear.

He tore at the straps, got free and leaped for the suit locker. He dressed in frantic haste, cycled the air lock...and found himself on the surface of a planet.

He had been returned to Ganymede.

Panicked, he fled; then abruptly, where nothing had been, there was something solid in his path. He turned his face to avoid the impact and tried to get his arms in front of him. He crashed into something that did not yield. His arms slid around something, and without opening his eyes he knew the robot had him. He tried to fight, but his strength was pitiful. He relaxed and tried to think.

In his suit helmet radio the voice of the robot said, "We will put you to sleep now."

He fought frantically to break loose. His mind screamed. No! If you go to sleep now you'll never...

He was wrong. His first waking sensation was delicious comfort. He felt good all over. He came a little more awake and his spaceman's mind began to reason. There's light gravity, and I'm supported by the armpits. No acceleration. I'm breathing something heavier than air, but it feels good in my lungs, and tastes good.

His eyelids unlocked themselves, and the shock of seeing was like a knife in his middle.

He was buried in the ice, looking out at the place where he and Waverill had stayed. He was far into the ice and could only see distortedly. Between him and the open were various things; rocks, eroded artifacts. At the edge of his vision on the right was a vaguely animal shape.

Terror made him struggle to turn his head. He couldn't; he was encased in something just tight enough to hold him. His nose and mouth were free, and a draft of the cloying atmosphere moved past them so that he could breath. There was enough space before his eyes for him to see the stuff swirling like a heavy fog. He thought, I'm being fed by what I breathe. I don't feel hungry. In horror, he forced the stuff out of his lungs. It was hard to exhale. He resisted taking any back in, but eventually he had to give up and then he fought to get it in. He tried to cry out, but the sound was a muffled nothing.

He yielded to panic and struggled for a while without accomplishing anything, except that he found that his casing did yield, very slowly, if he applied pressure long enough. That brought a little sanity, and he relaxed again until the exhaustion wore off.

There was movement in the vague shape at his right, and he felt a compulsion to see it more plainly. Even after it was in his vision, horrified fascination kept him straining until his head was turned toward it.

It was alive; obscenely alive, a caricature of parts of a man. There was no proper skin, but an ugly translucent membrane covered it. The whole was encased as Murdoch himself must be and from the casing several pipes stretched back into the dark ice. The legs were entirely gone, and only stubs of arms remained, sufficient for the thing to hang from in its casing. Bloated lungs pulsed slowly, breathing in and out a misty something like what Murdoch breathed. The stomach was shrunken to a small repugnant sack, hanging at the bottom with what might be things evolved from liver and kidneys. Blood moved from the lungs through the loathsome mess, pumped by an overgrown heart that protruded from between the lungs. A little blood circulated up to what had once been the head. The skull was gone. The nose and mouth were one round hole where the nutrient vapor puffed in and out. The brain showed horrible and shrunk through the membrane. A pair of lidless idiot eyes stared unmovingly in Murdoch's direction. The whole jawless head was the size of Murdoch's two fists doubled up, if he could judge the size through the distortion of the ice.

Sick but unable to vomit, Murdoch forced his eyes away from the thing. Now the aliens spoke to him, from somewhere, "Pretty isn't he, Murdoch. He makes a good bank for the virus. You were right you know, it does offer great longevity but it has its own ideas of what a host should be."

Murdoch produced a garbled sound and the aliens spoke again, "Your words are indistinct but perhaps you are asking how long it took him to become this way. He was one of our first visitors, the very first who tried to steal from us. His plan was not as clever as your own, which we found diverting, though of course you had no chance against our science, which is beyond your understanding." And, in answer to his moan, they said, "Do not be unphilosophical Murdoch you will find many thoughts to occupy your time."

I'll go mad, he thought. That's the way out!

But he doubted that even the escape of madness would be allowed.

THE END

THE HOUSE IN THE VALLEY

By August Derleth

Once more the epic struggle between the Elder Gods and the Ancient Ones was having repercussions on one of Earth's seemingly most peaceful valleys.

CHAPTER ONE

I, JEFFERSON BATES, make this deposition now, in full knowledge that, whatever the circumstances, I have not long to live. I do so in justice to those who survive me, as well as in an attempt to clear myself of the charge of which I have been unjustly convicted. A great, if little-known American writer in the tradition of the Gothic once wrote that "the most merciful thing in the world is the inability of the human mind to correlate all its contents." I, have had ample time for intense thought, and reflection, and I have achieved an order in my thoughts I would never have thought possible only so little as a year ago.

For, of course, it was within the year that my "trouble" began. I put it so, because I am not yet certain what other name to give it. If I had to set a precise day, I suppose in all fairness, it must be the day on which Brent Nicholson telephoned me in Boston to say he had discovered and rented for me the very place of isolation and natural beauty I had been seeking, for the purpose of working at some paintings I had long had in mind. It lay in an almost hidden valley beside a broad stream, not far from, yet well in from the Massachusetts coast, in the vicinity of the ancient settlements of Arkham and Dunwich, which every artist of the region knows for their curious gambrel structure, so pleasing to the eye, however forbidding to the spirit.

True, I hesitated. There were always fellow artists pausing for a day in Arkham or Dunwich or Kingston, and it was precisely fellow-artists I sought to escape. But in the end, Nicholson persuaded me, and within the week I found myself at the place. It proved to be a large, ancient house—certainly of the same vintage as so many in Arkham—which had been built in a little valley which ought to have been fertile but showed no sign of recent cultivation. It rose among gaunt pines, which crowded close on the house, and along one wall ran a broad, clear brook.

Despite the attractiveness it offered the eye at a distance, up close it presented another face. For one thing, it was painted black. For another, it wore an air of forbidding formidableness. Its curtainless windows stared outward gloomily. All around it on the ground floor ran a narrow porch which had been stuffed and crammed with bundles of sacking tied with twine, half-rotted chairs, highboys, tables, and a singular variety of old-fashioned household objects, like a barricade designed either to keep someone or something inside or to prevent it from getting in. This barricade had manifestly been there a long time, for it showed the effects of exposure to several years of weather. Its reason for being was too obscure even for the agent, to whom I wrote to ask, but it did help to lend the house a most curious air of being inhabited, though there was no sign of life, and nothing, indeed, to show that anyone had lived there for a very long time.

But this was an illusion which never left me. It was plain to see that no one had been in the house, not even Nicholson or the agent, for the barricade extended across both front and back doors of the almost square structure, and I had to pull away a section of it in order to make an entry myself.

ONCE inside, the impression of habitation was all the stronger. But there was a difference—all the gloom of the black-painted exterior was reversed inside. Here everything was light and surprisingly clean, considering the period of its abandonment. Moreover, the house was furnished, scantily, true, but furnished, whereas I had received the distinct impression that everything which had once been inside had been piled up around the house on the veranda outside.

The house inside was as box-like as it appeared on the outside. There were four rooms below—a bedroom, a kitchen-pantry, a dining-room, a sitting-room; and upstairs, four of exactly the same dimensions—three bedrooms, and a storeroom. There were plenty of windows in all the rooms, and especially those facing north, which was gratifying, since the north light is best for painting.

I had no use for the second story; so I chose the bedroom on the northwest corner for my studio, and it was there that I put in my things, without regard for the bed, which I pushed aside. I had come, after all, to work at my paintings, and not for any social life whatever. And I had come amply supplied, with my car so laden that it took me most of the first day to unload and store my things, and to clear away a path from the back door, as I had cleared the front, so that I might have access to both north and south sides of the house with equal facility.

Once settled, with a lamp lit against the encroaching darkness, I took out Nicholson's letter and read it once more, as it were, in the proper setting, taking note again of the points he made.

"Isolation will indeed be yours. The nearest neighbors are at least a mile away. They are the Perkinses on the ridge to the south. Not far past them are the Mores. On the other side, which would make it north, are the Bowdens.

"The reason for the long-term desertion is one which ought to appeal to you. People did not want to rent or buy it simply because it had once been occupied by one of those strange, ingrown families which are common in obscure and isolated rural areas— the Bishops, of which the last surviving member, a gaunt, lanky creature named Seth, committed a murder in the house. This one fact the superstitious natives allow to deter them from use of either the house or the land, which, as you will see—if you had any use for it—is rich and fertile. Even a murderer could be a creative artist in his way, I suppose—but Seth, I fear, was anything but that. He seems to have been somewhat crude, and killed without any good reason—a neighbor, I understand. Simply tore him apart. Seth was a very strong man. Gives me cold chills, but hardly you. The victim was a Bowden.

"There is a telephone, which I ordered connected.

"The house has its own power plant, too. So it's not as ancient as it looks. Though this was put in long after the house was originally built. It's in the cellar, I am told. It may not be working now.

"No waterworks, sorry. The well ought to be good, and you'll need some exercise to keep yourself fit—you can't keep fit sitting at an easel.

"The house looks more isolated than it is. If you get lonely, just telephone me."

The power plant. Of which he had written, was not working. The lights in the house were dead. But the telephone was in working order, as I ascertained by placing a call to the nearest village, which was Aylesbury.

I was tired that first night, and went to bed early. I had brought my own bedding, of course, taking no chances on anything left for so long a time in the house, and I was soon asleep. But every instant of my initial day in the house I was aware of that vague, almost intangible conviction that the house was occupied by someone other than myself, though I knew how absurd this was for I had made a thorough tour of the house and premises soon after I had first entered it, and had found no place where anyone might be concealed.

EVERY house, as no sensitive person needs to be told, has its own individual atmospheres. It is not only the smell of wood, or of brick, old stone, paint—no, it is also a sort of residue of people who have lived there and of events which have transpired within its walls. The atmosphere of the Bishop house challenged description. There was the customary smell of age, which I expected, of dampness rising from the cellar, out there was something beyond and of greater importance, something which actually lent the house itself an aura of life, as if it were a sleeping animal waiting with infinite patience for something, which it knew must happen, to take place.

It was not, let me say at once, anything to prompt uneasiness. It did not seem to me in that first week to have about it any element of dread or fear, and it did not occur to me to be at all disquieted until one morning in my second week—after I had already completed two imaginative canvases, and was at work outside on a third. I was conscious that morning of being scrutinized; at first I told myself, jokingly, that of course the house was watching me, for its windows did look like blank eyes peering out of that somber black; but presently I knew that my observer stood somewhere to the rear, and from time to time I flashed glances toward the edge of the little woods which rose southwest of the house.

At last I located the hidden watcher. I turned to face the bushes where he was concealed, and said. "Come on out; I know you're there."

At that a tall, freckle-faced young man rose up and stood looking at me with hard, dark eyes, manifestly suspicious and belligerent.

"Good morning," I said.

He nodded, without saying anything.

"If you're interested, come on up and have a look," I said.

He thawed a little and stepped out of the bushes. He was, I saw now, perhaps twenty. He was clad in jeans, and was barefooted, a lithe young fellow, well muscled, and undoubtedly quick and alert. He walked forward a little way, coming just close enough so that he could see what I was doing, and there stopped. He favored me with a frank examination. Finally he spoke.

"Your name Bishop?"

Of course, the neighbors might understandably think that a member of the family had turned up in some remote corner of the earth and come back to claim the abandoned property. The name of Jefferson Bates would mean nothing to him. Moreover, I was curiously reluctant to tell him my name, which I could not understand. I answered civilly enough that my name was not Bishop, that I was not a relative, that I had only rented the house for the summer and perhaps a month or two in the fall.

"My name's Perkins," he said. "Bud Perkins. From up yonder." He gestured toward the ridge to the south.

"Glad to know you."

"You been here a week," Bud continued, offering proof that my arrival had not gone unnoticed in the valley. "You're still here."

There was a note of surprise, in his voice, as if the fact of my being in the Bishop house after a week was strange of itself.

"I mean," he went on, "nothing's happened to you. What with all the goin's-on in this house, it's a wonder."

"What goings-on?" I asked bluntly.

"Don't you know?" he asked, openmouthed.

"I know about Seth Bishop."

He shook his head vigorously. "That ain't near the all of it, Mister. I wouldn't set foot in that house if I was paid for it—and paid good. Makes my spine prickle jest to be standing this near to it." He frowned darkly. "It's a place shoulda been burned down long ago. What were them Bishops doing all hours of the night?"

"Looks clean," I said. "It's comfortable enough. Not even a mouse in it."

"Hah! If 'twas only mice! You wait."

With that he turned and plunged back into the woods.

I realized, of course, that many local superstitions must have arisen about the abandoned Bishop house; what more natural than that it should be haunted? Nevertheless, Bud Perkins' visit left a disagreeable impression with me. Clearly, I had been under secret observation ever since my arrival; I understood that new neighbors are always of interest to people, but I also perceived that the interest of my neighbors in this isolated spot was not of quite that nature. They expected something to happen; they were waiting for it to take place; and only the fact that nothing had as yet occurred had brought Bud Perkins within range.

That night the first untoward "incident" took place. Quite possibly Bud Perkins' oblique comments had set the stage by preparing me for something to happen. In any case, the incident was so nebulous as to be almost negative, and there were a dozen explanations for it; it is only in the light of later events that I remember it at all. It happened perhaps two hours after midnight.

I was awakened from sleep by an unusual sound. Now, anyone sleeping in a new place grows accustomed to the sounds of the night in that region, and, once accustomed to them, accepts them in sleep; but any new sound is apt to obtrude. Just as a city dweller spending several nights on a farm may accustom himself to the noises of chickens, birds, the wind, frogs, may be awakened by the new note of a toad trilling because it is strange to the chorus, to which he has become accustomed, so I was aware of a new sound in the chorus of whippoorwills, owls, and nocturnal insects which invaded the night.

THE new sound was a subterranean one; that is, it seemed to come from far below the house, deep down under the surface of the earth. It might have been earth settling, it might have been fissure opening and closing, it might readily have been a fugitive temblor, except that it came and went with a certain regularity, as if it were made by some very large thing moving along a colossal cavern far beneath the house. It lasted perhaps half an hour; it seemed to approach from the east and diminish in the same direction in a fairly even progression of sounds. I could not be sure, but I had the uncertain impression, that the house trembled faintly under these subterranean sounds.

Perhaps it was this which impelled me on the following day to poke about in the storeroom in an effort to find out for myself what my inquisitive neighbor had meant by his questions and hints about the Bishops. What had they been doing that their neighbors thought was so bad?

The storeroom, however, was less crammed than I had expected it to be, perhaps largely because so many things had been put out on the veranda. Indeed, the only unusual aspect of it that I could find was a shelf of books which had evidently been in the process of being read when tragedy had obliterated the family.

These were of various kinds.

Perhaps chief among them were several gardening texts. They were extremely old books, and had been long in disuse, quite possibly hidden away by an earlier member of the Bishop family, and only recently discovered. I glanced into two or three of these, and found them to be completely useless for any modern gardener, since they described methods of raising and caring for plants which were unknown to me, for the most part—hellebore, mandrake, nightshade, witch hazel, and the like; and such of the pages which were given over to the more familiar vegetables were filled with bits of lore and superstition which held utterly no meaning for anyone in this modern world.

There was also one paper-covered book devoted to the lore of dreams. This did not appear to have been much read, though its condition was such for dust and lint, that it was impossible to draw any conclusions about it. It was one of those inexpensive books which were popular two or three generations ago, and its dream interpretations were the most ordinary; it was, in short, just such a book as one might expect a rather ignorant countryman to pick up.

Indeed, of them all, only one interested me. This was a most curious book indeed. It was a monumental tome, entirely copied in longhand, and bound by hand in wood. Though it very probably had no literary worth whatsoever, it could have existed in any museum as an item of curiosa. At that time I made little attempt to read it, for it seemed to be a compilation of gibberish similar to the nonsense in the dream book. It had a crudely lettered title which indicated that its ultimate source must have been some private old library—*Seth Bishop. His Book... Being Excerpts from the "Nekronomicon" and the "Cultes des Ghouls" and the "Pnakootic Manuscripts" and the "R'lyeh Text" Copied in His Own Hand by Seth Bishop in the Yrs. 1919 to 1923.* Underneath in a spidery hand which did not seem likely for one known to be so uneducated, he had scrawled his signature.

In addition to these, there were several works allied to the dream book. A copy of the notorious *Seventh Book of Moses,* a text much prized by certain oldsters in the Pennsylvania hex country— which, thanks to newspaper accounts of a recent hex murder, I knew about. A slender prayer-book in which all the prayers seemed to be mockeries, for all were directed to Asarael and Sathanus, and other dark angels.

There was nothing of any value whatsoever, apart from being simply curious items, in the entire lot. Their presence testified only to a diversity of dark interests on the part of succeeding generations of the Bishop family, for it was fairly evident that the owner and reader of the gardening books was very probably Seth's grandfather, while the owner of the dream book and the hex text was most likely a member of Seth's father's generation. Seth himself seemed interested in more obscure lore.

The works from which Seth had copied, however, seemed appreciably more erudite than I had been led to believe a man of Seth's background would be likely to consult. This puzzled me, and at the first opportunity I traveled into Aylesbury to make such inquiries as I could at a country store on the outskirts of the village, where, I reasoned, Seth might most probably have made purchases, since he had had the reputation of being a reclusive individual.

THE proprietor, who turned out to be a distant relative of Seth's on his mother's side, seemed somewhat loath to speak of

Seth, but did ultimately reveal something in his reluctant answers to my persistent questions. From him, whose name was Obed Marsh, I gathered that Seth had "at first"—that is, presumably as a child and young man—been as "backward as any of that clan." In Seth's later teens, he had grown "queer," by which Marsh meant that Seth had taken to a more solitary existence; he had spoken at that time with frequency of strange and disturbing dreams he had had, of noises he had heard, of visions he believed he saw in and out of the house; but, after two or three years of this, Seth had never mentioned a word of these things again. Instead, he had locked himself up in a room—which had certainly been the storeroom, judging by Marsh description—and read everything he could lay his hands on, for all that he never "went past the fourth grade." Later on, he had gone into Arkham, to the library of Miskatonic University, to read more books. After that "spell," Seth had come home and lived as a solitary until the time of his outbreak—the horrible murder of Amos Bowden.

All this, certainly, added up to little save a tale of a mind ill-equipped for learning, trying desperately to assimilate knowledge, the burden of which seemed to have ultimately snapped that mind. So, at least, it appeared at this juncture of my tenure of the Bishop house.

CHAPTER TWO

THAT night events took a singular turn. But, like so many other aspects of that strange sojourn, I was not aware immediately of the full implications of what happened. Set down baldly, it seems absurd that it should have given me any cause for second thought. It was nothing more than a dream which I experienced in the course of that night. Even as a dream, it was not particularly horrifying or even frightening, rather more awesome and impressive.

I dreamed simply that I lay asleep in the Bishop house, that while I so lay a vague, indefinable, but somehow awesome and powerful cloud—like a fog or mist—took shape out of the cellar, billowed up through the floors and walls, engulfing the furniture, but not seeming to harm it or the house, taking shape, meanwhile, as a huge, amorphous creature with tentacles flowing from its monstrous head, and swaying like a cobra back and forth all the while it gave voice to a strange ululation, while from somewhere in the distance a chorus of weird instruments played unearthly music, and a human voice chanted inhuman words which, as I subsequently learned, were written thusly:

Ph'nglui mglw'nafh Cthulhu R'lyeh
Wgah' nagl fhtagn

In the end, the amorphous creature billowed even farther upward and engulfed also the sleeper who was I. Thereupon it seemed to dissolve into a long dark passageway, down which came at a frantically eager lope a human being who was certainly similar in appearance to descriptions I had had of the late Seth Bishop. This being grew in size, too, looming almost as large as the amorphous fog, and vanished even as it had done, coming straight at the sleeping figure in the bed in that house in the valley.

Now, on the face of it, this dream was meaningless. It was a nightmare, beyond question; but it lacked any capacity for fear. I seemed to be aware that something of tremendous importance was happening to me or about to happen to me, but, not understanding it, I could not fear it; moreover, the amorphous creature, the chanting voice, the ululations, and the strange music all lent a ritual impressiveness to the dream.

ON AWAKENING in the morning, however, I found it readily possible to recall the dream, and I was obsessed with a persistent conviction that all its aspects were not really strange to me. Somewhere I had heard or seen the written equivalent of that fantastic chanting, and, so thinking, I found myself once more in the storeroom, poring over that incredible book in Seth Bishop's handwriting; reading here and there and discovering with wonder that the text concerned an ancient series of beliefs in Elder Gods and Ancient Ones and a conflict between them, between the Elder Gods and such creatures as Hastur and Yog-Sothoth and Cthulhu. This, at last, struck a familiar note, and seeking farther, I discovered what was certainly the chant I had heard—with, moreover, its translation in Seth Bishop's hand, which read:

In his house at R'lyeh dead Cthulhu waits dreaming

The one disturbing factor in this discovery was that I had most certainly not seen the line of the chant on occasion of my examination of the room. I might have seen the name "Cthulhu," but nothing more in that cursory glance at the Bishop manuscript. How then could I have duplicated a fact which was not part of my conscious or subconscious store of knowledge? It is not commonly believed that the mind can duplicate in a dream state or any other any experience which is utterly alien to it. Yet I had done so.

What was more, as I read on in that often shocking text of queer survivals and hellish cults, I found that hints in vague descriptive passages described just such a being as I had seen in my dream—not of fog or mist, but of solid matter, which was a second occurrence of the duplication of something utterly alien to my experience.

I had, of course, heard of psychic residue—residual forces left behind at the scene of any event, be it major tragedy or any powerful emotional experience common to Mankind—love, hate, fear—and it was possible that something of this sort had brought about my dream, as were it the atmosphere of the house itself invading and possessing me while I slept, which I did not regard as completely impossible, since certainly it was strange and the events which had taken place there were experiences of impressive power.

Now, however, though it was noon and the demands of my body for food were great, it seemed to me that the next step in pursuit of my dream lay in the cellar. So to it I made my way at once, and there, after a most exhaustive search, which included the moving away from the walls of tiers of shelves, some still with ancient jars of preserved fruit and vegetables on them, I discovered a hidden passageway which led out of the cellar into a cave-like tunnel, down part of which I walked. I did not go far, before the dampness of the earth underfoot, and the wavering of my light, forced me to return—but not before I had seen the disquieting whiteness of scattered bones, embedded in that earth.

When I returned to that subterranean passageway after replenishing my flashlight, I did not quit it before ascertaining beyond reasonable doubt that the bones were those of animals—for, clearly, there had been more than one animal. What was disturbing about their discovery was not their being there, but the puzzling question of how they had got there.

But I did not at the time give this much thought. I was interested in pushing deeper into that tunnel, and I did so, going as far in the direction, I thought, of the seacoast, as I could before my passage was blocked by a fall of earth. When at last I left the tunnel it was late in the afternoon, and I was famished; but I was reasonably certain of two things—the tunnel was not a natural cave, at least at this end; it was clearly the work of human hands; and it had been used for some dark purpose, the nature of which I could not know.

Now for some reason, these discoveries filled me with excitement. Had I been fully in control of myself, I have no doubt that I would have realized that this in itself was unlike me, but at the moment I was faced and challenged with a mystery which seemed to me insistently of the greatest importance, and I was determined to discover all I could of this apparently hitherto unknown part of the Bishop property. This I could not very well do until another day, and in order to find my way through the cave, I would need implements I had not yet found on the property.

ANOTHER trip to Aylesbury was unavoidable. I went at once to the store of Obed Marsh and asked for a pick and shovels. For some reason, this request seemed to upset the old man beyond all reason. He paled and hesitated to wait on me.

"You aimin' to dig, Mr. Bares?"

I nodded.

" 'Taint none o' my business, but maybe you'd like to know that was what Seth took to doin' for a spell. Wore out three, four shovels, diggin'." He leaned forward, his intense eyes glittering. "And the queerest thing about it was nobody could find out where he was diggin'—never see a shovelful of dirt anywhere."

I was somewhat taken aback by this information, but I did not hesitate. "That soil there around the house looks rich and fertile," I said.

He seemed relieved. "Well, if you're aimin' to garden, that's a different thing."

One other purchase I made puzzled him. I needed a pair of rubber boots to shield my shoes from the muck and mud of many parts of the tunnel floor, where, doubtless, the nearness of the brook outside caused seepage. But Marsh said nothing about this. As I turned to go, he spoke again of Seth.

"Ain't heard tell anything more, have you, Mr. Bates?"

"People hereabouts don't talk much."

"They ain't all Marshes," he replied, with a furtive grin. "There's some that do say Seth was more Marsh than Bishop. The Bishops believed in hexes and such-like. But never the Marshes."

With this cryptic announcement ringing in my ears, I took my leave. Prepared now for the tunnel, I could hardly wait for the morrow to come, so that I could return once more to that subterranean place and carry on my explorations into a mystery which must certainly have been related to the entire legendry surrounding the Bishop family.

Events were now moving forward at an increasing tempo. That night two more occurrences were recorded.

The first came to my attention just past dawn, when I caught sight of Bud Perkins lurking about outside the house. I was needlessly annoyed, perhaps, since I was making ready to descend into the cellar; just the same, I wanted to know what he was after; so I opened the door and stepped out into the yard to confront him.

"What are you looking for, Bud?" I asked.

"Lost a sheep," he said laconically.

"I haven't seen it."

"It come this way," he answered.

"Well, you're welcome to look."

"Sure hate to think this's all settin' up to start again," he said.

"What do you mean?"

"If you don't know, 'twon't do any good to say. If you do, it's better I don't say a thing, anyway. So I'm not sayin'."

This mystifying conversation baffled me. At the same time, Bud Perkins' obvious suspicion that somehow his sheep had come to my hands was irritating. I stepped back and threw open the door.

"Look in the house if you like."

But, at this, his eyes opened wide in positive horror. "Me set foot in there?" he cried. "Not for my life," he added. "Why, I'm the only one's got gumption enough to come this close to this place. But I wouldn't step in there for all the money you could pay me. Not me."

"It's perfectly safe," I said, unable to conceal a smile at his fright.

"Maybe you think so. We know better. We know what's waitin' there behind them black walls, waitin' and waitin' for somebody to come. And now you've come. And now things are startin' up again, jest like before."

WITH that, he turned and ran, vanishing as on his previous visit into the woods. When I had satisfied myself that he was not coming back, I turned and re-entered the house. And there I made a discovery which ought to have been alarming, but which seemed to me then only vaguely unusual, since I must clearly have been in a lethargic state, not yet fully awake. The new boots I had bought only yesterday for my use had been used; they were caked with mud. Yet I knew indisputably that they had been clean and unused yesterday.

At sight of them, a growing conviction took form in my mind. Without putting on the boots, I descended into the cellar, opened the wall into the tunnel, and walked rapidly to the area of the barrier. Perhaps I had a premonitory certainty of what I would find, for I found it—the cave-in of earth had been dug partially away, sufficiently for a man to squeeze through. And the tracks in the wet earth were clearly made by the new boots I had bought, for the stamped trademark in the sole of those boots was plainly to be seen in the glow of my flashlight.

I was thus faced with one of two alternatives—either someone had used my boots in the night to effect this change in the tunnel, or I myself had walked in my sleep to bring it about. And I could not much doubt which it had been—for, despite my eagerness and anticipation, I was fatigued in a way which would have been accounted for only by my having spent a considerable portion of my sleeping hours digging away at this blockade in the passageway.

I cannot escape the conviction now that even then I knew what I should find when I pursued my way down that tunnel—the ancient altar-like structures in the subterranean caverns into which the tunnels opened, the evidence of further sacrifice—not alone animals this time, but undeniably human bones, and at the end, the vast cavern opening downward and the faint glimmering far below of waters, surging powerfully in and out through some opening far down, the Atlantic Ocean itself, beyond doubt, which had made its way to this place by means of subsurface caverns on the coast. And I must have had a premonition, too, of what else I should see there at the edge of that final descent into the aquatic abyss—the tufts of wool, the single hoof with its portion of torn and broken leg—all that remained of a sheep, fresh as the night just past!

I turned and fled, badly shaken, unwilling to guess how the sheep had got there—Bud Perkins' animal, I felt certain. And had it, too, been brought there for the same purpose as the creatures whose remains I had seen before those dark and broken altars in the lesser caverns between this place of constantly stirring waters and the house I had left not long ago?

I did not tarry in the house long, either, but made my way into Aylesbury once again, apparently aimlessly, but, as I know now, pressed by my need to know yet more of what legend and lore had accumulated about the Bishop house. But at Aylesbury I experienced for the first time the full force of public disapproval, for people on the street averted their eyes from me and turned their backs to me. One young man to whom I spoke hurried past me as if I had not spoken at all.

Even Obed Marsh had changed in his attitude. He was nothing loath to take my money, but was surly in his manner and obviously wished that I would leave his store as soon as possible. But here I made it clear I would not move until my questions had been answered.

What had I done, I wanted to know, that people should shun me as they did?

"It's that house," he said finally.

"I'm not the house," I retorted, dissatisfied.

"There's talk," he said then.

"Talk? What kind of talk?"

"About you and Bud Perkins' sheep. About the way things happened when Seth Bishop was alive," Then he leaned forward with a dark, beetling face, and whispered harshly, "There's them that say Seth's come back."

"Seth Bishop's dead and buried this long time."

He nodded. "Aye, part of him is. But part of him maybe ain't. I'll tell you, best thing in the world is for you to clear out now. You got time yet."

I reminded him coldly that I had leased the Bishop place and had paid the rent for at least four months, with an option to complete a year there. He clammed up at once and would say nothing further about my tenure. I pressed him, nevertheless, for details about Seth Bishop's life, but all he would or could tell me was clearly the summation of vague, uncertain hints and dark suspicions which had been common in the vicinity, so that I left him at last not with any picture of Seth Bishop as a man to be feared, but rather of him as a man to be pitied, kept at bay in his black-walled house in the valley like an animal by his neighbors on the ridge and the people of Aylesbury, who were at one in hating and fearing him, without any but the most circumstantial evidence that he had committed any crime against the safety or peace of the environs.

What, in fact, had Seth Bishop knowingly done—apart from the final crime of which he had been proved guilty? He had led a recluse's existence, abandoning even the strange garden of his ancestors, turning his back, certainly, on what was reputed to be his grandfather's and his father's sinister interest in wizardry and the lore of the occult, instead of which he had interested himself obsessively in a far more ancient lore which appeared to me to be fully as ridiculous as that of witchcraft. One might expect such interests not to falter in such isolated areas, and, in particular, among families as ingrown as the Bishop family was.

Perhaps somewhere in the old books of his forebears Seth had found certain obscure references which had sent him to the library at Miskatonic, where, in his consuming interest, he had undertaken the monumental task of copying great portions of books, which, presumably, he could not get permission to withdraw from the library.

This lore which was his primary concern was, in fact, a distortion of ancient Christian legend; reduced to its most simple terms, it was a record of the cosmic struggle between forces of good and forces of evil.

HOWEVER difficult it was to summarize, it would appear that the first inhabitants of outer space were great beings, not in human shape, who were called the Elder Gods and lived on Betelgeuse, at a remote time. Against these certain elemental Ancient Ones, also called the Great Old Ones, had rebelled—Azathoth, Yog-Sothoth, the amphibious Cthulhu, the bat-like Hastur the Unspeakable, Lloigor, Zhar, Ithaqua, the wind-walker, and the earth beings, Nyarlathotep and Shub-Niggurath; but, their rebellion failing, they were cast out and banished by the Elder Gods—locked away on far planets and stars under the seal of the Elder Gods—Cthulhu deep under the sea in the place known as R'lyeh, Hastur on a black star near Aldebaran in the Hyades, Ithaqua in the icy Arctic barrens, still others in a place known as Kadath in the Cold Waste, which existed in time and space conterminously with a portion of Asia.

Since this initial rebellion—which was basically in a legend pattern paralleling the rebellion of Satan and his followers against the arch-angels of Heaven—the Great Old Ones had continually sought to regain their power to war against the Elder Gods, and there have grown up on Earth and other planets certain cultists and followers—like the Abominable Snowmen, the Dholes, the Deep Ones, and many others, all dedicated to serve the Ancient Ones, and often succeeding in removing the Elder Seal to free the forces of ancient evil, which had then to be put down again either by direct intervention of the Elder Gods or by the alert watchfulness of human beings armed against them.

This was the sum total of what Seth Bishop had copied from very old and very rare books, much of it repetitive, and all surely the wildest kind of fantasy. True, there were certain disturbing newspaper clippings appended to the manuscript of what happened at Devil Reef off Innsmouth in 1928, of a supposed sea serpent in Rick's Lake, Wisconsin, of a terrible occurrence at nearby Dunwich, and another in the wild of Vermont, but these, beyond question, I felt to be coincidental accounts which happened to strike a parallel chord. And, while it was also true that there was as yet no explanation for the subterranean passage leading toward the coast, I felt comfortably certain that it was the work of some distant forebear of Seth Bishop's, and only appropriated for his own use at a considerably later date.

All that emerged from this was the portrait of an ignorant man striving to improve himself in the directions which appealed to him. Gullible and superstitious he may have been, and at the end, perhaps deranged—but evil, surely not.

CHAPTER THREE

IT WAS at about this time that I became aware of a most curious fancy.

It seemed to me that there was someone else in the house in the valley, an alien human being who had no business there, but intruded from outside. Though his occupation seemed to be to paint pictures, I was reasonably certain that he had come to spy. I caught only the most fugitive glimpses of him—on occasion a reflection in a mirror or in a windowpane when I was near, but I saw in the north room of the ground floor the evidence of his work—one unfinished canvas on his easel and several that had been completed.

I did not have the time to look for him, for the One below commanded me, and each night I descended with food, not for him, for he devoured what no mortal man knew, but for those of the deeps who accompanied him, and came swimming up out of that cavernous pit, and were to my eyes like a travesty born of men and batrachian things, with webbed hands and feet, and gilled, and wide, frog-like mouths, and great searing eyes made to see in the darkest recesses of the vast seas about the place where He lay sleeping, waiting to rise and come forth once more and take possession again of his kingdom, which was on Earth and in the space and time all about this planet, where once he had ruled above all others until the casting-down.

Perhaps this was the result of my coming upon the old diary, which now I settled down to read, as were it a book I had treasured since childhood. I found it by accident in the cellar, mildewed and showing the effects of having been long lost—a fortunate thing, for there were in it things no outsider should see.

The early pages were gone, having been torn out and burned in an access of fear, before any self-confidence had come. But all the others were still there, and plain to be read in their spidery script...

"Jun. 8. Went to the meeting-place at eight, dragging the calf from Mores.

Counted forty-two of the Deep Ones. Also one other, not of them, which was like an octopus, but was not. Remained there three hours."

That was the first entry I saw. Thereafter the entries were similar—of trips underground to the water pits, of meetings with the Deep Ones and occasionally other water beings. In September of that year, a catastrophe...

"Sept. 21. The pits crowded. Learned something terrible had happened at Devil Reef. One of the old fools at Innsmouth gave things away, and the Federal men came with submarines and boats to blast Devil Reef and the waterfront at Innsmouth. The Marsh crowd got away, most of them. Many Deep Ones killed. Depth charges did not reach R'lyeh where He lies dreaming...

"Sept. 22. More reports from Innsmouth. 371 Deep Ones killed. Many taken from Innsmouth, all those who were given away by the Marsh 'look'. One of them said what was left of the Marsh clan had fled to Ponape. Three of the Deep Ones here to-night from that place; they say they remember how old Captain Marsh came there, and what a compact he made with them, and how he took one of them and married her, and had children who were born of man and the Deep Ones, tainting the whole Marsh clan forever, and however since the Marsh ships fared well, and all their sea enterprises succeeded beyond their wildest dreams; they grew rich and powerful, the wealthiest of all the families at Innsmouth, to which they took their clan to live by day in the houses and by night, slipping away to be with the other Deep Ones off the reef. The Marsh houses in Innsmouth were burned. So the Federal men knew. But the Marshes will be back, say the Deep

Ones, and all will begin again toward that day when the Great Old One below the sea will rise once more.

"Sept. 23. Destruction terrible at Innsmouth.

"Sept. 24. It will be years before the Innsmouth places will be ready again. They will wait till the Marshes come back."

They might say what they liked of Seth Bishop. No fool, he. This was the record of a self-educated man. All that work at Miskatonic had not been in vain. He alone of all who lived in the Aylesbury region knew what lay hidden in the Atlantic depths off the coast; none other even suspected...

This was the direction of my thoughts, the preoccupation of my days at the Bishop house. I thought thusly. I lived so. And by night?

Once darkness had come to the house, I was more keenly aware than ever that something impended. But somehow memory rejects what must have happened. Could it be otherwise? I knew why that furniture had been moved out on the veranda—because the Deep Ones had begun to come back along the passage, had come up into the house. They were amphibious. They had literally crowded the furniture out and Seth had never taken it back.

EACH time I left the house to go any distance, I seemed to see it once again in its proper perspective, which was no longer possible while I occupied it. The attitude of my neighbors was now quite threatening. Not only Bud Perkins came to look at the house, but some of the Bowdens and the Mores, and certain others from Aylesbury. I let them all in, without comment—those who would come. Bud would not, nor would any of the Bowdens. But the others searched in vain for what they expected to find and did not.

And what was it they expected to find? Certainly not the cows, the chickens, the pigs and sheep they said had been taken. What use would I have for them? I showed them how frugally I lived, and they looked at the paintings. But one and all went away sullenly, shaking their heads, unconvinced.

Could I do more? I knew they shunned and hated me, and kept their distance from the house.

But they disturbed and troubled me, nevertheless. There were mornings when I woke near to noon, and woke exhausted, as if I had not slept at all. Most troubling of all, often I found myself dressed, whereas I knew I had gone to bed undressed, and I found blood spattered on my clothing and covering my hands.

I was afraid to go back into that subterranean passage by day, but I forced myself to do so one day, just the same. I went down with my flashlight, and I examined the floor of that tunnel with care. Wherever the earth was soft, I saw the marks of many feet, passing back and forth. Most of them were human footprints, but there were disquieting others—naked feet with blurred toes, as if they were webbed! I confess I turned the light away from them, shuddering.

What I saw at the edge of the water pits sent me fleeing back along the passage. Something had climbed out of those watery depths—the marks were plain to see and understand, and what had taken place there was not difficult to imagine, for all the evidence scattered there in the mute remains which lay gleaming whitely under the glow of my flashlight.

I knew it could not be long before the neighbors allowed their resentment to boil over. There was no peace capable of achievement in that house, nor, indeed, in the valley. Old hatreds, old enmities persisted, and thrived in that place. I soon lost all sense of time; I existed in another world, literally, for the house in the valley was surely the focal point for entry into another realm of being.

I DO not know how long I had been in the house—perhaps six weeks—perhaps two months—when one day the sheriff of the county, accompanied by two of his deputies, came grim-faced to the house with a warrant for my arrest. He explained that he did not wish to use the warrant, but that nevertheless, he wished to question me, and if I did not accompany him and his men willingly, he would have no alternative but to use the warrant, which, he confided, was based on a serious charge, the nature of which seemed to him grossly exaggerated and entirely unmotivated.

I went along willingly enough—all the way to Arkham, in which ancient, gambrel-roofed town I felt strangely at ease and completely unafraid of what was to come. The sheriff was an amiable man who had been driven to this deed, I had not the slightest doubt, by my neighbors. He was almost apologetic, now that I found myself seated opposite him in his office, with a stenographer to take down notes.

He began by wanting to know whether I had been away from the house night before I last.

"Not to my knowledge," I answered.

"You could hardly leave your house and not know it."

"If I walked in my sleep, I could."

"Are you in the habit of walking in your sleep?"

"I wasn't before coming here. Since then, I don't know."

He asked meaningless questions, always skirting the central point of his mission. But this emerged presently. A human being had been seen in charge of a company of some kind of animals, leading the pack to an attack on a herd of cattle in night pasture. All but two of the cattle had been literally torn to pieces. The cattle had belonged to young Sereno More, and it was he who had made the charge against me, an act in which he was abetted by Bud Perkins, who was even more insistent than Sereno.

Now that he had put the charge into words, it seemed more ridiculous than ever. He himself apparently felt so, for he became more than ever apologetic. I myself could hardly forbear laughing. What motive could I have for so mad an act? And what "animals" could I have led? I owned none, not even a dog or cat.

Nevertheless, the sheriff was politely persistent. How had I come by the scratches visible on my arms?

I seemed to be aware of them for the first time and gazed at them thoughtfully.

Had I been picking berries?

I had, and said so. But I added also that I could not recall having been scratched.

The sheriff seemed relieved at this. He confided that the scene of the attack on the cattle was bordered on one side by a hedge of blackberry bushes, the coincidence of my bearing scratches was bound to be noticed, and he could not ignore it. Nevertheless, he appeared to be satisfied, and, being satisfied that I was no more than I pretended to be, he became somewhat more loquacious;

thus I learned that once before a similar event had occurred, with the charge that time being leveled at Seth Bishop, but, like this, it had come to nothing, the Bishop house had been searched, nothing had been found, and the attack was so baseless and unmotivated that no one could be brought to trial on the suspicions, however dark, of the neighbors.

I assured him that I was perfectly willing that my house be searched, and he grinned at this, and told me in all friendliness that it had been searched from roof to cellar while I was in his company, and once again nothing had been found.

Yet, when I returned to the house in the valley, I was uneasy and troubled. I tried to keep awake and wait upon events, but this was not to be. I fell asleep, not in the bedroom, but in the storeroom, poring over that strange and terrible book in Seth Bishop's hand.

That night I dreamed again, for the first time since my initial dream.

And once again, I dreamed of a vast, amorphous being, which rose out of the water pit in the cavern beyond the passage under the house; but this time it was no misty emanation, this time it was horribly, shockingly real, built of flesh that seemed to have been created out of ancient rock, a vast mountain of matter surmounted by a neckless head, from the lower edges of which great tentacles writhed and curled, reaching out to singular lengths; this came rising out of the waters, while all around it flowed the Deep Ones in an ecstasy of adoration and subservience, and once again, as before, the weirdly beautiful music which had accompanied it rose, and a thousand batrachian throats called harshly *"Ia! Ia! Cthulhu fhtagn!"* in accents of worship.

And once again came the sound of great footfalls below the house, in the bowels of the earth…

At this juncture I woke, and to my terror, heard still the subterranean footfalls, and felt the shuddering of the house and the earth in the valley, and heard distantly the incredible music fading away into the depths below the house. In my terror, I ran and burst from the house, running blindly to get away, only to face into still another danger.

Bud Perkins stood there, his rifle aimed at *me.*

"Where you think you're goin'?" he demanded.

I stopped running, not knowing what to say. Behind me, the house was silent.

"Nowhere," I said finally. Then, my curiosity overcoming my dislike of this gaunt neighbor, I asked. "Did you hear anything, Bud?"

"We all been hearin' it, night after night. Now we're guardin' our stock. You might as well know it. We don't aim to shoot, but if we have to, we'll do it."

"It's not my doing," I said.

"Tain't nobody else's," he answered laconically.

I could feel his animosity.

"That's the way it was when Seth Bishop was here. We ain't sure he's not still here."

I felt a curious coldness come over me at his words, and at that instant, the house behind me, for all its looming terrors, seemed more inviting than the darkness outside, where Bud and his neighbors stood vigil with weapons as lethal as anything I might find within those black walls. Perhaps Seth Bishop, too, had met this kind of hatred; perhaps the furniture had never been moved back into the house because it made a barrier against bullets.

I turned and went back into the house without a further word.

Inside, all was now quiet. There was not a sound anywhere. I had previously thought it somewhat unusual that not a sign of mouse or rat had existed in the abandoned house, knowing how quickly these small animals take over a house; now I would have welcomed the sound of their scampering to and fro or gnawing. But there was nothing, only a deathly, pregnant stillness, as if the house itself knew it was ringed around with grim, determined men armed against a horror they could not know.

It was late when at last I slept that night.

CHAPTER FOUR

MY SENSE of time was not effective in those weeks, as I have already set down. If my memory now serves me rightly, there was a lull of almost a month after that night. I discovered that, gradually, the guards had been withdrawn; only Bud Perkins remained, and he stayed grimly night after night.

It must have been at least five weeks later when I woke from sleep one night and found myself in the passage below the house, walking toward the cellar, away from the yawning chasm at the far end. What had awakened me was a sound to which I was unaccustomed—a screaming which could have come only from a human voice, far behind me. I listened in cold horror, and yet somewhat lethargically, while the screams of fright rose and fell, and were cut off terribly at last. Then I stood for a long time in that place, unable to move forward or back, waiting for a resumption of that frightening sound. But it did not come again, and at last I made my way back to my room and fell exhausted on my bed.

I woke that next morning with a premonition of what was to come.

And in mid-morning, it came. A sullen, hateful mob of men and women, most of them armed. Fortunately, they were in charge of a deputy-sheriff, who kept them in a semblance of order. Though they had no search warrant, they demanded the right to search the house. In the face of their mood, it would have been folly to deny them; so I made no attempt to do so. I stepped outside and left the door stand open for them. They surged into the house, and I could hear them going through room after room, upstairs and down, moving and throwing things about. I made no protest, for I was stoutly guarded by three men, one of whom was Obed Marsh, the storekeeper from Aylesbury.

It was to him I finally addressed myself in as calm a voice as I could muster, "May I ask what this is all about?"

"You sayin' you don't know?" he asked scornfully.

"I don't."

"Jared More's boy disappeared last night. Walkin' home from a school party up the road a piece. He had to come by here."

There was nothing I could say. It was patent that they believed the boy had vanished into this house. However much I wanted to protest, I could not rid my thoughts of the memory of that terrible screaming I had heard in the tunnel. I did not know who had screamed, and I knew now that I did not want to learn. I felt reasonably sure that they would not find the entrance to the tunnel, for it was artfully concealed behind shelving in that small cellar space, but from that moment forward I stood in an agony of suspense, for I had little doubt about what would happen to me if by some chance anything belonging to the missing boy should be found on the premises.

But again a merciful Providence intervened to prevent any discovery—if there were one to be made; I dared to hope that my own fears were groundless. In truth, I did not know, but horrible doubts were now beginning to assail me. How came I in the tunnel? And whence? When I had awakened, I had been on the way back from the water's edge. What had I done there? And *had I left anything behind?*

By twos and threes, the mob came out of the house again, empty-handed. They were no less sullen, no less angry—but they were somewhat dubious and bewildered. If they had expected to find anything, they were sharply disappointed. If the missing boy had not been taken to the Bishop house they could not imagine where he might have gone.

Urged by the deputy-sheriff, who had given them their way, they now drew back from the house and began to disperse all but Bud Perkins and a handful of equally grim men, who remained on guard.

Then for days I was aware of the oppressive hatred which was directed toward the Bishop house and its lone occupant.

Thereafter came an interval of comparative quiet.

And then that final catastrophic night!

IT BEGAN with faint intimations of something stirring below. I suppose I was subconsciously aware of movement even before I was conscious of it. At the time I was reading in that hellish manuscript book of Seth Bishop's—a page devoted to the minions of Great Cthulhu, the Deep Ones who devoured sacrifice of warm-blooded animals, being themselves coldblooded, and waxing fat and strong on what would seem a kind of pagan cannibalism; I was reading this, I say, when without warning I became conscious of the stirrings below, as if the very earth were becoming animated, trembling faintly, rhythmically, and there began immediately thereafter a faint far-away music, exactly similar to that which I had heard in my first dream in that house, rising from instruments unknown to human hands, but resembling a fluting or piping sound heard in chorus, and accompanied once more by an occasional ululation which came from the throat of some living entity.

I cannot adequately describe the effect that this had on me. At the moment, engrossed as I was in an account clearly related to the events of the past weeks, I was, as it were, conditioned to such an occurrence, but my state of mind was one of nothing short of exaltation, and I was filled with a compelling urgency to rise and serve Him who lay dreaming far below. Almost as in a dream, I put out the light in the storeroom, and slipped out in darkness, possessed by caution against the enemies who waited beyond the walls.

As yet, the music was too faint to be heard outside the house. I had no way of knowing how long it would remain so faint; so I made haste to do that which was expected of me before the enemy could be warned that the dwellers in the watery chasm below were once again rising toward the house in the valley. But it was not to the cellar that I moved. As if by pre-ordained plan, I slipped out the back door of the house and made my way stealthily in the darkness to the protecting shrubbery and trees.

There I began to make slow but steady progress forward. Somewhere up ahead Bud Perkins stood on guard...

OF WHAT happened after that, I cannot be sure. The rest was nightmare, certainly. Before I reached Bud Perkins, two shots rang out. That was his signal to the others to come. I was less than a foot away from him in the darkness, and his shots startled me out of my wits. He, too, had heard the sounds from below, for now I could hear them outside in this darkness as well.

So much I remember with reasonable clarity.

It was what happened after that that baffles me even now. Certainly the mob came, and if the men from the sheriff's office had not been waiting, too, I would not now be alive to make this deposition. I remember the screaming, furious mob; I remember that they set fire to the house. I had been back there. I had run out, escaping the flames. From where I looked back, I saw not only the flames, but that other sight—those shrilly crying Deep

Ones, falling victim to flame and terror, and at the last that gigantic being which reared up out of the flames flailing its tentacles, before it dropped defiantly back down, compacting into a great sinuous column of flesh, and vanished without trace! It was then that someone in the mob threw dynamite into the flaming house. But even before the echo of the blast had died away, I heard, as did all the others encircling all that remained of the Bishop house, that chanting voice which cried, *'Ph'nglui mglw'nafh Cthulhu R'lyeh wgah'nagl fhtagn!'*—announcing to all the world that Great Cthulhu still lay dreaming in his subaqueous haven of R'lyeh!

They said of me that I was crouched beside the torn remains of Bud Perkins, and they intimated hideous things. Yet they must have seen, even as I saw, what writhed in that flaming ruin, though they deny that there was anything at all there but myself. What they say I was doing is too horrible to repeat. It is the fiction of their diseased, hate-filled brains, for surely they cannot deny the evidence of their own senses. They witnessed against me in court, and sealed my doom.

Surely they must understand that it was not I who did all the things they say I did! Surely they must know that it was the life-force of Seth Bishop, which invaded and took possession of me, which again restored that unholy link to those creatures of the deep, bringing them their food, as in the days when Seth Bishop had an existence in the body of his own and served them, even as the Deep Ones and those countless others scattered over the face of the earth. Seth Bishop who did what they say I did to Perkins' sheep and Jared More's boy and all those missing animals and finally to Bud Perkins himself, for all that he made them believe it was I, for I could not have done such things, it was Seth Bishop come back from hell to serve again those hideous beings who came to his watery pit from the depths of the sea. Seth Bishop, who had discovered their existence and summoned them to do his bidding and who lived to serve them in his own time and in mine and who may still lurk deep in earth below that place where the house stood in the valley, waiting for another vessel to inhabit and so serve them in time to come, forever.

THE END

FATHER'S VAMPIRE

By Len J. Moffatt

Father collected things—but he wasn't at all in a rut as to what he collected.

FATHER is a little mad, of course, and someday I suppose I will have to have *him* put away too. He is quite harmless right now, however, and as long as I'm around to keep an eye on him he shouldn't cause anyone any real trouble.

Father collects things. Even when we were poor as church-mice and Father was earning a meager living for Mother and me by digging wells, cesspools and graves around the town...yes, even when we were on relief during the depression years Father collected things.

One thing about Father, though. He wasn't in a rut like many collectors are. He didn't specialize in any one thing. He would bring home odds and ends, old books, torn halves of magazines, bits of string and rope, used ice cream sticks, pieces of metal from worn-out machines and so on.

And, of course, after we became fabulously wealthy there seemed to be no end to Father's collecting. We became wealthy when Uncle Henry died. Uncle Henry was Father's brother who struck it rich in Texas or some such God-forsaken place and for some reason or other (we were never on very friendly terms with Uncle Henry) he willed us his vast fortune. It was a little disconcerting because we weren't used to having all that money and we didn't quite know what to do with it. It was then that Father went a little mad.

Oh, he was practical enough at first. We had the old house done over and he bought Mother a pretty new cotton dress and gave me a ten-dollar bill to do with just whatever I pleased. I gave some of it to Mother to buy groceries with and am afraid I spent the rest of it rather foolishly on a girl.

Then Aunt Mabel came to live with us. She was Uncle Henry's widow. The lawyer who came with her (he didn't stay very long although Mother was polite enough when she invited him to stay for supper) said we had inherited the money all right but there was a provision in the will which said we must look after Aunt Mabel until she died if we wanted to *keep* the money.

Mother said, "I knew there was a catch to it, but of course, Mabel is welcome here anytime."

Father said, "I always did dislike you less than I did Henry, Mabel." He gave me a look which meant I was supposed to say something nice to Aunt Mabel so I told her she could have one of my pet rats. Not the pregnant one, however, as I wanted the little rats from it to use in my home laboratory experiments.

Aunt Mabel didn't seem too happy with us at first but I think she got used to our dull, normal way of living after a while. I suppose she was used to a more adventurous life in Texas and just didn't feel at home with us right away. Anyway she didn't have to live with us very long because we found her dead in bed one morning.

Father sent for a doctor right away. As I said he can be practical when he wants to be and he knew a doctor would have to pronounce her dead, make out a certificate, and so on. The doctor called in the constable and some other authorities because he said Aunt Mabel had been murdered.

This made Mother hysterical. She began to scream that she didn't do it and no one could prove she did it. But the constable claimed that the tiny pricks in Aunt Mabel's throat were caused by Mother's hatpin and the doctor said there was hardly a drop of blood in Aunt Mabel's body.

They were a little put out though because there was no blood in the bedclothes or anywhere in the room. They searched the entire house and grounds, but they couldn't find Aunt Mabel's blood anywhere.

So Father signed the papers and had Mother put away in the asylum just up the road from here. We buried Aunt Mabel in the old churchyard. We asked Reverend Worthy in to say a few words over her as Aunt Mabel had been a religious woman, always quoting the Bible or a bit now and then from the Decameron of Boccaccio.

IT WAS several days after the funeral when Father called me into his study and gave me his best chair to sit in. He perched his lanky frame on the edge of a table and smiled knowingly. I smiled knowingly back at him. I know how to humor Father.

"Being a bright and intelligent young man you no doubt have some idea concerning what I am about to reveal," said Father. I kept on smiling.

"Of course," he said. "Your own Father's son. Well you realize then that it wasn't your Mother who killed poor dear Mabel."

"Oh?" I said quietly.

"Of course not," said Father. "It was the vampire I am keeping in the cellar. I couldn't very well tell the authorities I had collected a vampire, coffin and all, now could I? Your mother knew about it, naturally. It was always hard to keep secrets from her. But then that is the way it is with people who are a little—er—demented? I'm afraid the strain of Mabel's demise was just too much for your poor Mother, so it is just as well that she is where she is and that things have turned out so nicely without me having to give up my vampire."

I was fascinated. Vampires have always fascinated me. I couldn't control my eagerness as I questioned Father.

"What does it look like? Is it in the form of a man or woman or what? Is it thin or fat? Does…"

Father raised a thin hand to ward off my questions.

"Please, son," he smiled. "One thing at a time. I really couldn't tell you about the nature of the vampire as I haven't seen it yet."

"You haven't? Then how do you know it killed Aunt Mabel?"

"The markings on her throat and the fact that we could not find the blood she obviously lost," said Father, impatiently. "Why it was so obvious that I was sorely afraid the authorities would suspect the presence of a vampire. They did not, however, or perhaps they assumed that your mother had gotten rid of the blood in some other way or drunk it herself. Authorities being what they are—politicians—are generally a stupid lot. Clever at times, but always stupid."

"If you really have a vampire, Father, I want to see it. I must see it!"

"Whatever for? They are dangerous, you know. I just collected this one for the curiosity of having one about. Besides it doesn't seem to get out of its coffin, lazy fellow that it is. Except for its escapade with Mabel. It is probably a very old vampire who prefers to sleep most of the time and needs little nourishment. Just as well though, as I considered inviting tramps and other such riff-raff in to supper now and then so it would not starve and thus not give us any trouble. One must be practical, you know."

"Of course," I agreed. "But I really do want to see it and talk with it. I have always wanted to interview a vampire. I could write it up for the local paper and then maybe Editor Stanley would put me on his staff."

"Why on earth do you want to write for that two-bit rag?" said Father, frowning. "And if you did write such an interview you would have to present it as fiction and use a pseudonym. I don't want notoriety, you know. I want to be alone with my collection."

Father was beginning to weep. I handed him my handkerchief and tried to change the subject. One of Father's pet peeves is the town's weekly paper which stirred up such a fuss when we inherited the money. Such inaccurate reporting! If Stanley had let me write it up as I wanted to and offered to but...

"Look, Father," I said. "Please let me visit the vampire. I'll be very polite and I'll write the interview for some other publication. One of the 'little magazines', perhaps. They don't pay much but they are awfully literary. Lord knows we don't need the money."

"Well," said Father, managing a weak smile. "I guess it will be all right. I doubt if you will get to see it, though. I admit I was a little curious when the coffin arrived. I even tapped on the box and asked it to come out but nothing happened at all. I tried to lift the lid but it is evidently locked or bolted from the inside. Very clever vampire. The coffin is made of wood which must be six inches thick. I thought once of prying it open, forcing the lock or bolt or whatever it is but I was afraid of ruining the coffin itself. It's a wonderful piece of woodcarving. I know there is a vampire in there all right because I have the papers that go with the box—a kind of written guarantee. And then, of course, there was Mabel..."

I waited impatiently for Father to dismiss me. He had given his permission and there was nothing on earth I wanted more to see than a real undead vampire. I thought of all the questions I could ask and of other things, too, for I must admit I have peeked into some of Father's old books when he wasn't around...

Finally Father let me go with a parting warning to be very careful, and above all, to be polite. I thanked him heartily and left him playing with his collection of hand-painted cockroaches. He painted them himself—all the colors of the rainbow. Father really has the soul of an artist.

*   *   *

AS I DESCENDED the cellar steps I thought I heard a bumping noise but wasn't sure where it was corning from. I was carrying a flashlight, my notebook and ballpoint pen and two cold cans of beer. I had thought of wearing some garlic or a crucifix but decided that wouldn't be very polite, though it struck me as humorous at the time. I knew the vampire wouldn't hurt me any. I have made a study of vampires and although I hate to appear immodest I believe I probably know more about them than any other being in the world. Even more than Father because I know he hasn't read all of his books.

The coffin was indeed beautiful, obviously hand-carved. It was covered with engravings depicting all sorts of fascinating rites as well as scenes from the private lives of famous beauties of history. There were also some very patriotic scenes showing the battle of Bunker Hill, the Spanish-American War and so on with a likeness of George Washington in bas-relief smiling down upon it all.

I knocked quietly on the coffin lid. There was a noise inside.

"Maybe just an echo," I thought, but I knocked again—harder.

"Oh, go away and let me sleep!" said a voice from inside the coffin.

"You're there!" I shouted with joy. "You're really there! A real true vampire at last! Please come out and talk to me."

"Why should I?" muttered the voice, definitely masculine.

I decided to fib a bit. It seemed the only way to get it out of its coffin.

"I've heard a lot about you, Mr. Vampire. I understand you have lived a fascinating life and that when you died your life after death—if I may call it that—was even more fabulous. But I would like to hear the details from your own lips. I'm sure you are a genius at storytelling and can thrill me with tales of the places you have been, the women you have known, the people you have dined with and dined on…"

I could hear it moving about inside its coffin.

"Naturally," came the voice. "But why do you want to know?"

"I have always been fond of vampires and vampire stories," I replied promptly. "But most of the stories were silly fiction and I want to hear the truth from a real vampire. I want my facts from an authority. In short, I want to interview you. I can promise you a very nice write-up in all of the Sunday papers. If you wish, I'll use a pseudonym and will not reveal your location so no one will come around and bother you…"

I heard a clicking sound inside the coffin and then the lid rose up. The vampire, in the form of a fat, healthy-looking man, climbed out, stretched and yawned.

"So you want the story of my life and undeath," it grinned, showing white, pointed teeth. "Aren't you afraid I'll attack you?"

"Why should I be afraid?" I smiled, ever so innocently. "You belong to my father and besides you have recently dined on Aunt Mabel who must have had enough blood to satisfy you for weeks to come."

"Perhaps," said the vampire, sitting down on the coffin's edge beside me. "You look like an interesting morsel though…"

"Oh, skip that nonsense," I said. "Let's get to your history. Now, first give me the basic facts, statistics, you know. Birth date. Where born? And so on up to time of death, cause of same and the like. You just talk away and I'll take it down in shorthand…"

"Very well," it said, trying to keep its eyes away from my neck. They were rather nice blue eyes, though. "I was born on April 9, 1652…"

It began to give a very boring account of its life in a small Hungarian village going into some detail regarding its various conquests of girls and the amount of wine it could consume in one evening. But I patiently took it all down. While it talked it kept gazing at me as though hypnotized and when it began to drool I moved away a little.

It must have noticed my moving for it immediately stopped talking and edged closer to me.

"Do not sit so far away," it whispered, placing a cold hand on my shoulder.

"Please continue your story," I said as quietly as possible.

"Another time," murmured the vampire. "You can best enjoy it when you become one of us. Your poor aunt is having the devil's own time trying to get out of that churchyard, but perhaps you will be more fortunate. In fact, I will take the trouble to instruct your father to let your coffin rest here with mine. We can be death-long companions. But first you must let me…"

His face was close to mine now and I could feel his cold breath on my throat. This wouldn't have been so bad but he had a bad case of halitosis. I stood up and stepped away from him, fingering the flashlight and letting the notebook and pen drop to the floor. It arose and moved towards me.

"The light will not help you," it smiled. "It won't hurt much, really. Just a little nip, a little pressure and you will be dead, and I will be fed. Then you will evolve into undeadness and join me forever…"

"Not interested, really," I said, insistently enough.

"But why not? You said you have always been fascinated by vampires. Why not become one? It is so easy and so much fun after all…"

"I am not going to be a vampire," I told it firmly. "I have a definite interest in them but I would never think of being one, believe me. I'm happy the way I am."

"Please do not be difficult," said the vampire. It was close to me now and I could feel the wall behind me. Somehow it had got between me and the stairs. "If I want to I can force you into submission. I am stronger than a mere mortal man, you know."

I smiled right into its leering face.

"You may as welt know," I said. "It is impossible for me to become a vampire. The most powerful vampire in existence cannot harm me. I know."

The vampire began to look a little unsure of itself. But it managed a grin combined with a sneer.

"And why can't you become a vampire? All I have to do is attack you, drink your blood..."

"You just can't do it," I said. "Perhaps you're not as bright as I thought. But surely all vampires know about *druds* and have learned to fear them."

The vampire shuddered.

"Druds! There are no *druds* here. *Druds* are rare; perhaps one is born every few centuries, but...

"I'm a drud," I said. "I found out by reading one of Father's old books. Even Father doesn't know about me or about *druds*, for that matter, as he doesn't read half the stuff he collects. I might never have known if I hadn't read that book. Or perhaps I would have learned about myself naturally once I met you or some other vampire. I know I have often felt the hunger, the thirst but I always tried to satisfy it with a sandwich or a glass of beer. I assumed it was an unusual hunger but I hate to bother with doctors and as I appeared to be quite healthy otherwise..."

THE vampire was leering again. "You are not a *drud,"* it said. "You may have read about the accursed creatures in some old book but you couldn't be a *drud*. A *drud* is a vampire's vampire. It drinks the blood of vampires after the vampire has dined on some mortal being. *Druds* have the disgusting taste for distilled blood...the blood of my kind after we have taken it from some human. But you are not a *drud* and now I shall have your life!"

I ducked just in time to avoid its grabbing arms and clicking teeth.

"I am too a *drud!"* I shouted. "What makes you think I'm not? You better look out or *I'll* have *your* blood. I'm awfully thirsty, you know. I didn't come down here just to get a story from you. That was just to get you out of your coffin so I could get at you!"

"You cannot be a *drud,"* grinned the vampire, closing in again. "You have eyebrows. *Druds* do not have eyebrows!"

"Of course, they haven't," I said, reaching up and pulling off the fake eyebrows I had been wearing. I advanced on the vampire.

It screamed horribly, I'm sure, and ran from me to its coffin. I raced madly after it but stumbled over an empty beer can. By the time I got to my feet the vampire was in its coffin and I could hear the lock clicking on the inside.

"You can't reach me now!" it cried. "You'll never get me! I'll stay here forever! You can't reach me now!"

I hammered heavily on the coffin lid and could hear it weeping hysterically inside. Finally, I picked up my notes and pen and found my way to the stairs. As I climbed up into the house I smiled and thought that I really hadn't gotten much of a story for all my trouble. Shaving off my eyebrows had been a nuisance but, oh well, they will grow back in a little while.

Father is peeved at me for frightening the vampire so that it won't come out of its coffin, but he'll get over it eventually. Of course, we'll have to find some other use for the hobo Father invited in to supper tonight.

THE END

THE OTHER WING

By Algernon Blackwood

One of the almost legendary figures among ghost story writers, Algernon Blackwood is justly famous for his oft-reprinted classics, "The Willows," and "The Wendigo." But here is a remarkable tale not often seen in print. "The Other Wing" is a strange, haunting tale of an imaginative child in a huge, lonesome mansion.

CHAPTER ONE

It used to puzzle him that, after dark, someone *would* look in around the edge of the bedroom door, and withdraw again too rapidly for him to see the face. When the nurse had gone away with the candle this happened: "Good night, Master Tim," she said usually, shading the light with one hand to protect his eyes; "dream of me and I'll dream of you." She went out—slowly. The sharp-edged shadow of the door ran across the ceiling like a train. There came a whispered colloquy in the corridor outside, about himself, of course, and—he was alone. He heard her steps going deeper and deeper into the bosom of the old country house; they were audible for a moment on the stone flooring of the hall; and sometimes the dull thump of the baize door into the servants' quarters just reached him, too—then silence. But it was only when the last sound, as well as the last sign of her had vanished, that the face emerged from its hiding-place and, flashed in upon him round the corner. As a rule, too, it came just as he was saying, "Now I'll go to sleep. I won't think any longer. Good night, Master Tim, and happy dreams." He loved to say this to himself; it brought a sense of companionship, as though there were two persons speaking.

The room was on the top of the old house, a big, high-ceilinged room, and his bed against the wall had an iron railing round it; he felt very safe and protected in it. The curtains at the other end of the room were drawn. He lay watching the firelight dancing on the heavy folds, and their pattern, showing a spaniel chasing a long-tailed bird towards a bushy tree, interested and amused him. It was repeated over and over again. He counted the number of dogs, and the number of birds, and the number of trees, but could never make them agree. There was a plan somewhere in that pattern; if only he could discover it, the dogs and birds and trees would "come out right." Hundreds and hundreds of times he hid played this game, for the plan in the pattern made it possible to take sides, and the bird and dog were against him. They always won, however; Tim usually fell asleep just when the advantage was on his own side. The curtains hung steadily enough most of the time, but it seemed to him once or twice that they stirred—hiding a dog or bird on purpose to prevent his winning. For instance, he had eleven birds and eleven trees, and, fixing them in his mind by saying, "that's eleven birds and eleven trees, but only ten dogs," his eyes darted back to find the eleventh dog, when—the curtain moved and threw all his calculations into confusion again. The eleventh dog was hidden. He did not quite like the movement; it gave him questionable feelings, rather, for the curtain did not move of itself. Yet, usually, he was too intent upon counting the dogs to feel positive alarm.

Opposite to him was the fireplace, full of red and yellow coals; and, lying with his head sideways on the pillow, he could see directly in between the bars. When the coals settled with a soft and powdery crash, he turned his eyes from the curtains to the grate, trying to discover exactly which bits had fallen. So long as the glow was there the sound seemed pleasant enough, but sometimes he awoke later in the night, the room huge with darkness, the fire almost out—and the sound was not so pleasant then. It startled him. The coals did not fall of themselves. It seemed that someone poked them cautiously. The shadows were very thick before the bars. As with the curtains, moreover, the morning aspect of the extinguished fire, the ice-cold cinders that made a clinking sound like tin, caused no emotion whatever in his soul.

And it was usually while he lay waiting for sleep, tired both of the curtain and the coal games, on the point, indeed, of saying, "I'll go to sleep now," that the puzzling thing took place. He would be staring drowsily at the dying fire, perhaps counting the stockings and flannel garments that hung along the high fender-rail when, suddenly, a person looked in with lightning swiftness through the door and vanished again before he could possibly turn his head to see. The appearance and disappearance were accomplished with amazing rapidity always.

It was a head and shoulders that looked in, and the movement combined the speed, the lightness and the silence of a shadow. Only it was not a shadow. A hand held the edge of the door. The face shot round, saw him, and withdrew like lightning. It was utterly beyond him to imagine anything more quick and clever. It darted. He heard no sound. It went. But—it had seen him, looked him all over, examined him, noted what he was doing with that lightning glance. It wanted to know if he were awake still, or asleep. And though it went off, it still watched him from a distance; it waited somewhere; it knew all about him. *Where* it waited no one could ever guess. It came probably, he felt, from beyond the house, possibly from the roof, but most likely from the garden or the sky. Yet, though strange, it was not terrible. It was a kindly and protective figure, he felt. And when it happened he never called for help, because the occurrence simply took his voice away.

"It comes from the Nightmare Passage," he decided; "but it's *not* a nightmare." It puzzled him.

Sometimes, moreover, it came more than once in a single night. He was pretty sure—not *quite* positive—that it occupied his room as soon as he was properly asleep. It took possession, sitting perhaps before the dying fire, standing upright behind the heavy curtains, or even lying down in the empty bed his brother used when he was home from school. Perhaps it played the curtain game, perhaps it poked the coals; it knew, at any rate, where the eleventh dog had lain concealed. It certainly came in and out; certainly, too, it did not wish to be seen. For, more than once, on waking suddenly in the midnight blackness, Tim knew it was standing close beside his bed and bending over him. He felt, rather than heard, its presence. It glided quietly away. It moved with marvelous softness, yet he was positive it moved. He felt the difference, so to speak. It had been near, him, now it was gone. It came back, too—just as he was falling into sleep again. Its midnight coming and going, however, stood out sharply different from its first shy, tentative approach. For in the firelight it came alone; whereas in the black and silent hours, it had with it—others.

And it was then he made up his mind that its swift and quiet movements were due to the fact that it had wings. It flew. And the others that came with it in the darkness were "its little ones." He also made up his mind that all were friendly, comforting, protective, and that while positively *not* a Nightmare, it yet came somehow along the Nightmare Passage before it reached him. "You see, it's like this," he explained to the nurse, "the big one comes to visit me alone, but it only brings its little ones when I'm *quite* asleep."

"Then the quicker you get to sleep the better, isn't it, Master Tim?"

He replied, "Rather! I always do. Only I wonder where they come *from!*" He spoke, however, as though he had an inkling.

But the nurse was so dull about it that he gave her up and tried his father. "Of course," replied this busy but affectionate parent, "it's either nobody at all, or else it's Sleep coming to carry you away to the land of dreams." He made the statement kindly but somewhat briskly, for he was worried just then about the extra taxes on his land, and the effort to fix his mind on Tim's fanciful world was beyond him at the moment. He lifted the boy on to his knee, kissed and patted him as though he were a favorite dog, and planted him on the rug again with a flying sweep. "Run and ask your mother," he added; "she knows all that kind of thing. Then come back and tell me all about it—another time."

Tim found his mother in an armchair before the fire of another room; she was knitting and reading at the same time—a wonderful thing the boy could never understand. She raised her head as he came in, pushed her glasses onto her forehead, and held her arms out. He told her everything, ending up with what his father said.

"You see, it's *not* Jackman, or Thompson, or anyone like that," he exclaimed. "It's someone real."

"But nice," she assured him, "someone who comes to take care of you and see that you're all safe and cozy."

"Oh, yes, I know that. But—"

"I think your father's right," she added quickly. "It's Sleep, I'm sure, who pops in round the door like that. Sleep *has* got wings, I've always heard."

"Then the other thing—the little ones?" he asked. "Are they just sorts of dozes, you think?"

Mother did not answer for a moment. She turned down the page of her book, closed it slowly, put it on the table beside her. More slowly still she put her knitting away, arranging the wool and needles with some deliberation.

"Perhaps," she said, drawing the boy closer to her and looking into his big eyes of wonder, "they're dreams!"

Tim felt a thrill run through him as she said it. He stepped back a foot or so and clapped his hands softly. "Dreams!" he whispered with enthusiasm and belief; "of course! I never thought of that."

His mother, having proved her sagacity, then made a mistake. She noted her success, but instead of leaving it there, she elaborated and explained. As Tim expressed it she "went on about it." Therefore he did not listen. He followed his train of thought alone. And presently, he interrupted her long sentences with a conclusion of his own:

"Then I know where She hides," he announced with a touch of awe. "Where She lives, I mean." And without waiting to be asked, he imparted the information: "It's in the Other Wing."

"Ah!" said his mother, taken by surprise. "How clever of you, Tim!"—and thus confirmed it.

Thenceforward this was established in his life—that Sleep and her attendant Dreams hid during the daytime in that unused portion of the great Elizabethan mansion called the Other Wing. This other wing was unoccupied, its corridors untrodden its windows shuttered and its rooms all closed. At various places green bare doors led into it, but no one ever opened them. For many years this part had been shut up; and for the children, properly speaking, it was out of bounds. They never mentioned it as a possible place, at any rate; in hide-and-seek it was not considered, even; there was a hint of the inaccessible about the Other Wing. Shadows, dust, and silence had it to themselves.

But Tim, having ideas of his own about everything, possessed special information about the Other Wing. He believed it *was* inhabited. Who occupied the immense series of empty rooms, who trod the spacious corridors, who passed to and fro behind the shuttered windows, he had not known exactly. He had called these occupants "they," and the most important among them was "The Ruler." The Ruler of the Other Wing was a kind of deity, powerful, far away, ever present yet never seen.

And about this Ruler he had a wonderful conception for a little boy; he connected her, somehow, with deep thoughts of his own, the deepest of all. When he made up adventures to the moon, to the stars, to the bottom of the sea, adventures that he lived inside himself, as it were—to reach them he must invariably pass through the chambers of the Other Wing. Those corridors and halls, the Nightmare Passage among them, lay along the route; they were the first stage of the journey. Once the green baize doors swung to behind him and the long dim passage stretched ahead, he was well on his way into the adventure of the moment; the Nightmare Passage once passed, he was safe from capture; but once the shutters of a window had been flung open, he was free of the gigantic world that lay beyond. For then light poured in and he could see his way.

The conception, for a child, was curious. It established a correspondence between the mysterious chambers of the Other Wing and the occupied, but unguessed chambers of his Inner Being. Through these chambers, through these darkened corridors, along a passage, sometimes dangerous, or at least of questionable repute, he must pass to find all adventures that were *real*. The light—when he pierced far enough to take the shutters down—was discovery. Tim did not actually think, much less say, all this. He was aware of it, however. He felt it. The Other Wing was inside himself as well as through the green baize doors. His inner map of wonder included both of them.

But now, for the first time in his life, he knew who lived there and who the Ruler was. A shutter had fallen of its own accord; light poured in; he made a guess, and Mother had confirmed it. Sleep and her Little Ones, the host of dreams, were the daylight occupants. They stole out when the darkness fell. All adventures in life began and ended by a dream—discoverable by first passing through the Other Wing.

CHAPTER TWO

And, having settled this, his one desire now was to travel over the map upon journeys of exploration and discovery. The map inside himself he knew already, but the map of the Other Wing he had not seen. His mind knew it, he had a clear mental picture of rooms and halls and passages, but his feet had never trod the silent floors where dust and shadows hid the flock of dreams by day. The mighty chambers where Sleep ruled he longed to stand in, to see the Ruler face to face. He made up his mind to get into the Other Wing.

To accomplish this was difficult; but Tim was a determined youngster, and he meant to try; he meant, also, to succeed. He deliberated. At night he could not possibly manage it; in any case, the Ruler and her host all left it after dark, to fly about the world; the Wing would be empty, and the emptiness would frighten him. Therefore he must make a daylight visit; and it was a daylight visit he decided on. He deliberated more. There were rules and risks involved; it meant going out of bounds; the danger of being seen; the certainty of being questioned by some idle and inquisitive grownup: "Where in the world have you been all this time," and so forth. These things he thought out carefully, and though he arrived at no solution, he felt satisfied that it would be all right. That is, he recognized the risks. To be prepared was half the battle, for nothing then could take him by surprise.

The notion that he might slip in from the garden was soon abandoned; the red bricks showed no openings; there was no door; from the courtyard, also, entrance was impracticable; even on tiptoe he could barely reach the broad window-sills of stone. When playing alone, or walking with the French governess, he examined every outside possibility. None offered. The shutters, supposing he could reach them, were thick and solid.

Meanwhile, when opportunity offered, he stood against the outside walls and listened, his ear pressed against the tight red bricks; the towers and gables of the Wing rose overhead; he heard the wind go whispering along the eaves; he imagined tiptoe movements and a sound of wings inside. Sleep and her Little Ones were busily preparing for their journeys after dark; they hid, but they did not sleep; in this unused Wing, vaster alone than any other country house he had ever seen. Sleep taught and trained her flock of feathered Dreams. It was very wonderful. They probably supplied the entire county. But more wonderful still was the thought that the Ruler herself should take the trouble to come to his particular room and personally watch over him, all night long. That was amazing. And it flashed across his imaginative, inquiring mind: "Perhaps they take me with them! The moment I'm asleep! That's why she comes to see me!"

Yet his chief preoccupation was...how Sleep got out. Through the green baize, doors, of course! By a process of elimination he arrived at a conclusion: he, too, must enter through a green baize door and risk detection.

Of late, the lightning visits had ceased. The silent, darting figure had not peeped in and vanished as it used to do. He fell asleep too quickly now, almost before Jackman reached the hall, and long before the fire began to die. Also, the dogs and birds upon the curtains always matched the trees exactly, and he won the curtain game quite easily; there was never a dog or bird too many; the curtain never stirred. It had been thus ever since his talk with Mother and Father. And so he came to make a second discovery: His parents did not really believe in his Figure. She kept away on that account. They doubted her; she hid. Here was still another incentive to go and find her out. He ached for her, she was so kind, she gave herself so much trouble—just for his little self in the big and lonely bedroom. Yet his parents spoke of her as though she were of no account. He longed to see her, face to face, and tell her that he believed in her and loved her. For he was positive she would like to hear it. She cared. Though he had fallen asleep of late too quickly for him to see her flash in at the door, he had known nicer dreams than ever in his life before—travelling dreams. And it was she who sent them. More—he was sure she took him out with her.

One evening, in the dusk of a March day, his opportunity came; and only just in time, for his brother Jack was expected home from school on the morrow, and with Jack in the other bed, no Figure would ever care to show itself. Also it was Easter, and after Easter, though Tim was not aware of it at the time, he was to say goodbye finally to governesses and become a day-boarder at a preparatory school for Wellington. The opportunity offered itself so naturally, moreover, that Tim took it without hesitation. It never occurred to him to question, much less to refuse it. The thing was obviously meant to be. For he found himself unexpectedly in front of a green baize door; and the green baize door was—swinging! Somebody, therefore, had just passed through it.

It had come about in this wise. Father, away in Scotland, at Inglemuir, the shooting place, was expected back next morning; Mother had driven over to the church upon some Easter business or other; and the governess had been allowed her holiday at home in France. Tim, therefore, had the run of the house, and in the hour between tea and bedtime he made good use of it. Fully able to defy such second-rate obstacles as nurses and butlers, he explored all manner of forbidden places with ardent thoroughness, arriving finally in the sacred precincts of his father's study. This wonderful room was the very heart and centre of the whole big house; he had been birched here long ago; here, too, his father had told him with a grave yet smiling face: "You've got a new companion, Tim, a little sister; you must be very kind to her." Also, it was the place where all the money was kept. What he called "father's jolly smell" was strong in it—papers, tobacco, books, flavored by hunting crops and gunpowder.

At first he felt awed, standing motionless just inside the door; but presently, recovering equilibrium, he moved cautiously on tiptoe towards the gigantic desk where important papers were piled in untidy patches. These he did not touch; but beside them his quick eye noted the jagged piece of iron shell his father brought home from his Crimean campaign and now used as a letter-weight. It was difficult to lift, however. He climbed into the comfortable chair and swung round and round. It was a swivel-chair, and he sank down among the cushions in it, staring at the strange things on the great desk before him, as if fascinated. Next he turned away and saw the stick-rack in the corner—this, he knew, he was allowed to touch. He had played with these sticks before. There were twenty, perhaps, all told, with curious carved handles, brought from every corner of the world; many of them cut by his father's own hand in queer and distant places. And, among them, Tim fixed his eye upon a cane with an ivory handle, a slender, polished cane that he had always coveted tremendously. It was the kind he meant to use when he was a man. It bent, it quivered, and when he swished it through the air it trembled like a riding-whip, and made a whistling noise. Yet it was very strong in spite of its elastic qualities. A family treasure, it was also an old-fashioned relic; it had been his grandfather's walking stick. Something of another century clung visibly about it still. It had dignity and grace and leisure in its very aspect. And it suddenly occurred to him: "How grandpapa must miss it! Wouldn't he just love to have it back again!"

How it happened exactly, Tim did not know, but a few minutes later he found himself walking about the deserted halls and passages of the house with the air of an elderly gentleman of a hundred years ago, proud as a courtier, flourishing the stick like an Eighteenth Century dandy in the Mall. That the cane reached to his shoulder made no difference; he held it accordingly, swaggering on his way. He was off upon an adventure. He dived down through the byways of the Other Wing, inside himself, as though the stick transported him to the days of the old gentleman who had used it in another century.

It may seem strange to those who dwell in smaller houses, but in this rambling Elizabethan mansion there were whole sections that, even to Tim, were strange and unfamiliar. In his mind the map of the Other Wing was clearer by far than the geography of the part he travelled daily. He came to passages and dim-lit halls, long corridors of stone beyond the Picture Gallery; narrow, wainscoted connecting-channels with four steps down and a little later two steps up; deserted chambers with arches guarding them— all hung with the soft March twilight and all bewilderingly unrecognized. With a sense of adventure born of naughtiness he went carelessly along, farther and farther into the heart of this unfamiliar country, swinging the cane, one thumb stuck into the armpit of his blue serge suit, whistling softly to himself, excited yet keenly on the alert—and suddenly found himself opposite a door that checked all further advance. It was a green baize door. And it was swinging.

He stopped abruptly, facing it. He stared, gripping his cane more tightly. He held his breath. "The Other Wing!" he gasped in a swallowed whisper. It was an entrance, but an entrance he had never seen before. He thought he knew every door by heart; but this one was new. He stood motionless for several minutes, watching it; the door had two halves, but one half only was swinging, each swing shorter than the one before; he heard the little puffs of air it made; it settled finally, the last movements very short and rapid; it stopped. And the boy's heart, after similar rapid strokes, stopped also—for a moment.

"Someone's just gone through," he gulped. And even as he said it he knew who the someone was. The conviction just dropped into him. "It's Grandfather; he knows I've got his stick. He wants it!" On the heels of this flashed instantly another amazing certainty. "He sleeps in there. He's having dreams. That's what being dead means."

His first impulse, then, took the form of, "I must let Father know; it'll make him burst for joy"; but his second was for himself—to finish his adventure. And it was this, naturally enough, that gained the day. He could tell his father later. His first duty was plainly to go through the door into the Other Wing. He must give the stick back to its owner. He must *hand* it back.

The test of will and character came now. Tim had imagination, and so knew the meaning of fear; but there was nothing craven in him. He could howl and scream and stamp like any other person of his age when the occasion called for such behavior, but such occasions were due to temper roused by a thwarted will, and the histrionics were half "pretended" to produce a calculated effect. There was no one to thwart his will at present. He also knew how to be afraid of Nothing, to be afraid without ostensible cause, that is—which was merely "nerves." He could have "the shudders" with the best of them.

But, when a real thing faced him, Tim's character emerged to meet it. He would clench his hands, brace his muscles, set his teeth—and wish to heaven he was bigger. But he would not flinch. Being imaginative, he lived the worst a dozen times before it happened, yet in the final crash he stood up like a man. He had that highest pluck—the courage of a sensitive temperament. And at this particular juncture, somewhat ticklish for a boy of eight or nine, it did not fail him. He lifted the cane and pushed the swinging door wide open. Then he walked through it—into the Other Wing.

CHAPTER THREE

The green baize door swung to behind him; he was even sufficiently master of himself to turn and close it with a steady hand, because he did not care to hear the series of muffled thuds its lessening swings would cause. But he realized clearly his position, knew he was doing a tremendous thing.

Holding the cane between fingers very tightly clenched, he advanced bravely along the corridor that stretched before him. And all fear left him from that moment, replaced, it seemed, by a mild and exquisite surprise. His footsteps made no sound, he walked on air; instead of darkness, or the twilight he expected, a diffused and gentle light that seemed like the silver on the lawn when a half-moon sails a cloudless sky, lay everywhere. He knew his way, moreover, knew exactly where he was and whither he was going. The corridor was as familiar to him as the floor of his own bedroom; he recognized the shape and length of it; it agreed exactly with the map he had constructed long ago. Though he had never, to the best of his knowledge, entered it before, he knew with intimacy its every detail.

And thus the surprise he felt was mild and far from disconcerting. "I'm here again!" was the kind of thought he had. It was *how* he got here that caused the faint surprise, apparently. He no longer swaggered, however, but walked carefully, and half on tiptoe, holding the ivory handle of the cane with a kind of affectionate respect. And as he advanced, the light closed softly up behind him, obliterating the way by which he had come. But this he did not know, because he did not look behind him. He only looked in front, where the corridor stretched its silvery length towards the great chamber where he knew the cane must be surrendered. The person who had preceded him down this ancient corridor, passing through the green baize door just before he reached it, this person, his father's father, now stood in that great chamber, waiting to receive his own. Tim knew it as surely as he knew he breathed. At the far end he even made out the larger patch of silvery light which marked its gaping doorway.

There was another thing he knew as well—that this corridor he moved along between rooms with fast-closed doors, was the Nightmare Corridor; often and often he had traversed it; each room was occupied. "This is the Nightmare Passage," he whispered to himself, "but I know the Ruler—it doesn't matter. None of them can get out or do anything." He heard them, none the less, inside, as he passed by; he heard them scratching to get out. The feeling of security made him reckless; he took unnecessary risks; he brushed the panels as he passed. And the love of keen sensation for its own sake, the desire to feel "an awful thrill," tempted him once so sharply that he raised his stick and poked a fast-shut door with it!

He was not prepared for the result, but he gained the sensation and the thrill. For the door opened with instant swiftness half an inch, a hand emerged, caught the stick and tried to draw it in. Tim sprang back as if he had been struck. He pulled at the ivory handle with all his strength, but his strength was less than nothing. He tried to shout, but his voice was gone. A terror of the moon came over him, for he was unable to loosen his hold of the handle; his fingers had become a part of it. An appalling weakness turned him helpless. He was dragged inch by inch towards the fearful door. The end of the stick was already through the narrow crack. He could not see the hand that pulled, but he knew it was terrific. He understood now why the world was strange, why horses galloped furiously, and why trains whistled as they raced through stations. All the comedy and terror of nightmare gripped his heart with pincers made of ice. The disproportion was abominable. The final collapse rushed over him when, without a sign of warning, the door slammed silently, and between the jamb and the wall the cane was crushed as flat as if it were a bulrush. So irresistible was the force behind the door that the solid stick just went flat as a stalk of a bulrush.

He looked at it. It *was* a bulrush.

He did not laugh; the absurdity was so distressingly unnatural. The horror of finding a bulrush where he had expected a polished cane—this hideous and appalling detail held the nameless horror of the nightmare. It betrayed him utterly. Why had he not always known really that the stick was not a stick, but a thin and hollow reed...?

Then the cane was safely in his hand, unbroken. He stood looking at it. The Nightmare was in full swing. He heard another door opening behind his back, a door he had not touched. There was just time to see a hand thrusting and waving dreadfully, familiarly, at him through the narrow crack—just time to realize that this was another Nightmare acting in atrocious concert with the first, when he saw closely beside him, towering to the ceiling, the protective, kindly Figure that visited his bedroom. In the turning movement he made to meet the attack, he became aware of her. And his terror passed. It was a nightmare terror merely. The infinite horror vanished. Only the comedy remained. He smiled.

He saw her dimly only, she was so vast, but he saw her, the Ruler of the Other Wing at last, and knew that he was safe again. He gazed with a tremendous love and wonder, trying to see her clearly; but the face was hidden far aloft and seemed to melt into the sky beyond the roof. He discerned that she was larger than the Night, only, far, far softer, with wings that folded above him more tenderly even than his mother's arms; that there were points of light like stars among the feathers, and that she was vast enough to cover millions and millions of people all at once. Moreover, she did not fade or go, so far as he could see, but spread herself in such a way that he lost sight of her. She spread over the entire Wing...

And Tim remembered that this was all quite natural really. He had often and often been down this corridor before; the Nightmare Corridor was no new experience; it had to be faced as usual. Once knowing what hid inside the rooms, he was bound to tempt them out. They drew, enticed, attracted him; this was their power. It was their special strength that they could suck him helplessly towards them, and that he was obliged to go. He understood exactly why he was tempted to tap with the cane upon their awful doors, but, having done so, he had accepted the challenge and could now continue his journey quietly and safely. The Ruler of the Other Wing had taken him in charge.

A delicious sense of carelessness came on him. There was softness as of water in the solid things about him, nothing that could hurt or bruise. Holding the cane firmly by its ivory handle, he went forward along the corridor, walking as on air.

The end was quickly reached. He stood upon the threshold of the mighty chamber where he knew the owner of the cane was waiting; the long corridor lay behind him, in front he saw the spacious dimensions of a lofty hall that gave him the feeling of being in the Crystal Palace, Euston Station, or St. Paul's. High, narrow windows, cut deeply into the wall, stood in a row upon the other side; an enormous open fireplace of burning logs was on his right; thick tapestries hung from the ceiling to the floor of stone; and in the centre of the chamber was a massive table of dark, shining wood, great chairs with carved stiff backs set here and there beside it. And in the biggest of these throne-like chairs there sat a figure looking at him gravely—the figure of an old, old man.

Yet there was no surprise in the boy's fast-beating heart; there was a thrill of pleasure and excitement only, a feeling of satisfaction. He had known quite well the figure would be there, known also it would look like this exactly. He stepped forward on to the floor of stone without a trace of fear or trembling, holding the precious cane in two hands now before him, as though to present it to its owner. He felt proud and pleased. He had run risks for this.

And the figure rose quietly to meet him, advancing in a stately manner over the hard stone floor. The eyes looked gravely, sweetly down at him, the aquiline nose stood out. Tim knew him perfectly: the knee-breeches of shining satin, the gleaming buckles on the shoes, the neat dark stockings, the lace and ruffles about neck and wrists, the colored waistcoat opening so widely—all the details of the picture over father's mantelpiece, where it hung between two Crimean bayonets, were reproduced in life before his eyes at last. Only the polished cane with the ivory handle was not there.

Tim went three steps nearer to the advancing figure and held out both his hands with the cane laid crosswise on them.

"I've brought it, Grandfather," he said, in a faint but clear and steady tone; "here it is."

And the other stooped a little, put out three fingers half concealed by falling lace, and took it by the ivory handle. He made a courtly bow to Tim. He smiled, but though there was pleasure, it was a grave, sad smile. He spoke then; the voice was slow and very deep. There was a delicate softness in it, the suave politeness of an older day.

"Thank you," he said; "I value it. It was given to me by my grandfather. I forgot it when I—" His voice grew indistinct a little.

"Yes?" said Tim.

"When I—left," the old gentleman repeated.

"Oh," said Tim, thinking how beautiful and kind the gracious figure was.

The old man ran his slender fingers carefully along the cane, feeling the polished surface with satisfaction. He lingered specially over the smoothness of the ivory handle. He was evidently very pleased.

"I was not quite myself—er—at the moment," he went on gently; "my memory failed me somewhat." He sighed, as though an immense relief was in him.

"You know I forget things, too—sometimes," Tim mentioned sympathetically. He simply loved his grandfather. He hoped—for a moment—he would be lifted up and kissed. "I'm *awfully* glad I brought it..." He faltered. "...that you've got it again."

The other turned his kind grey eyes upon him; the smile on his face was full of gratitude as he looked down.

"Thank you, my boy. I am truly and deeply indebted to you. You courted danger for my sake. Others have tried before, but the Nightmare Passage,—er—" He broke off. He tapped the stick firmly on the stone flooring, as though to test it. Bending a trifle, he put his weight upon it. "Ah!" he exclaimed with a short sigh of relief. "I can now—"

His voice again grew indistinct; Tim did not catch the words.

"Yes?" he asked again, aware for the first time that a touch of awe was in his heart.

"—get about again," the other continued very low. "Without my cane," he added, the voice failing with each word the old lips uttered, "I could not...possibly...allow myself...to be seen. It was indeed deplorable…unpardonable of me…to forget in such a way. Zounds, sir! I—I…"

His voice sank away suddenly into a sound of wind. He straightened up, tapping the iron ferrule of his cane on the stones in a series of loud knocks. Tim felt a strange sensation creep into his legs. The queer words frightened him a little.

The old man took a step towards him. He still smiled, but there was a new meaning in the smile. A sudden earnestness had replaced the courtly, leisurely manner. The next words seemed to blow down upon the boy from above, as though a cold wind brought them from the sky outside.

Yet the words, he knew, were kindly meant, and very sensible. It was only the abrupt change that startled him. Grandfather, after all, was but a man. The distant sound recalled something in him to that outside world from which the cold wind blew.

"My eternal thanks to you," he heard, while the voice and face and figure seemed to withdraw deeper and deeper into the heart of the mighty chamber. "I shall not forget your kindness and your courage. It is a debt I can, fortunately, one day repay… But now you had best return and with dispatch. For your head and arm lie heavily on the table, the documents are scattered, there is a cushion fallen…and my son is in the house… Farewell! You had best leave me quickly. See! *She* stands behind you, waiting. Go with her! Go now…!"

The entire scene had vanished even before the final words were uttered. Tim felt empty space about him. A vast, shadowy Figure bore him through it as with mighty wings. He flew, he rushed, he remembered nothing more—until he heard another voice and felt a heavy hand upon his shoulder.

"Tim, you rascal! What are you doing in my study? And in the dark, like this!"

He looked up into his father's face without a word. He felt dazed. The next minute his father had caught him up and kissed him.

"Ragamuffin! How did you guess I was coming back tonight?" He shook him playfully and kissed his tumbling hair. "And you've been asleep, too, into the bargain. Well—how's everything at home—eh? Jack's coming back from school tomorrow, you know, and…"

CHAPTER FOUR

Jack came home, indeed, the following day, and when the Easter holidays were over, the governess stayed abroad and Tim went off to adventures of another kind in the preparatory school for Wellington. Life slipped rapidly along with him; he grew into a man; his mother and his father died; Jack followed them within a little space; Tim inherited, married, settled down into his great possessions—and opened up the Other Wing. The dreams of imaginative boyhood all had faded; perhaps he had merely put them away, or perhaps he had forgotten them. At any rate, he never spoke of such things now, and when his Irish wife mentioned her belief that the old country house possessed a family ghost, even declaring that she had met an Eighteenth Century figure of a man in the corridors, "an old, old man who bends down upon a stick," Tim only laughed and said:

"That's as it ought to be! And if these awful land-taxes force us to sell some day, a respectable ghost will increase the market value."

But one night he woke and heard a tapping on the floor. He sat up in bed and listened. There was a chilly feeling down his back. Belief had long since gone out of him; he felt uncannily afraid. The sound came nearer and nearer; there were light footsteps with it. The door opened—it opened a little wider, that is, for it already stood ajar—and there upon the threshold stood a figure that it seemed he knew. He saw the face as with all the vivid sharpness of reality. There was a smile upon it, but a smile of warning and alarm. The arm was raised. Tim saw the slender hand, lace falling down upon the long, thin fingers, and in them, tightly gripped, a polished cane. Shaking the cane twice to and fro in the air, the face thrust forward, spoke certain words, and vanished. But the words were inaudible; for, though the lips distinctly moved, no sound, apparently, came from them.

And Tim sprang out of bed. The room was full of darkness. He turned the light on. The door, he saw, was shut as usual. He had, of course, been dreaming. But he noticed a curious odor in the air. He sniffed it once or twice—then grasped the truth. It was a smell of burning!

Fortunately, he awoke just in time…

He was acclaimed a hero for his promptitude. After many days, when the damage was repaired, and nerves had settled down once more into the calm routine of country life, he told the story to his wife—the entire story. He told the adventure of his imaginative boyhood with it. She asked to see the old family cane. And it was this request of hers that brought back to memory a detail Tim had entirely forgotten all these years. He remembered it suddenly again—the loss of the cane, the hubbub his father kicked up about it, the endless, futile search. For the stick had never been found, and Tim, who was questioned very closely concerning it, swore with all his might that he had not the smallest notion where it was. Which was, of course, the truth.

THE END

THE LIVING EYES

By Justin Dowling

Mrs. Weir might die; her eyes would live forever...

I WAS fifteen years old when I first saw Mrs. Weir's eyes, and her useless hands.

If I shut my eyes, I can still see her house, standing apart from others in the village on a hill overlooking the sea on a wild coast.

But above all I can still see Mrs. Weir's eyes and the useless hands, lying across a special board fixed on her wheel chair.

My father, a widower, knew Mrs. Weir and took me to stay with her one winter. "Remember," he said to me, "pass no rude remarks. Mrs. Weir is a queer woman. She has paralyzed legs and hands. Don't stare at her eyes, whatever you do."

"Why are we going, father?" I asked.

"Mrs. Weir has money. She may want to help me. I was a very good friend of hers."

"Will anyone else be there?" I went on.

"Yes," he answered, "her two sons live with her, while a niece will probably be there, with her husband."

The house had the squat, uncomfortable appearance of an old prison. At our knock, the door opened and a large man appeared. "What do you want?" he asked.

"We want," my father replied, "to see Mrs. Weir. Tell her Mr. Rowlands and his son are here."

The servant said, "Of course, sir. She is expecting you. Come in." As an afterthought he added, "My name is Leonard."

We were ushered into the great hall, and led across to the lounge. "So you have come, Richard," a voice said.

We were both startled because we had thought the room empty. Then we saw a wheel chair, with the dim outline of a figure in it.

"I hope we find you well, Mrs. Weir?" said my father.

"Well enough, Richard," said the voice. "Put on the light."

I sat on the edge of a stiff-backed chair when the light came on. Remembering what my father had said, I stared at her feet. She had on black slippers. Then I looked at her chin and wanted to laugh at her whiskers. But her mouth, thin and bloodless, choked my mirth. I paused. Then I lifted my head. The shock nearly made me cry out!

I stared into eyes so prominent, grotesque, hideous and terrifying, that I wanted to run from the room.

They protruded from their wide sockets as if on sticks. The white parts were a mass of red veins entangled in a million tiny threads, writhing and twitching, expanding and shrinking, as she blinked.

They were alive in a manner strangely apart from the rest of her.

I dropped my glances to the useless hands, lying on the board fixed across her chair. There was nothing unusual about them. They lay on their backs, with the fingers slightly curled. I wanted to pull the fingers straight; to whip some action from them; stir life into them; to make them move. That they could not do so without aid, chilled me; fascinated me; frightened me.

ALL this time my father and Mrs. Weir had been talking, but I had not heard a word of it. Then I heard Mrs. Weir say to me, "You will sleep in the west wing. Leonard will unpack your clothes. Remember to dress for dinner, wash your hands and face and do not be late. Do not stare so, boy!"

I ran from the room. Finding my bedroom, I flung myself down upon the fourposter bed. I covered my face with my hands, but could still see the protruding eyes, with the veins twisting and turning, knotting and untying—and the useless hands lying on their backs.

I was introduced to the other guests. The sons, who were as old as my father, lifelessly shook my hand without looking at me.

Mrs. Weir's niece was thin and short, beside her lanky husband. At dinner Mrs. Weir sat at the top of the table, her useless hands on a board. One son sat at an angle to the table, so that he could feed his mother.

By candlelight, her eyes were even more startling than before. I had resolved not to look at them, if possible. I might as well have tried to walk on water. The veins had gathered in a blotch, and throbbed. Then they quickly flowed back in all directions, twisting and entangling themselves in a mad flurry. Again I was aware of their aliveness, which was so apart from the rest of her. Eyes that lived in a dead face.

It was obvious to me, even though I was so young at the time, that Mrs. Weir's eyes dominated everybody with whom she came into contact. They cowered all opposition. Those who spoke did so in a low tone. Heads were raised and dropped hurriedly. People full of life and vigor, happy and strong, dried up under those eyes like an orange left in the sun.

Leonard took great delight in frightening me. He told me about a pretty girl of fourteen, who had once insulted Mrs. Weir at a flower show. She cried, "Oh, Mummy, look at those awful eyes!"

Leonard said that Mrs. Weir had been very angry. She never forgot or forgave. When the child had grown into the full blossom of beautiful womanhood, she had been invited to stay at Doonside, Mrs. Weir's house. She was as beautiful as a rose until Mrs. Weir crushed her; crumpled her until her senses left her. Leonard said that she still screamed in her room at the asylum: "The eyes! They are eating me!"

I could imagine them doing that, and how the little veins would leap in excitement in the process.

Leonard hated Mrs. Weir. "She's not human," he said.

During a meal the son fed her carefully. He did not eat himself until he was sure she had finished. All the time her eyes lashed him as effectively as a whip. Head sunken on his chest he would, each time he lifted the spoon to her mouth, gaze into her eyes.

After dinner, that first night, I went out and down the path through some tall trees. I went to a place where I could see the water spraying against the rocks. The sound of the sea soothed me—I almost forgot the eyes. A rustling behind made me spin around. It was Leonard.

He grinned and said, "Mrs. Weir says you must go to bed."

I was furious. What right had she to tell me what to do?

He went on: "Mrs. Weir said that if you refused I was to bring you to her."

The prospect of facing her eyes again that night decided me. I went to bed.

The next day, when my father told me, he was going to marry Mrs. Weir. I threw myself on my bed and cried.

"You'll get used to her," he said. "She won't live forever."

She lived for another three years.

The wedding ceremony was performed in the lounge. I could never forgive my father for such an act. To think that Mrs. Weir was to be my stepmother! That I was to live under the permanent lash of the eyes. They would crush me; eat me alive!

The only consolation I had was that I was to go to a boarding school. I would be home only in the holidays.

Mrs. Weir was dressed entirely in black, except for a white veil. My father looked grim and handsome in his frock coat and knife-edged trousers. Mrs. Weir sat in her wheel chair, propped up straight with cushions. Her hands lay on their backs on the board. I only saw her eyes once. The mass of veins were taking a leading part in the ceremony. They leapt and fought each other in a whirl of excitement, brilliantly red. The eyeballs protruded further from their taut sockets.

Then I knew what was really happening...*Mrs. Weir's eyes were being married!*

There could be no other explanation. The rest of her was dead.

Then I glanced at the hands, lying on their backs. On one of the fingers was now a ring—glittering. Mrs. Weir had moved her fingers! Impossible! Incredible! But it was true.

The eyes were married!

The next three years of my life were ones of happiness at school and horror at "home." Every holiday I came under the merciless lashing of the eyes. Every time it became worse.

My father hardly spoke to me. He was now a constant attendant on my stepmother.

One holiday the relatives came, carbon copies of each other, dejected, miserable people with one thing on their minds—the death of Mrs. Weir and whether my father was now going to be left the vast Weir fortune.

One night, when I was in the library, I heard Mrs. Weir raise her voice, passionately. She said, "I know what you are all thinking! You wish me dead. And now I warn you. Should I die unnaturally, I shall return to strangle my murderer, and the marks of my fingers shall be upon his, or her, throat. My eyes shall follow the rest of you until death."

Ten months later she was dead.

I WAS home for the holidays, and most of the relatives were there. My father called me into the room, with the others.

She was dead, but the eyes were open, staring. Alive—as if they refused to die. My father tried to pull the lids down, but they shot up each time, like a blind.

The veins continued to writhe and twist, turn and contract expand and leap.

I do not know what made me say it. But I startled the others in the room. I said, softly, *"Mrs. Weir is dead, but her eyes will live forever."*

Then everybody remembered her dreadful warning. All were afraid.

The next few days were ones of tramping police feet. The doctor had been suspicious. A post mortem was held. Poison was found in her stomach. A fat detective asked questions. His pig eyes suspected everyone, but most of all, Leonard.

When they arrested him he cursed and swore at them. He shouted to us from the police car, "She'll be back for the real murderer. She said so. She's in'uman."

On the last night we slept at the house, screams awoke us at midnight. We tumbled out into the great hall.

Someone said, "Where's Rowlands?"

He was missing—and there had been screams!

We rushed to my father's room and burst through the door. He lay on his back, staring up at the ceiling, but not seeing. He was dead.

He had been strangled. There were finger marks on his throat.

Someone shouted, "Look! Look!" as the lights failed.

In the gloom we saw Mrs. Weir's eyes. They were hanging in mid air, staring at us, bright, horrifying *and alive.* Like they had been on her wedding day.

Then they were gone.

We tried to convince ourselves that it was a hallucination. We took a fainting woman to the lounge. One of the sons moaned, "It can't be! We imagined it! It's against the laws of nature."

Mrs. Weir's niece suddenly shouted: "She said she would come back and strangle the one…"

Leonard got off. There was not enough evidence. I was glad.

THIRTY years have passed since the death of Mrs. Weir and my father, but the eyes are still alive. They haunt me. Alive, they are destroying me.

My doctor says it is my imagination, and I never actually see them. That my mind was so vividly impressed when I was young that I now project them from my subconscious mind into reality.

The two sons are dead. Mrs. Weir's niece is in an asylum. Her husband shot himself.

I know the doctor is wrong. Mrs. Weir's eyes will come again. I hope this document is found.

Her eyes will come again. And I will be waiting. I have made up my mind.

This time I will tell them. Tell them to bring the hands. The hands for my throat. The hands to leave their finger marks. Hands that were useless in life, deadly in death.

I will tell the eyes they were wrong. Wrong about my father. He did not kill Mrs. Weir.

It was me. I put the poison in her glass of wine. The poison I found in my father's bag.

THE END

SOMETHING IN THE WIND

By Gregory Luce

The rolling terrain of northeastern Oregon has an irregular, sometimes peculiar look to it. Take a drive on any dusty country road and you'll often witness swift transformations in the character of the land. One can become mesmerized by the seemingly endless sea of wheat, flowing along mile after mile; but pass a fence border and suddenly the rolling waves of grain can give way to vast expanses of sagebrush-ridden landscape. These undeveloped wastelands invoke a disquieting, sometimes ominous feeling when passing through their remotest sections.

Being an eastern Oregon wheat farmer, I lived in just such a remote area on the eastern side of Antelope Valley. My farm was settled near the bottom of a large bluff where the entrance of Cobb's Canyon junctioned with the valley floor. There was a county road that worked its way up from the south end of the valley. Starting a few miles outside Pine City, the road edged its way north, crossing the mouth of Cobb's Canyon and running directly toward my place where it veered sharply and continued up the canyon, dead-ending at Earl Stevers' place.

It was about mid-August, and the weekend was a real scorcher. Earl phoned early Saturday afternoon and jawed with me about a truck load of second hand stuff he'd picked up over at the Grimsley estate near Echo.

Earl, not usually the effervescent type, seemed a little excited. "Got somethin' to show you," he said, "somethin' unusual."

Around mid-afternoon, I climbed into my old, weather-beaten Buick station wagon and headed up Cobb's Canyon toward Stevers' place. A few minutes later, I swung into Earl's driveway and saw the aging Oregonian standing amidst a clutter of items on the back of an old flatbed truck. As I climbed out of the wagon, I saw Earl hop up on a large object in the middle of the truck bed.

It was a large, rust-covered iron container.

I knew it was just another piece of junk, something he'd picked up at the Grimsley estate sale; but to Earl it was a real find, another piece of metallic debris he could break down into scrap metal and pawn off to one of his local farm cronies. Earl, however, didn't have a clue as to what Grimsley had used it for.

Amos Grimsley had, in fact, lived in virtual obscurity for years, rarely venturing outside except for occasional trips into Echo for supplies. Most of the townsfolk had considered him a harmless crackpot who collected spiritualistic paraphernalia; but others had branded him a warlock, a practitioner of satanic rites and evil deeds. They'd speak in whispers and cast disapproving glances in his direction whenever his aging sedan rumbled into town.

Grimsley had died sometime back, apparently with no last will and testament. After waiting the period required by law for any next of kin to surface, the State had held an auction to sell off the estate. Earl picked up the remains of Grimsley's personal belongings that hadn't sold during the bidding, one item of which was the large iron container.

It looked like a big iron bread box—four feet wide, three feet tall, and four feet deep, standing on four short metal legs. An incredibly heavy object, it was completely sealed all the way around except for the front side, which had a top-hinged iron door that appeared to swing outward and up from the bottom. There was just one problem: no handle. There was however, a long lever protruding out of a narrow slit on the top side of the container. On one side of the slit was a series of slots—settings for the lever. The lever itself extended down, disappearing into the black interior of the container. Earl figured it connected to some inner-mechanism that was used in opening the container and if pulled all the way back, would cause the front door to swing open.

So there he was, standing atop this curious metal contraption on the back of his flatbed truck.

I yelled out a greeting as I walked up the dusty driveway. "Hey, old man!"

"Gil Page…is that you?" he called back, squinting in my direction. "Come and take a look at this…"

"Better climb down before you have a heart attack."

"Never mind that. Ever seen anything like this before?"

"Can't say I have," I answered, approaching the side of the truck. "What is it?"

"Haven't been able to figure that out yet," Earl replied. His face had a look of perplexity on it. "I'm not sure what to make of it."

"Maybe it's not complete."

"What d'ya mean?"

"You know—maybe it's part of something else. Something bigger."

"Well..." Earl leaned over and spat, "...I've never seen any piece a' farm equipment that had a contraption like this attached to it."

Earl squatted down and began to pull back on the lever. It didn't budge. He strained hard, beads of sweat popping out of his forehead, but it still didn't move.

While Earl struggled and strained, I leaned an arm against the truck and looked the place over. It was a big junkyard out in the middle of the tumbleweeds—second hand stuff was strewn all over the grounds.

Earl wasn't a farmer anymore. He'd given it up and sold off most of his farmland after Suzy had passed back in the winter of '79. Since then he'd become something of a pack rat, picking up lots of stuff that nobody else wanted, making a small income from selling used items such as equipment parts and scrap metal to other local farmers.

"You know, you've got more junk lyin' around here than you'll ever know what to do with," I commented. "Why do you keep bringing more of it in here?"

I looked up and saw Earl was ignoring me. He was struggling with the lever, which still resisted his efforts. I shook my head.

"You're just gonna give yourself a stroke."

There was a hammer lying on top of the cab, so I hoisted myself up and grabbed it. I moved over to the container. "Here...I'll loosen that thing up for you. Lemme take a whack at it."

Earl jumped off the container and pulled a dirty red handkerchief out of his back pocket, wiping it across his glistening forehead.

"Darned thing's bein' stubborn," he said, taking a deep breath.

I took the hammer and gave the container a good rap on the side. My ears were greeted with a deep, hollow sound, far too deep for the size of the object. It resonated for several seconds before fading.

Earl looked surprised. "Will you listen to that..."

My forehead wrinkled. "Knowing Amos Grimsley, it won't surprise me if we find some old lady's corpse inside."

I banged on the lever several times with the hammer; then I climbed up on top and dropped to one knee, wrapping both hands around the lever.

Just as I was about to pull, something caught my eye. Painted on top, near the front end of the slit where the lever was stuck, was a faded set of words: KEEP LOCKED IN THIS POSITION. At the other end of the slit, next to the rear slot, were more painted words. These were just as faded and read: FULL OPEN. Then I noticed something curious under the rust. Leaning in closer, I saw what appeared to be several words, barely noticeable, scratched into the container's iron surface near the middle of the slit. They seemed to have been carved into the metal with a sharp-ended instrument like a nail or knife; I couldn't quite make them out. I licked my index finger and wiped away the rust: Beneath the oxidation were the words, HALFWAY TO HELL.

I whistled softly. "I'll be damned. Take a look at this."

Earl leaned over the top of the container and looked down at the strange inscription. Both of us stared at it for several seconds.

"Somebody's idea of a joke," I said.

Earl looked intently at the peculiar writing. "Yeah…s'pose so."

"What the hell's inside this thing?"

"Dunno…" Earl shook his head slowly. "…dunno." He climbed back onto the container and motioned me back a little. "Scoot over just a bit and we'll both give it a try."

We positioned ourselves on either side of the lever, wrapping our hands around it. We pulled and jerked as hard as we could, but the lever refused to budge. I could feel the heat bearing down on us as we struggled to free it. The sun's rays were like dancing pinpoints of fire on my forehead. Suddenly the handle gave a little. The lever began sliding, ever so slightly, toward the rear. As it inched back, there was a high-pitched metal on metal grating sound as the front door began to swing forward. The lever slipped over the next slot and dropped in.

Out of nowhere, a sudden, strong gust of wind swirled up around us. My eyes became flooded with dust.

"Darned wind! Hold on just a minute." I jumped off over the front side of the container and squatted down, cupping my hands over my eyes. Through the tiny slits between my cupped fingers, I could see the bottom of the iron door. It had opened outward just a crack—maybe an inch or more from the bottom. Then I saw—or thought I saw—something very curious. For just an instant the dust seemed to kick up off the surface of the flatbed, right below the opening at the bottom of the door; and it appeared the wind had gusted outward from *inside* the container.

"Hmmm, that's funny...must have blown up through the cracks in the floorboard," I muttered.

"What's that, Gil?" asked Earl, who was still squatting on top of the container, his right hand clutching the lever.

"Nothin'...Nothin'," I responded, shaking my head.

The swirling gust subsided a little but as it faded I noticed a slight breeze had taken its place.

The two of us kept up our efforts for awhile, but the lever had locked up again, refusing to move out of the second slot. Presently, we gave up and began examining some of the other contents on the flatbed. Most of it was hardware and kitchenware. There were a few items of clothing and a small box of books containing several old, musty volumes written in foreign languages.

After a while I glanced at my watch—it was getting late. I stepped over to Earl, who was bent over, going through the contents of an old toolbox.

"Listen old man, I hate to run out on you, but I gotta get back to the house. Promised I'd take Martha and Jenny into Pilot Rock for an early dinner. Goin' to Chub's Diner."

"Always thinkin' with your stomach," Earl said without glancing up. "I'll give you a call later and let you know what I find inside this thing...if I ever get it open."

"If it's cash, we split fifty-fifty...right?"

Earl looked up. "In your dreams..."

I laughed and jumped down off the truck. Earl did likewise, waving goodbye as he disappeared into a small storage shed next to the house.

As I slid behind the steering wheel of the Buick, I gazed through the bug-covered windshield. Earl had re-emerged from the shed and was climbing back onto the flatbed, an oil can in one hand.

"Crazy old coot," I muttered as the engine roared to life. I shot a glance in the rearview mirror as the car bounced down the uneven driveway. Earl was pouring oil down the length of the lever near the opening of the slit. The station wagon went over a slight rise in the bumpy road and Earl disappeared from sight. I headed down Cobb's Canyon toward home, a cloud of dust flying from the rear.

EARLY EVENING found my family back from a pleasant meal at Chub's Diner. My daughter Jenny practiced line-dancing upstairs while Martha and I sipped on glasses of homemade lemonade, relaxing in wicker chairs on our old-style front porch.

The farmhouse was up a bit from the valley floor. Facing in a southwesterly direction, it provided a wide view of the surrounding terrain. Straight in front were miles of golden wheat fields, while to the left was the rugged, uncultivated rangeland of Cobb's Canyon, teeming with sagebrush, tumbleweeds, jackrabbits, and rattlesnakes. Looking due south at the other side of the canyon mouth we could see the Connors' ranch, while further to the right was the Stimmons' farmhouse, sitting in the middle of the wheat-lands about a quarter-mile off the main county road.

It was nearly seven-thirty and the searing summer heat was just starting to fade as the sun crept closer to the horizon. I got up to go in the house for a refill of Martha's lemonade. As I pulled open the squeaky screen door, I noticed the breeze stiffening a bit. It was blowing down the canyon, from the direction of Earl's place, which was somewhat unusual. Normally it came rushing in from the southwest, across the valley floor. I stepped into the living room, the rickety door slamming shut behind me. The sound of the phone ringing took me into the kitchen. I reached over and picked up the receiver—it was Earl, his voice was high-pitched and excited:

"Gil—get up here as soon as you can! I got that blasted thing open—you've gotta help me get it closed!"

"Closed? Wait a minute Earl—get what closed? What are you talkin' about—the container?"

There was no response, but I could hear a racket in the background on the other end of the line.

"Earl...are you there? What's going on?"

There was still no response, but a few seconds later Earl's voice finally came back on the line. It was frantic.

"Gil—get up here right now! I can't do it myself—the wind's too strong. This thing has to be closed—it's the only way to cut it off! Dear God—we've gotta stop it. There's somethin'—somethin'—in the wind! Do ya hear me? *There's somethin' in the wind!*"

Crackle, click. The line went dead.

I picked up the phone and redialed, but there was no response at the other end of the line—no ringing, no busy signal, just the soft whistle of static. I pushed down the receiver button and tried again; this time I got a loud, wowing electronic sound, indicating something was wrong with the line. I was about to dial again when I heard a high-pitched scream from the front porch. It was Martha. I bolted across the living room and threw open the screen door.

Martha was standing there, her hair and dress blowing in the stiffening wind, looking up the canyon. Her eyes were wide with terror. One hand covered her mouth while the other arm raised slowly, pointing up Cobb's Canyon. I stepped out further onto the porch and saw something that sent a shock wave through me.

Up in the canyon—near the location of Earl's ranch—was a gigantic cloud of dust, so thick it was almost black. It appeared to be swirling around like a spread-out funnel cloud, as though it was a huge, fat tornado. It towered hundreds of feet above the ground and connected to a layer of low-lying black clouds that had suddenly appeared from nowhere.

My daughter, Jenny, burst onto the porch. She looked up the canyon and tried to scream, but nothing came out except a choking gasp of sudden panic. She ran over and grabbed my arm. The three of us stood there, riveted to the front porch, dumbstruck by what we were seeing. It was a nightmare of nature, a gyrating wall of destructive force; and what was worse—it seemed to be moving down the canyon toward the valley floor.

I ran back into the house, reappearing a moment later with a set of binoculars. Stepping down the porch steps, I trained the lenses on the approaching menace. The giant cloud of dust was cutting a swath along the bottom of the opposite side of the canyon—about two miles distance, moving rapidly. I realized this path would take it directly through the Connors' ranch.

"Dear Lord…" I croaked.

I leaped back up the steps. Martha called to me as I ran past her toward the screen door.

"Gil! Where are you going? What are we going to do?"

I've gotta call John," I answered without looking back. I ran into the kitchen and picked up the phone. My trembling fingers frantically dialed John Connors' number. It rang three times before a voice answered.

"Hello."

"John, it's Gil. Have you looked out your window!?"

"No, we've got the curtains closed. Startin' to get quite a blow out there, though. Why? What's goin'—"

"John—shut up and listen! Get Bonnie, get Tom, and get the hell out of there!"

"What are you talkin' about?"

"Go look out your window—*now!*"

I heard the receiver rattle down on a counter. A few moments later there was a commotion in the background—shouting and screaming. Seconds later the phone was picked up again; Connors' voice was panic-stricken.

"What is that thing!?"

"I don't know—just get in your car and get outa there—fast!"

"We can't!" John cried out.

"What?"

"Tom's in Pine City with the pickup, and the Ford's jacked up in the driveway—a busted U-joint!"

"Haven't you got anything else? Anything that moves?"

"All I got is that old Massey Ferguson sittin' out by the barn. I don't think it'll do over a few miles an hour, though."

"Get on it and start heading toward my place. I'll meet you on the road in the station wagon. Get moving! That thing'll be on top of you in a couple of minutes!"

I slammed down the receiver and ran back out on the porch. The wind was screaming. Martha and Jenny were standing there, arms around each other, watching the giant dust cloud as it moved steadily toward the Connors' ranch. It was now less than a mile away.

"I want you and Jenny to get in the cellar and stay there 'til I get back," I commanded, running down the steps.

"Gil—where are you going?" Martha shouted.

"I gotta get Bonnie and John. They're stuck over there without a car."

"But Gil—"

"Just do as I say!"

"Dad! Wait a min—" Jenny was cut off by the door of the station wagon as it slammed shut. I turned the key and the V-8 engine roared to life. My foot punched the gas pedal to the floor. The Buick lurched down the driveway and onto the main road, dust and rocks shooting out behind it.

From my place to the Connors' ranch was a straight shot, just over a mile, right across the mouth of the canyon. I could feel the wind pushing against the side of the station wagon. As I gained speed I thought it would blow me off the road. I fought hard to keep the car from sliding into the ditch. Dozens of tumbleweeds went flying in front of me from the left, skipping over onto the rippling surface of the wheat fields that lay to the right of the roadway. The wheat itself looked like a stormy sea of endless waves, rising and falling.

I passed the turn-off to the Stimmons' farm. Up ahead and to the left I could see the spinning cloud of dust slashing across the landscape. It was huge, probably three hundred feet across at its base and even wider as it rose toward the layer of black clouds that hovered a half-mile or so above it. As it cut a path through the rangeland, I could see soil and vegetation flying into the air. The black clouds above seemed to be spreading out over the entire canyon, casting an eerie ambiance of semi-darkness over the countryside.

The dust cloud was almost to Connors' livestock barns on the backside of the property when I saw something straight ahead of me. Plodding up the roadway was an ancient Massey Ferguson tractor with two windblown figures clinging to its topside. John Connors clutched desperately to the steering wheel while Bonnie hung by his side, her arms locked tightly around his waist. It looked like they would be blown off at any second.

I slammed on the brakes and slid through the gravel, coming to a stop a few yards in front of the approaching tractor. Oddly enough, the wind still seemed to be blowing down from the upper part of the canyon, and not from the direction of the giant dust cloud almost directly in front of me. I could barely get the driver door open because of the wind pressure.

I managed to squeeze out of the car just as the tractor came to a stop. John and Bonnie climbed down and made their way toward the station wagon, fighting for every step against the terrific crosswind. When they reached the car's front left fender, I pointed my arm back toward their ranch.

"Look!"

The two of them braced against the side of the Buick and looked back. The dark cloud of swirling dust was descending upon the Connors' livestock barns. As it hit the buildings, they literally exploded, flying apart as though blasted by dynamite. It was incredible.

Bonnie and John both screamed in disbelief. Bonnie turned away and buried her face into her husband's shoulder. My eyes were transfixed on the scene of destruction.

Then I felt a new wave of horror. As the dust cloud enveloped the livestock barns, *it stopped its forward movement.* It hovered there, swirling around for a good thirty seconds or more, as though making sure the job was finished before advancing further. When the buildings were completely destroyed, it moved on. Seconds later it swallowed up the Connors' ranch house, pausing again while it annihilated the structure.

Bonnie glanced up just in time to see her home explode. Her eyes went blank for a moment, then she turned her face into her husband's shoulder and started to sob.

We stood there and watched, the wind whipping hard against our bodies. Then the dust cloud began to move again, this time in a westerly direction. It headed out onto the valley floor, cutting a swath through the rippling waves of grain. A minute or so later it had moved off a safe distance.

John looked back at me. "Let's get out of here," he said, his voice cracking. We climbed into the Buick. Suddenly Bonnie shouted frantically.

"John—Gil—look over there!"

John and I looked out over the valley. A tremor of eye-opening horror shook us both.

The dark cloud of swirling dust had changed direction.

It was moving northeast—directly toward the Stimmons' farm and my place beyond that.

I shouted into the wind, "Lord all mighty…Martha and Jenny!"

Bonnie covered her mouth in a gasp of horror. "Look at that!" she cried, her finger pointing ahead to the left.

The dust cloud was picking up speed.

I turned the key, slammed the car into gear, and punched the gas pedal to the floor. A wave of realization came over me. There was something *in* that swirling cloud—*something alive.*

I gripped the steering wheel hard as the car shot up the road toward the farmhouse. I could see it in the distance, sitting there in the path of impending destruction. Jenny and Martha were there in the cellar, probably out of their minds with fear. A lump came to my throat and I swallowed hard.

Over to the left, the swirling cloud of death was descending upon the Stimmons' farm with frightening speed. As it engulfed the outer buildings, the same explosion of spiraling destruction ensued. A prayer went through my mind, hoping my longtime neighbors had been out running errands in town; taking a drive through the foothills; visiting relatives for the weekend—anything, as long as they hadn't been home.

Bonnie suddenly cried out again—a ring of terror was in her voice. *"No, no, no!"*

She had caught sight of a vehicle coming around the driveway from behind the Stimmons' farmhouse. It was moving slowly, as though trying to fight its way through the blasting pressure of the wind demon that was almost on top of it. Before it had traveled ten yards it was completely swallowed up by the spinning cloud of dust. The car disappeared for a second or two, only to re-emerge as it was hurled through the air, smashing into the side of the farmhouse. A moment later the structure itself was consumed, erupting into a flying mass of splintered fragments.

John Connors put his hand over his eyes and lowered his head. "Dear God," he muttered under his breath.

The station wagon rushed past the side entrance to the Stimmons' property, streaking up the road toward home. The dust cloud was now directly to the left. John and Bonnie carefully watched its progress. It had paused once more while annihilating the Stimmons' house and grounds. Then it began advancing again, on a direct collision course with the Page place—my place.

I pressed down on the gas pedal even harder. I figured I could beat the dust giant to the farm. I'd grab Martha and Jenny, then take off back down the valley before it could descend upon the house. Then I saw that the dust cloud seemed to sense the station wagon's increase in speed and was trying to match it. In raw panic, I slammed the gas pedal all the way to the floor. The car flew along the gravel roadway, fighting against the crosswind. The dust cloud began to fall back, behind and to the left.

As the car roared up to the house, I slammed on the brakes hard. The station wagon skidded sideways into the driveway, smashing through the wooden fence that ran along side of it.

I laid on the horn.

Seconds later, Martha and Jenny came running out, stumbling down the hill as the wind swirled about them. The two women jumped into the back seat with Bonnie.

The dust demon was closing fast.

I backed the car off the fence and swung it around toward the main road.

"Dammit!" I yelled.

In a matter of seconds the dust cloud had moved over—*onto the roadway.* It was now headed directly toward us, cutting off any chance of escape down the valley. It was less than two hundred yards away.

"Hang on!" I cried. I jerked the wheel hard to the left and headed up the only remaining avenue of escape—straight up Cobb's Canyon.

The other occupants of the car looked back at the towering funnel of dust that was stalking us. As soon as the station wagon started up the canyon, the dust cloud changed its course again. It crossed into the canyon, skirting the edge of my property, hot in pursuit of our fleeing automobile.

The Buick sped up the road. It was about two and a half miles to Earl's place. The contour of the road from this point on was much more uneven and perilous, making it like a real-life high-speed roller coaster ride. The station wagon scraped bottom several times, banging frighteningly as it flew over dips and rises.

The frontal wind pressure on the car was incredible as I struggled to hold the steering wheel steady. It was still blowing straight down the canyon, even though the dust demon was pursuing us from behind.

John Connors was dumbfounded. "I don't believe it. That thing's *following* us. We're bucking a head wind and that thing is still following us. That's impossible—it's moving against the wind itself!"

"That doesn't make any difference," I responded. "None of this is natural. This head wind we're bucking...and that thing behind us...it's like they're working together somehow. It'll follow us until it catches us...or until we outrun it."

Jenny was in near hysterics in the back seat. "We're all gonna die! *We're all gonna die!*"

Martha grabbed the wriggling teenager and pulled her close.

"None of this—can be happening," Bonnie declared in disbelief. "John—Gil—it's just not possible."

"Yes it is," I answered, "and I know how it started—that iron contraption on the back of Earl's truck."

"What contraption?" asked John, "What are you talking about? What the hell is that thing behind us?"

"I don't know what it is...but I think I know how to stop it." My voice trembled with grim determination. I knew what must be done. We had to get to Earl's place and shut the door on that horrendous iron container. I knew our swirling pursuer was nothing from nature and nothing from God. It was something Earl had released when he'd pulled back that lever. I shook my head. What kind of devil's play had Amos Grimsley been involved in, anyway? A bizarre scene flashed through my mind. I could see the wizened figure of Grimsley, sitting on top of the container, roaring with sardonic laughter.

The station wagon came over the small rise just before Earl's place. Where the house had once stood now looked like a bombsight—twisted wreckage was everywhere. Most of the equipment parts and other items that habitually surrounded the premises were gone—vanished. Even Earl's pickup was nowhere in sight.

The car skidded into the driveway. All of us were rocked to and fro as it slid to a halt. The flatbed truck was still sitting there, untouched by the wind. On top of it was the iron container, its front-side door wide open. We were astonished by what we saw spewing forth from it. An enormous, twisting shaft of black wind was blasting out of the container.

Earl's barn, which had stood directly in front of the container, was nowhere in sight—disintegrated by the explosion of wind that had burst forth. What a sight that must have been, I thought. For just a moment my mind beheld the frightening scene. I could see my aged friend, sitting there in amazement, his hands still wrapped around the lever, watching his barn being blown to smithereens. Poor Earl, I thought, poor Earl.

I leaned back and spoke to the women. "Stay in the car until we get back...and keep your seatbelts on!" I looked at John Connors. "C'mon...let's shut this thing down."

The two of us climbed out and looked to the rear. The cyclonic demon had followed us up the canyon, charging like a predator in pursuit. It was less than half a mile away and moving quickly.

Avoiding the blast of wind that bellowed from the front, we came around the backside of the container and leaped up on the flatbed. The handle on the container was set in the last slot, all the way back to "full open."

I jumped up and straddled the handle, attempting to dislodge it from the slot and push it forward. I strained hard, but was unable to budge it.

"Get up here and give me a hand!" I yelled at John.

The dust demon was nearer, a few hundred yards away.

John climbed up on the container to help. We both gripped the lever and pushed, straining and straining to bring the door down against the flow of air that was belching out of the front of the container.

The dust cloud was hitting the perimeter of Earl's property, and the wreckage from the earlier round of destruction went flying back into the air. A broken wooden beam went sailing into the rear window of the station wagon, shattering it. A moment later a rock smashed into the side passenger window. Even through the shriek of the wind we could hear the women screaming from inside the car. The twisting cloud of death was only a few yards away from it. John and I mustered all of our strength and pushed.

The lever began to move.

As it slid forward out of the rear slot, we heard an unearthly roar from above. I looked up and saw something that rocked my senses. John Connors saw it too. Within the funnel of swirling wind was *a huge, monstrous face!* It was peering at us through the wall of dust. The face itself was not of an actual physical nature, but seemed to be a nebulous, almost transparent image with fluid-like features that were totally unaffected by the volatile winds. It appeared to be scowling down at us in a look of rage.

I glanced over at the station wagon—it had become engulfed by the wall of dust!

"Push!" I screamed.

John and I gave one final push. As the lever slid forward, the door below began to creak and rumble as it started closing downward, slowly cutting off the screaming shaft of wind that still cascaded out of the container.

The entity above issued another hideous bellow that cut through the howl of the rushing wind.

The door slammed shut; the flow of wind from the container ceased instantly.

Suddenly the swirling dust cloud—along with the demonic creature within—began to shoot skyward, spiraling toward the black clouds above. It was as though the string on a helium balloon had been cut, allowing the creature and the swirling dust cloud to escape into the upper atmosphere. As it all hurtled skyward, a funnel of suction pulled objects up along with it. John and I clung desperately to the lever. John's legs rose off the container, then mine. Within seconds both our bodies were being pulled straight up. Through squinted eyelids, I saw John's shoes go flying off his feet, shooting straight up into the whirling suction above—it was almost a comical sight. I felt sure we were going to die.

After an eternity of seconds, the suction began to subside and both of us settled slowly back down onto the container. We regained our footing and looked up to see saw the cloud of dust still ascending into the heavens. It was getting smaller and smaller as it moved away from the Earth. The surrounding wind was rapidly subsiding.

I stared through the settling dust—the station wagon was still there, sitting about ten yards farther back. It had been rocked about by the powerful wind force and had done a complete one-eighty. The three women were all crying in the back seat. The strain and stress caught up with John Connors at that moment; he broke down and began to weep, crying like an infant.

As the black clouds of destruction faded into the heavens, I looked down again at the container. The hellish contraption was now shut, but whatever kind of demonic entity had been contained within its iron walls was no longer a prisoner. Strangely enough, the container now seemed curiously harmless. Covered with oxidation and rust, it looked totally benign.

A curious feeling came over me. On sudden impulse, I started pulling back the lever again.

"Gil—what are you doing?" John shouted.

The metal screeched loudly as the door flew open.

Nothing happened.

OUR BATTERED station wagon made its way slowly down Cobb's Canyon. The Page farmhouse, my farmhouse, was still standing—the lone structural survivor of the windblown carnage that had descended upon the upper end of Antelope Valley. I silently thanked God for saving my family and friends. But Earl and the Stimmons family were gone. Their lives had come to a horrifying end.

And what about the wind? We all knew the comfort of a gentle summer breeze was lost to us forever. It would always act as a grim reminder of the horror of that day. But more than that, it would serve perpetual notice that the cyclonic abomination that had reeked such wanton destruction on our community was still out there, hiding in the winds that circle the Earth. Any news report of a hurricane or tornado would give us pause, making us wonder if the tempestuous horror had returned. Even a blustery day would accentuate the latent fear that would forever remain in the back of our minds.

As the station wagon rolled into the driveway, one final prayer sprang into my mind. It was a vengeful, heartfelt plea. I prayed that Amos Grimsley would burn in Hell...

Forever!

THE END

HAND OF DEATH

By Marjorie Murch Stanley

"I couldn't do anything about it; he had found the answer to interchangeable human parts."

I CAN tell this story now…without hurting Tom.

First of all, you must understand that I loved him very much. Nothing that happened to him, or ever could have happened, would have changed that. Perhaps if I'd gotten to him in time, I could have made him understand. But that was the trouble from the beginning… I couldn't get to him.

We had been very close to each other for more than a year. We were going to be married as soon as he and his father, Professor Martin, finished one final experiment. And suddenly, Tom and I were like strangers. You might say it all began on a Friday night in October.

"Darling, darling," Tom whispered. "Just a few more weeks and we'll be together forever. Dad wants to get this one last experiment out of the way. The minute he can spare me from the lab, we'll be married."

"Tom, I hope it's soon. We've waited so long!"

We were walking through Clifton Park where we came as often as we could for our hurried meetings. Tom had so few spare moments. I knew better than to ask what the experiments were. Even Tom didn't know all the details, although he told me once they would revolutionize medicine.

He walked me back to my apartment, held me tightly and kissed me good night.

"Now don't forget Wednesday night," he warned me.

"As if I could," I laughed.

I went into my apartment alone and, not turning on the light, I went to the window and watched him walk down the dark street.

To all intents and purposes…I never really saw Tom again.

I ATE Wednesday afternoon. I was ironing the skirt of my best black formal when the phone rang. Tom and I were planning a big evening out, our first real date in weeks. He had tickets to a new play and we were going to meet some friends for supper afterwards. After so many hurried meetings, quick lunches near his laboratory, short phone calls, a walk now and then, it was heaven to think I'd be with him all evening. I'd had a quick, almost curt, call from him Monday at the office, just to say he'd pick me up at seven-thirty on Wednesday. Other than that we'd had no contact since Friday night.

My nails were shiny, my hair in pin curls, and my heart very light as I answered the phone.

"Margaret? This is Paul."

"Yes, Paul. How are you?" My voice was warm. There are a lot of nice guys in the world, I thought, but Dr. Paul Holbrook is one of the best. He and Tom had been roommates in pre-med school. But while Paul had gone on with medicine, and taken his degree, Tom had elected to work with his father along a different line.

"Fine. Listen. Is Tom there with you?"

"No. I'm not expecting him until seven-thirty. Why?"

"Funny. Nobody answers at the laboratory. I thought someone was always there in the afternoon. Oh, well, it can wait."

"You sound funny, Paul. Is there something wrong?"

"Nothing, really. I saw Tom this morning, out near the lab. I was driving past, and I stopped. He was walking his dog."

I laughed. "That big mutt. Honestly, the housekeeper could just as well do it, but Tom's so crazy about Siegfried, you know..."

"It wasn't Siegfried. It was a little dachshund. The poor little thing was limping and Tom was talking to it like a mother. I kidded him about it and he told me to mind my own business."

"Why, Paul," I said slowly, "that doesn't sound like Tom. He doesn't have a dachshund. That is...well, there was one in the laboratory three or four weeks ago. Tom found him in the road one night with a leg so badly smashed it had to be amputated."

"This was a dachshund all right. Probably a different one. Even in school Tom was always picking up stray dogs. Oh, well, I was just taking a long chance on his being at your place, Margaret. I'll see you after the show tonight. Right?"

"That's right, Paul."

WE HUNG up. I went back to my ironing. As I look back on that time, just before the roof of my little world fell in, I don't believe I had even an inkling of what was ahead. I was excited about that evening, eager to have a good time, and odd facts like a closed laboratory, a limping dachshund and Tom's being rude to his best friend, just didn't tie together. I didn't go to the laboratory often. Tom's father was a queer sort—a cheerful, gay, whistling little man given to sudden silences and fits of brooding. The two of them lived in an apartment over their laboratory in the quieter section of town, almost on the outskirts. A housekeeper, a Mrs. Vernon, took care of them. The place was really off the main road, their street going on for a block or two and then meandering off into a dirt road into the countryside. It was so different from my tiny apartment, right in the center of town.

But, as I said, on that particular Wednesday afternoon, I don't believe I gave a thought to anything except making myself as pretty as possible for Tom.

Tom was late. Seven-thirty came and went. At eight-fifteen I decided to phone his apartment. At that moment, I heard a loud, almost belligerent pounding on the door. It didn't sound like Tom, but when I opened the door, there he was. He had a peculiar look on his face…vague…or perhaps puzzled is a better word. He mumbled an apology as he came in. He didn't kiss me.

"I don't mind your being late, darling, but is something wrong?" I asked hesitantly.

"No." He swung to face me. "What makes you say that? What could be wrong?"

"Nothing. I didn't mean anything. I guess, I…I'm just a little impatient to get going."

I thought he might say something nice about my looks. My black dress fitted me perfectly. My light brown hair was smooth and shining from the rinse I'd given it. And while I'll never be beautiful, Tom always said he liked green eyes and a turned up nose. But he didn't say anything. He just stood there in his bulky topcoat, his brown eyes with a bewildered look in them…and his dark hair a little too long.

It was a warm evening for this late in the summer, but Tom didn't seem to notice, so after a moment, I took my own coat from the closet and we left.

I CAN'T remember much of the play. Tom didn't hold my hand. In fact he seemed to be trying not to touch me at all. During intermission he sat staring straight ahead, with his coat folded in his lap so that people had to clamber over us on their way to the lobby.

When the play was over, we took a cab to the supper club.

"Hi, kids," I greeted Paul and his date, Bettina. Paul introduced another couple at the table, as Tom and I sat down.

"We're a little ahead of you," Bettina told us seriously, setting her glass down carefully in front of her.

"Not for long," Tom assured her, signaling the waiter.

It was then I noticed Tom was wearing an old suit from his college days. It brought back forcibly to me, how terribly thin and run down looking he was. In college, of course, he'd gotten a bit too heavy—he was on the football team—but really this old suit hung like a sack on him.

Tom took his first drink at a gulp, and the second and third. Paul and I exchange glances. Tom had a poor head for liquor and seldom drank at all. Paul started to apologize for the episode with the dachshund, but Tom brushed his words aside and went on talking to Bettina. He hadn't paid the slightest attention to me since leaving the theatre.

In another hour, Tom was so drunk he could hardly stand. We started to leave. The other man and Paul tried to get Tom to his feet without creating a disturbance. And yet the oddest thing happened. When Paul tried to put his arm around Tom, Tom suddenly gave a lunge, got to his feet, and was out of the door before we could do anything. When we reached the street, Tom was just driving away in a cab.

We all followed in Paul's car, but we lost him in traffic. We drove out to the laboratory. It was locked and there was no light inside, although we could hear dogs barking somewhere toward the back. Paul took me home, and I cried myself to sleep.

For three days, Paul and I tried to get in touch with Tom. If he heard our phone calls, he didn't answer. If he and the professor were at the laboratory, they paid no attention to our ringing and knocking at the door. Where Mrs. Vernon was I don't know, but we always heard the dogs.

I went to work every day. I'm secretary to the head of a chemical firm, but I had a hard time keeping my mind on my job. When I quit work at noon on Saturday, I hurried back to the apartment. No sooner had I stepped in the door when the phone rang.

"Thought I'd catch you, Margaret." Paul's voice came thinly over the wire. "Look, I've got some bad news. No...no..." I had gasped audibly. "No...it's not Tom. It's his father...the professor. He's been strangled."

My knees gave way and I sank into a chair. "Strangled? But who...who could have done such a thing... Why?"

"Nobody knows. Tom found him and notified the police. It must have happened about six this morning, but Tom didn't find him until about eight. The professor was on the laboratory floor."

"How...how horrible," I breathed. "Where's Tom now? Can I see him? He must be sick over this."

"He'll be at the inquest this afternoon. Mrs. Vernon is taking care of him. She's the one who called me. The inquest will be held at the coroner's office at four o'clock. You could see Tom there. Do you want me to pick you up?"

"Yes. Yes. I'll be ready. Oh, Paul, Professor Martin was such a little...inoffensive man. Who'd want to hurt him?"

And that was the question they tried to find the answer to at the inquest.

TO THE strangers who didn't know Tom, I suppose his actions seemed normal. He sat in a corner of the room with his head in his hand and his elbows on his knees. He was wearing the long loose laboratory coat as he habitually did. He answered everything they asked him in an especially loud voice. To me, it seemed to hold suppressed fury. He never once met my eyes. Instead he asked why all the "extra people" were there.

Someone asked him if we weren't friends of his. He said we were, but did we need to get mixed up in this.

Of course they told him the hearing was open, that anyone could come. At first his coldness puzzled me...then I wanted to cry. Paul squeezed my hand sympathetically and that helped me keep the tears back.

Tom's story was perfectly straightforward and the housekeeper corroborated it. He awakened at, eight o'clock, shaved, dressed and went downstairs as he always did. He said the professor often spent the night on the cot in the laboratory and had done so the night he was killed. No, the professor hadn't had any visitors. In fact the last person to visit them had been Paul and that was nearly three weeks before.

The housekeeper said she lived in except on Saturday and Sunday nights when she stayed overnight with a married daughter. She awakened at seven-thirty as usual, and started breakfast in the kitchen. She hadn't heard anything in the night.

"Though I can't be saying as everything was perfectly normal, this past month or two. Tom and his pa were getting mysterious about their work. They even went so far as to lock the laboratory doors, something they've never done in the twelve years I've been caring for them. And they said I wasn't to answer the door, no matter who was there, nor the telephone either." Old Mrs. Vernon seemed put out, but when they questioned her further, she couldn't say exactly why things seemed "mysterious."

Tom admitted they'd been extra careful about their work. "My father was on the verge of a very important discovery. Even I didn't know just what it was. Only that it would be the means of stopping a great deal of the suffering of injured animals. That's about all I can say."

Did his father have any enemies?

Tom's eyes seemed to be seeing things that we couldn't. "None that I know of. You might even say he had no friends. Certainly since my mother died twelve years ago, he went nowhere. And we never entertained. The only people who came to the lab were friends of mine and they came very infrequently."

AS TOM spoke, his words sounded rational and calm, but I knew him. I knew that he was tense and uncertain, that he could hardly contain his impatience at being there, and that he was trying desperately to hold back his nervousness.

The police in charge said that the laboratory had been thoroughly checked for fingerprints. One large thumb print found on the laboratory table, which did not match those of the professor, Tom, or the housekeeper, had been forwarded to Washington for possible identification. I was watching Tom during these remarks and it seemed to me that his face took on a sickly look, as though someone had dealt him a blow in the pit of his stomach.

There seemed to be nothing more to discuss, and after Paul and I had answered a routine question or two, the coroner gave his verdict as death by strangulation caused by a person or persons unknown. And we were free to go.

I started towards Tom, but he got up and walked out the door without looking at me. And I spent another night crying myself to sleep.

I spent most of Sunday trying to get Tom on the phone, but no one answered. It was about eight o'clock when Paul phoned me.

"The police have identified the fingerprint. It belongs to a Gringo Mallardex—fighter, ex-convict. He got sent up once for manslaughter, by strangling!"

"Then that's the answer!" I cried. "Oh, Paul...let's go out to see Tom. Let's try again. Maybe we can get him to sell the house...turn the lab over to someone else...maybe..."

"Margaret, wait." Paul's voice cut in. "You didn't let me finish. The D. A. found out something else. Gringo Mallard is dead. He was killed in a brawl in a town two counties away. He was killed a week before the professor was strangled."

"Then...then...what does it mean? How could his fingerprints be on the lab table? Is there some mistake?"

"That's what the D. A. wants to know, Margaret. Tom knows something he isn't telling anyone. That's why he's acting so strangely. You know, it occurred to me last night; how could a stranger get near to that house without those dogs setting up a racket? And yet both Tom and Mrs. Vernon must have slept right through the murder. I think Tom is shielding someone."

"But who? Who would he possibly want to shield?"

"I don't know. The D. A. will be after him the first thing in the morning. We've got to get out there tonight, and try to talk to him. I'm going to break my way into the laboratory, if necessary. Do you want to come?"

IT WAS late in the evening when we drove up to Tom's place. It had been a raw, dull day. Summer was really over and we'd been having a spell of wet weather. Leaves were dropping and out on the lonely section where Tom lived, they had blown into soggy heaps. The place seemed more desolate than ever.

Paul rang the bell, then pounded on the door. We waited. The dogs in the kennels started barking.

"If he's not in there, where could he be?" I could hear the phone ringing in the back somewhere, and it rang and rang before it stopped.

"I guess Mrs. Vernon isn't back yet. I'm going in anyway, if I can make it." Paul started to poke around the doorway, then the window. Finally he told me to watch out. He stood at one side and smashed in a window with a stone. He did it carefully and thoroughly until he could reach in and turn the lock. Then he stepped inside and pulled up the frame. After a moment, he helped me through.

We were in the laboratory proper. We switched on a light. It was a weak one, and at first sight, the lab looked as it had on the few occasions I'd visited Professor Martin. I could almost see the round, pink face and stocky figure bending over his endless books or working at his strange assortment of test tubes. I shuddered and looked about me quickly. Where had they found his body? Here? I moved from the place where I was standing. The light seemed to dim even more. I stepped near a spot that was dark. Had it once been blood? I moved again. Then I remembered…there wouldn't have been blood, of course, at least not the professor's. He'd been strangled. Strangled! What a ghastly feeling that must be.

I was working myself to a fine state of hysteria, but I was ashamed to let Paul know my feelings. He was on the other side of the room, flipping through some ledgers, when a low voice from behind me, almost in my ear said:

"What do you want?"

I screamed before I could stop myself, although almost at the same instant I knew—it was Tom.

He just stood there looking at the two of us, at Paul, with a stack of papers in his I hand, and at me with my hands over my mouth.

"I said—what do you want?" Tom came toward us. Involuntarily I backed toward Paul. As Tom came under the light, I saw that he was muddy almost to his knees.

"Tom," I faltered, "we just had to see you."

"Why?" Tom cut in, almost with a snarl. I looked at him and he was an utter stranger. There was nothing left of the man I had known...the friendly, sweet person who had loved me.

"You needn't talk like that." Paul's voice was brisk with a false heartiness. "We're your friends. We want to talk to you. Something has come up that you've got to know about."

TOM looked from our faces to the broken window. When he saw the papers in Paul's hand, he made an angry snatch at them, crossing the room in a frenzy. He stopped mid-action, and slowly slumped down in a chair.

I sat down opposite him. Paul pulled up a lab stool, and leaning forward, he told Tom about Gringo Mallard.

So you see...there must be a mistake somewhere, Tom. Gringo couldn't have killed your father. He'd been dead for nearly a week."

Tom didn't look surprised. He was staring at Paul in an odd sort of way. I could say...wistfully. Then he said in a flat unemotional voice, "Yes, I know."

"You...know..." I stammered. "How do you know Gringo was dead? The police only found it out an hour ago."

"I know because I saw him a few minutes ago. He's dead all right." Tom laughed—the eeriest sound I ever heard. "Say, how would you two like to hear a story?" Tom sat up straight with a jerk. "Sure. I'll tell it to you and then it won't be a secret any more…I won't have to hide any more…I won't be alone anymore."

"Start from the beginning," I begged.

"The beginning? There isn't any beginning. I'm going to start at the end. Do you know where I've been?" He waved a finger impishly under our noses. "Don't guess. You wouldn't be right. I've been pushing a man back into his grave."

Paul's eye caught mine, and the same thought must have hit us both at once. *Humor him. He's out of his mind.*

"That's why I'm muddy. I went out into the swamps…down the road. All this rain. I thought it might wash him out and it had. There Gringo was…floating in the swamp…ugly and sodden and dead." Tom giggled. "I had to make sure. I pushed him back in the ground. Yes, everything that was out there was dead."

I was afraid to speak. Tom's eyes stared straight ahead. He didn't see us. "But he killed my father. He killed him. I didn't do it. They can't blame me."

AFTER a long moment, Tom went on in a more normal manner. "My father was a wonderful man, and he had a wonderful idea. For a while it worked. It's all there in the ledgers. You can read it…every little experiment. He started small. He wanted it kept a secret. He wanted to be absolutely sure. He had to prove it over and over to himself that he was right. I begged him to let the medical profession know, before someone else came up with the same idea, and got the glory, but he wouldn't listen. He started being away for hours at a time."

Tom got to his feet restlessly. He started to pace back and forth…so that his shadows swung from one wall to the other. "And then one afternoon…it was a few days before the night we went to the theatre…it happened. I guess my father had been planning it a long time. He was having one of his sullen moods. We quarreled about giving out the secret. For days he'd acted strangely. This day he was half-dazed from lack of sleep…he'd been out all night. I heard funny noises early in the morning. I knew it was too early for the housekeeper to be coming downstairs. I went down to see what was going on, and I saw my father coming out of the laboratory. He locked the door behind him, and he wouldn't let me in the room all day. Finally I tried to force in the door and my father came up behind me. I felt him jab me with a needle. I swung on him, and that's the last I remember until I woke up on the lab table."

Tom looked at the table in front of him, then covered his face with his hands and sat down. He was shaking, almost sobbing. Paul opened one of the cabinets and poured Tom a stiff drink.

"There's no way of telling you how I felt. I had the feeling that time had passed…hours. I felt light-headed; but not sick. I didn't hurt anywhere, and for a little while I didn't move. I was fully conscious, but I kept my eyes closed, trying to figure out why my father had given me a knock-out dose of whatever it was. The sheet was pulled up to my chin; my arms were crossed over my chest. Finally, I opened my eyes. My father was standing beside me.

"It worked," he told me, coming around so that we faced each other. "It worked. Now we can tell them. I've proved it finally."

Tom shifted to the edge of his chair. His voice dropped to a hoarse whisper. I could feel the hair prickling the back of my neck. Paul moved uneasily.

"And then my father told me to get up…to get up and walk around…that I was perfectly all right…that there wouldn't be any reaction." Tom stopped. The silence was heavy in the laboratory.

"Go on…go on…" Paul told him, harshly. "Get to the point."

Tom sprang to his feet. "All right! All right! Here's the point!" Tom grabbed me by the arm, and started pulling me toward the hall. Paul jumped to my side, and Tom shoved us both along. "There…" Tom pointed to the hallway. "See that mirror…I smashed it. I smashed the one upstairs. I did it in a drunken rage…when I saw what had happened to me. Look!" Tom turned back to the laboratory. He snatched off his coat…and flung it to the floor. Then he started ripping at his shirt. His body was bound tightly with strips of cloth. He tore at the knots. Finally he hacked at it with a scalpel. And then…as though released under terrific pressure…a heavy, hairy…twisting arm came into sight…not Tom's arm…but attached to him…struggling and squirming…throwing a thousand spidery shadows on the walls.

I SCREAMED and screamed...while Tom held the wiggling horror with both his arms...laughing at my terror...at Paul's stunned amazement...shrieking all the while... "See...see...this is why I got drunk...why I smashed the mirrors. My father did this to me. I was his best experiment...a real freak. If your dog got a smashed leg...he'd graft on a new one. If some punk lost an ear in a fight...he'd graft on a new one...and if you were all in one piece...maybe you'd like an extra arm...everybody can use another arm...like this...like mine...have another arm...just for the laughs." And Tom's choked laughter went on and on...over my screams...until the room swirled about me, and I lost consciousness.

I don't know how much later it was when I came to. I was on a sofa in Tom's apartment over the laboratory. Paul was sitting by me, holding ammonia under my nose.

"Margaret! Wake up! Wake up! I can't leave you alone unless you wake up."

I fought my way back to consciousness.

"Where is he?" I whispered.

"He's in the bedroom. No...no...lie down. It's all right. You won't have to see him again."

"How did you...?"

"I knocked him out. Then I bound up the arm again." I shuddered at Paul's words, but he kept a firm grip on my hands so that I couldn't sit up. "He's perfectly rational, although he's terribly depressed."

"Paul, I've got to go to him. You must let me. I can stand it now. Now that I've seen..."

"It's no place for a woman...with a maniac!"

"You mustn't say that about Tom. I...I love him..." The words came hard, yet even as I said them...the old tenderness swept over me. I had loved Tom too long and waited for him too long, not to have some of that feeling still alive no matter what. "Paul, what can we do for him? I don't care what he's like...this isn't the real Tom. He's just had too much of horror and disillusionment about his father...and..."

"There's just one thing to do and I'm going to try it, if he'll let me."

I sat up and this time Paul let me. "I'm not afraid of him, Paul... Let me see him again."

We went slowly into the bedroom. There was nothing violent looking about Tom. He was on the bed, with a blanket over him. His face was clean now, and the hair smoothed down. We sat down, one of us on either side of the bed, and this time Tom told the rest of his story in a flat, passionless voice, oddly out of focus with the violence of his words.

"Don't be afraid of me, Margaret. I didn't want you to know about this...ever. I wanted to kill myself. I wouldn't even answer the phone because it might be you, and I think I would have broken down, just talking to you. It takes a brave man to kill himself, and I'm not brave. I guess my father knew that. It's awful to think he'd do that to me, his own son...just to prove himself right. I suppose you've guessed the rest. The night of the theatre, I nearly went crazy. No matter what I put on, or how tightly I strapped the arm, it still showed. I only wanted to hide myself, along with the other animals. We were all freaks together. That's why I was so nervous when you caught me walking the dachshund that morning, Paul."

Paul stretched out his hand and patted Tom's shoulder... "I'm sorry about that...but it's OK now...forget it."

TOM went on. "But then I got a terrific yearning to see you, Margaret...and other people, normal people, I found my old college suit, and that covered the bump if I strapped the arm straight down my side. Oh, I'd tried everything, but father had done his work well...every muscle, every cord...I could feel it as though the arm was my own, but I didn't have any control over it. Even strapped as it was...it writhed. I begged my father...I pleaded with him to take it off. And he promised he would...if I'd wait just a little while...a week...a few days...so he could take notes. I promised. I couldn't do anything about it myself. And it was true. There was no reaction at all. He had found the answer to interchangeable human parts."

Tom shook his head slowly. "Perhaps those words occurred to my father... Perhaps that's what gave him the idea of spare parts. That idea should be funny, somehow. Anyway, you know I got drunk the night of the theatre. I found I couldn't face you after all, Margaret. When I got home in the cab, my father was waiting for me. He took notes, reams of notes...and my reactions to everything. When I finally sobered up we...we buried what was left of Gringo. Somehow, through some method he never revealed, he got the body of the man while it was still warm and brought it home, that night when he stayed out. It's all in the records, I suppose."

Tom stopped.

"Paul...if...if...I don't get through this thing in one piece...you take the records...take everything. There's a will...you won't have any trouble."

Paul reassured him. "That's nonsense...everything is settled. I'll amputate the arm. We'll bury it...or burn it...and no one on earth will ever know."

Tom shook his head. "They'll find Gringo. Or somebody will start putting two and two together. There will be people out here...crowds, maybe. They'll find him." His voice dropped eerily again, "I think Gringo wants to be found. He wants the rest of himself. And the arm...the arm...it keeps struggling."

"Stop that, Tom. That's just what you mustn't think about. Can you tell us how it happened...about the Professor?"

"So simple. I'd gotten up early on Saturday morning, so my father could help me take a bath. Someone had to hold the arm, you see. We had to do it while Mrs. Vernon was still asleep. The arm was quiet that morning, but you never could be sure. When I'd bathed, I went back to the lab, and my father was getting ready to strap it down, when it just...reached out for his throat. Father pulled at the arm...and I tried to break away. But the thing's in such a position...not really below my arm, but a little towards the back, that I couldn't get into a good position to hold it. When I broke loose, Father was dead. Then...then the arm quieted down, and I strapped it myself. Then I locked up all the ledgers and went back upstairs until my usual time for getting up. Then I went down and pretended to discover him, and I called the police."

"Tom...please listen to Paul," I said. "It's a chance worth taking. If this whole thing gets out, it might mean a long trial. You'll never live it down."

Paul stood up. "It's decided. I'm going to do it. Margaret, you'll have to help. We can do it here; we have everything we need. We'll do it tonight. There's no need to wait."

Tom watched us both. He must have seen the look Paul gave me, but he allowed himself to be persuaded. Paul said he should sleep a little while, and we'd wake him when everything was ready. Paul wanted to read everything Professor Martin had written on the case.

I waited quietly by Tom's side until he was asleep. I wasn't afraid, not even repulsed by what lay under the covers. I suppose I was just numb. I prayed that whatever reaction was coming to me would wait until the operation was over.

Finally I went downstairs to Paul and we made what preparations were necessary. He finished reading the ledgers, shaking his head in admiration and incredulity. We went into the cellar to look at the furnace. Paul decided against burning the arm. We would take it down the road to the woods and bury it before it grew light.

We each had a drink, and then arranged the table for operating, and sterilized the instruments. Then I went up to awaken Tom while Paul scrubbed his hands. Never, to my dying day, will I ever walk up a flight of stairs and open a bedroom door again, without the full horror of this moment returning to me.

TOM lay as we had left him. There had been no struggle. His eyes were wide and blank; his face a ghastly shade of blue. The arm...the big, hairy, dark arm had him by the throat. His own arms were by his side. He held the knife with which he had cut the straps. This time I did not scream. I looked at him until the picture was printed on my mind forever, and then I didn't remember anything for a long time.

So, as I said in the beginning, I can tell this story without hurting Tom. If I could have reached his mind...made him know I loved him no matter what...perhaps he would have called to us at last.

When my terrible weeks of blackout and illness were over, Paul was my only security. I knew he loved me, and so we were married. It was true...what Tom had said. Everything was left to

Paul to carry on as he saw fit. The whole story came out in every gruesome detail, and like everything of that nature, rapidly became yesterday's news. I began to forget. And yet, sometimes, just lately, I've been wondering if it is all over for me.

Paul and I were very close for a while after our marriage. What we had gone through together seemed a very strong tie. Recently Paul has spent less time at the hospital and in his office, and more time out at Tom's old laboratory. He's made quite a pet of Tom's little dachshund. Every once in a while I see him looking at me in a strange sort of way. Somehow, I don't feel so close to Paul any more.

THE END

PATTERN IN THE DUST

By Ivar Jorgensen

*The young man sobbed as he knelt at the desolate grave of the girl he'd loved—
and murdered—one hundred years ago…*

"IT MAY be the cure we're looking for and it may not," Dr. Frederick Lawrence said. "If you had waited another year before getting this fever, we could be entirely certain."

Lawrence was a handsome cap, dark, alert, and yet with a dreamer's eyes. He was looked upon in the medical profession as a comer. He paced back and forth past the foot of the white bed and seemed to direct his remarks more to Carol, who sat stroking her husband's head, than to Greg himself.

Greg's hot, glazed eyes were upon Carol also; eyes which appeared, not to see, so full were they of the burning languor this horrible fever had brought. But Greg did see, and his mind, under its blanket of sickness, still functioned normally. His thoughts of Carol were foremost, which was entirely natural. On the threshold of death a miser thinks of his money; a dictator of his power.

Greg thought of Carol: I don't want to go away from her. I am not afraid to die. The fading out, the emptiness, the passing over—these hold no terrors at all. But I've had Carol for such a short time. It isn't fair that I be forced to leave so soon. Not fair.

"Has the serum been tested at all, Doctor?" Carol asked the question as her cool hand continued to stroke Greg's brow.

Dr. Lawrence's compelling eyes rested on her for several silent moments. He made a deprecating gesture. "After a fashion. It worked satisfactorily upon rodents."

"But rodents are not human."

"That's true. On the basis of what I've already done with it, I'd say there's not even a fifty-fifty chance of its saving your husband. Its merit lies solely in the fact that without it—" Young Dr. Lawrence shrugged again, "—there's no chance whatever."

141

Greg couldn't see what the hesitation was about. Lawrence added it up neatly. Less than half a chance—no chance at all. Where was the point of dissension? He smiled, laid his hand on Carol's, and said, "You'd better get out your hypodermic, Doc."

TEARS WELLED into Carol's eyes. "But darling. If—if it doesn't work…"

"If it doesn't, we've lost nothing."

"And if it isn't administered pretty quick, it won't matter one way or another," Lawrence said.

Carol was crying softly now and Greg strove to buck her up. "It's going to work, honey. I've got a hunch, and you know my hunches. Remember that horse last year when we were at the track? He didn't have a chance. But I knew differently."

Dr. Lawrence had already started preparations. "As I told you," he said, "this formula is revolutionary in theory. It runs opposite some established medical concepts." He pushed the needle of the hypodermic through the cork of a sealed bottle and drew dark fluid up into the chamber. "While in my heart I'm also certain it will work. I still can't say what your reactions will be."

Greg smiled and patted Carol's hand. "I might become famous, honey. The first man to be saved by a new serum. Let's get it over with. The sooner I'm up and around, the sooner I can appear on radio and television."

Carol didn't have the courage to watch during the injection. Still holding Greg's hand, she turned her head away and cried softly into her handkerchief. Dr. Lawrence, tight-lipped, bared Greg's arm, and in a moment the latter felt the mild bee-sting of the needle entering his flesh.

Dead silence beat and echoed thunderously in the small hospital room. Lawrence withdrew the needle, stepped back, his whole attention riveted upon the patient in the bed.

Greg lay motionless for some moments, his chest rising and falling in an almost imperceptible rhythm. He opened his eyes. "Don't feel anything, Doc. Not a thing. It's like—"

Carol turned, screamed. In her hand was—nothing.

GREG'S FEVER was gone. That was the first knowledge that came to him as consciousness returned. The racking, retching pains had vanished. The flaming furnace in his chest had burned itself out. His next thought was: I am not the same person I was.

It did not occur to him to classify this condition as death. He felt such strength of life, such vigor, as to make such a conception unthinkable. So two facts became established in his mind: he was alive, and he had licked the fever.

But with the opening of his eyes, there came complete bewilderment. He lay, stark naked, upon a close-cropped lawn. It was a rather sheltered spot, bordered in a semicircle by a ring of close-set trees. Nearby stood a smart white building that could have been a residence, or possibly a garage. It was a severely designed building, a radical architectural departure from any structure Greg had ever seen.

But such things were noted only in passing, because Greg's attention was rooted mainly in his own nudity. Lying naked in someone's yard. It was like one of the old standard nightmares, except that Greg knew he was alive, awake, and that all this was very real. Before taking time to wonder about his surroundings, his nude state must be corrected.

He lay still for some minutes, waiting for a sound, for some sign of activity about him. There was none save the contented whisperings of the trees above him. Gradually a hope arose. There was a feeling of *absentia* about this strange house. A quiet waiting, as houses seem to wait for the return of their tenants.

Greg got slowly to his feet. After a few moments he realized he was holding his breath. He breathed deeply and the blood pounded in his ears. Still no break in the pastoral quiet about him. He compressed his lips grimly and took a step toward the house. Another—another. Only the leaves in the trees stirred, and they seemed to be urging him on, striving to give him confidence.

The flagstones of the winding walk were under the soles of his bare feet and the door to the strange house confronted him.

Magically, it opened. He started back in surprise. The door closed. Greg grinned in relief. Obviously he was breaking an electric eye beam with his body. He did not waste time trying to locate the electric eye, but stepped forward through the doorway into the house.

THE INTERIOR of the house completely eclipsed the exterior in daring originality. Greg wondered for a moment whether or not he had come inadvertently into some sort of futuristic exhibit, rather than a place where people lived. There seemed no rhyme or reason to the place; yet, taken overall, it presented an amazing picture of both beauty and convenience. Thin spider web cables were flung down from the high ceiling, upon which were suspended glass rectangles which were evidently rooms. These rooms were attained by following equally spidery circular staircases which gave the impression of winding off into infinity.

Greg waited, tense, for signs of life. There were none. Finally he built up the courage to go forward. Clothing was the problem of the moment. A bedroom seemed the logical answer.

He climbed one of the staircases and was surprised at coming directly into a room with a broad, low bed and a streamlined highboy, the cut of which was obviously masculine. He found the wardrobe and his nudity was soon a thing of the past.

At least, moderately so. The clothing he found was entirely functional. It reminded him of a beach getup done along startling lines. But he could find no other clothing and was not inclined to be choosy.

Still bewildered, but far more sure of himself than he had been before, Greg gave closer attention to the strange house. It occurred to him that he could easily get into trouble for illegal entry, and started to leave the bedroom. But near the exit he became intrigued with a panel of knobs and dials on the front of what could have been the latest thing in television sets; or, for that matter, far beyond the latest thing. There were about a dozen of the knobs, each with a notation underneath. These notations read: audio, visual, sensory, ultra perceptive, and so on.

Familiar with the first two only, he snapped the audio and instantly heard a voice coming from a hidden loudspeaker: "...thus it can be easily seen that our Union must be on the alert at all times. Preparedness is of course the watchword. At any moment some unimportant incident could be taken by the

Federation as an excuse for unleashing their lightning. While this crisis lasts, we must maintain a calm clear-headedness, but at the same time shun all forms of appeasement. And above all, let us fervently hope that this year of 2052 will not usher in a bloody holocaust which could easily be the end of civilization."

Stunned, Greg snapped off the broadcast. 2052! Then it was with surprising lack of panic that he remembered Carol and Doctor Lawrence and the hypodermic needle; that he knew what the serum had done. It had cured the fever, but that was not the extent of its powers.

ONE HUNDRED years! And, strangely, it was not the staggering miracle upon which his mind dwelt, but rather a puckish bemusement relative to the timetable involved. Why, he wondered, had it been exactly one hundred years? Why not ninety-nine, or one-hundred-one? And now came the most thundering realization of all.

Carol had been dead for many years.

Carol dead! The thought brought a heartsickness almost akin to the physical. Somehow he could not visualize that beautiful, vibrant body ever experiencing the changes of death. Nor did he want to visualize it.

His mind dotted with painful thought, Greg came back to the moment and realized he had left the strange house and was walking blindly down a street. People were passing him on the broad sidewalks; people dressed as he was dressed. Sleek, shining vehicles went by silently and he had the thought: one hundred years ago such automobiles would have been laughed at.

Other knowledge was garnered as he walked blindly down the wide, pleasant street. He had moved swiftly in time but not in distance, because there, old and ivy covered—but apparently still functioning—was the hospital in which he had received the injection of serum so long ago. Yes, there was the hospital, so of course this was still Mortonville, the quiet little suburban town where he and Carol had gone through the ecstasies of first love and marriage.

The town had changed, but it did not appear to have grown to any great extent. In fact, many of the old buildings remained as before. There was an arresting mixture here of the old and the obviously new.

But all these impressions came upon the back of his mind, so to speak. Overshadowing all else was his great sense of grief and loneliness. Carol was dead! All the people he had known existed no more. *Carol—Carol—Carol.*

Then came the next logical step in his thought sequence. As though it had happened but yesterday—which to him it had indeed—he felt an overwhelming urge to visit her grave. Swiftly he oriented himself and turned left at the next intersection. If the grave existed, he knew where to find it. Desperately he hoped it still did exist as he hurried across town to the tree-dotted cemetery where Mortonville had always placed its dead.

The cemetery had not changed greatly. The trees were larger, and some of them were gone now. Also, the cemetery was not too well kept up and gave the impression of long disuse. Possibly, he thought, the dead were no longer buried. But when would such a change in funeral procedure have taken place? In 1952, Carol had been twenty-three. If she had lived to an old age, there could easily be no grave. No grave to weep on. Only a memory for a man out of his time but not beyond the yearning for it.

BUT HE found the grave. Wandering in a part of the cemetery completely untended and long run down, he pulled the clinging ivy from a small, plain stone to read the words:

> *Carol Hempstead*
> *Born Aug. 7, 1929*
> *Executed for murder*
> *Nov. 17, 1954*
> *May She Rest In Peace*

Executed for murder. Greg blacked out.

And in the half-world of his unconsciousness was such an agony of mind as to be unbearable, as to act as a stimulant and bring back clear, torturing reality.

Executed! But why? How? Sweet little Carol hearing the pronouncement of death for murder! But whose murder? It was grotesque—unthinkable. But from the alchemy of this horrible knowledge and the agonies it brought, there was brewed an overpowering urge in Greg's mind. Nay, more than an urge. A certainty, an iron command.

He had to go back!

If I came here, he told himself, I can also go back from here. Doors open for those entering as well as those leaving. The same path that runs up the hill runs also down.

I must go back—back—back.

What Greg did he never knew nor cared. There was something in it of strength—a new strength he had felt when lying naked on the lawn beside that strange house. A power—but a blind power. Yet strong enough to achieve a purpose without knowing how. And Greg was standing in a familiar darkened room with the odor of heliotrope in his nostrils.

He had returned.

He stood for a moment filled with a great happiness, while the weakness of sudden and violent transition quivered through his body, faded, and gave place to strength. He moved toward the door and opened it. The hall was dimly lit from the floor lamp in the living room.

And there were voices. Old familiar voices. Greg stopped.

"I think it's about over, Carol. I can never practice again, of course, but there are other ways to make a living."

"It was so cruel—so unjust."

"It could have been worse. If they'd found a body, it would have meant the chair. For me—and possibly—"

"For me?"

"Probably not. But who can tell? We only know the absence of a *corpus delicti* saved our hides."

Carol's voice was empty—listless. "That would have been mere anticlimax. What they've done to us already—shunned—ostracized. Oh, Fred!"

GREG MOVED forward until he could look into the living room and see Carol press her body into Frederick Lawrence's arms and against his breast. Red rage flamed in Greg's brain.

So that was it! This man hadn't been a doctor. He'd been a devil! A fiend! He'd known all along what the serum would do! He had wanted Carol and he'd gotten her. Greg shook his head like a groggy fighter. How much actual time had elapsed? What day was this? What month? What year?

Lawrence's voice was tender, soothing. "I know, darling. I know. But we have each other. And the time has come to go away together. I'll make you forget all this. I swear it!"

Greg leaned against the wall for support. All the time this conniving blackleg had had this plan in his mind. An untried serum! What a ghastly lie. Greg could visualize the long months of research behind it. Lawrence had known exactly what that serum would do.

"You've been so good to me, Fred. If it hadn't been for you I think I'd have gone mad!"

"But you do love me?"

Carol did not answer and Lawrence said, "You need a drink, darling. And I'd like one myself. I'll get it."

"No. It's in the kitchen. You'd have to hunt. Sit still."

Carol got up and went out of the room.

Greg's rage was now of a crimson hue. The gun! It had been in the drawer under the winter blankets. Was it still there? He went like a raging shadow into the bedroom and opened the lower drawer of the chest. The gun was there.

He took the gun out into the living room and fired four bullets into the skull of Frederick Lawrence.

Four bullets and that was all because a pull of almost tidal proportions was dragging at him. And he knew his return had been a temporary thing; knew his place was a hundred years hence in a time not born, among people who did not yet exist, by a grave not yet dug.

The gun fell from his hand and the tidal wave, against which his will had stood for a time, swept him up and spun him like an atom in a vortex.

CHILLED in body and mind, he stood in the graveyard while the sun beat down and the trees whispered. But now their whisperings were hostile, sardonic, and he realized what he had done. Was it possible? Could such a grisly; bloodcurdling joke have existence in fact? He had to know.

Again he strode down the wide streets to a place he had known. The building of his other years was gone—the old, placid public library. But in its stead had arisen a grander, newer one. He stumbled up the broad steps, into the vast interior.

"The old newspaper files, please."

The girl behind the desk glanced up. Her gaze held for a moment—a questioning gaze. Then, "Newspaper files. Room Seven. Out the main door to your left."

He dug through the newer editions, back—back to where they became yellowed and long-forgotten. And there it was. An article by a sob-sister journalist of olden times:

They executed Carol Hempstead today for the pistol murder of her clandestine sweetheart, Frederick Lawrence. Carol walked to the chair with a firm step and a calm face.

Her conviction and execution vindicates, to a certain extent, those officials of the law who believed but could not prove the guilt of this pair in the disappearance of Carol's husband some months before the murder of Lawrence.

The truth or untruth of these accusations will never be known. It looked for a time like Carol would escape the chair on the grounds of insanity. She maintained to the very end that her husband killed Lawrence and then disappeared into thin air. The insanity plea was rejected, however, when experts testified Carol Hempstead was an excellent actress rather than a mentally deranged person.

A strikingly beautiful girl, Carol—

GREG GOT up from his chair and walked out into the street. He stared straight ahead and staggered somewhat. But—no one stopped him as he went on his unseeing way.

I did it. I executed her myself. It was not true when I read it on the stone. It was not true until I went back and made it true.

He was again in the cemetery, the long-unused part of it drawing him like a magnet.

I sat her down in the chair. I strapped her in.

He fell to his knees.

I pulled the switch.

And he grieved for a girl who had been dust one hundred years.

THE END

ASTRA

By Arthur J. Burks

…It looked like instantaneous transmission of material items; nothing could explain it.

MARY HALE opened her eyes slowly, knowing that the terror was with her again. It dribbled out of her hair in beads of sweat, though the time was winter and the big house always cold at night. Cold sweat made her feel as if all her taut body was a bleeding wound. She was instantly aware that Fred, behind her as she lay on her side; was awake, waiting, perhaps, for her to tell him again.

In her dream, which couldn't possibly be a dream and produce such definitely visible fearsome results, she preferred another man to her husband. Had she ever blurted it out while she slept? Didn't Fred behave strangely toward her? Hadn't he begun eyeing her with questions in his expression since the first of the…no, she simply couldn't call them dreams. Astral traveling? She simply couldn't believe in such nonsense. She could, of course, be going mad.

She turned to her husband, bursting into tearing sobs as his ready arms came about her, drawing her close.

"Again, Baby?" he asked softly.

"Yes, Fred, and if, when we go down to the kitchen—Fred, am I going mad?"

"Of course not, beloved. It isn't anything, not really, that is; nothing we can't handle. What was it this time?"

"Shopping! I went shopping in a darkened store, after midnight. In fact, Fred, I just returned. It's ten miles from here to the store…

"And if you just came back, I can testify that you haven't left this bed since you tucked yourself in beside me last night!"

"Well, then, this time I did something, Fred. I've tried things before, but nothing ever came of it. This time I put one of my calling cards under a can of kennel ration…well back in the shelf, so that it won't likely be found right away. If we go there, before the store opens…"

"We'll do it, Baby," said Fred Hale. "Now, what did you buy last night, or so early this morning?"

Should she, here and now, safe in his arms, tell him about George? George Bannett, who made her forget her husband completely, the instant he walked into her dream, astral travel, whatever it was? Awake, she knew no George Bannett, nor could she find him in any Lancaster-Lititz-Columbia-Ephrate-Elizabethtown-Marietta telephone book. He wasn't therefore, real. Yet, his *presents were.* At least, up until now they always had been.

"I bought three pounds of coffee, because it's cheaper, you know," said Mary Hale. Fred turned on the light, took down what she told him. "I bought a head of cabbage, a bag of Idaho potatoes, five pounds of sugar, three cans of evaporated milk, two cans of dog food, our usual kind, three cans of cat food, again our usual kind, four packages of frozen mixed vegetables, two pounds of sweet potatoes, three bunches of carrots, a bag of spinach, forty cents worth of bananas, altogether, it came to five dollars and twelve cents…"

"And you paid cash?"

"Yes, I had to. It's an A & P store, you know."

"That's one thing that gets me," said Fred slowly. "You always pay cash for this stuff you get somehow in the night, but no cash is ever missing from either your purse or mine. And all these stores, all through the neighborhood; which report, eerie nocturnal visitations, with unexplained cash rung up on their cash registers— and the cash in the dampers to match, and nothing stolen—report exactly the sum total you always tell me. Where does the money come from?"

Dared she tell her adored but inclined-to-be-jealous husband, that George Bannett always paid the bills? He was looking at her strangely now, preparing to answer himself somehow.

"Baby, in your dreams, where does the money come from?"

She would have been caught, flatly, if she hadn't been expecting the question.

"That's the mystery," she said. "I always know *then*, but never know *here*. I just know that the bill is always paid, in cash, and rung up on the cash register…"

"Maybe," said Fred softly, "there is something you're not telling?"

"*Fred!*"

"No need to disturb yourself about it—*is there?*" he asked.

She was flustered, of course. Who wouldn't have been, for in the dream, or astral journey, whatever it always was, George Bannett wasn't her husband; he was something just as intimate, though, half of a relationship that the world frowned, or affected to frown, upon. Yet that part of her weird life with George Bannett was only implied; no slightest part of it came into her nightly experience—*to be remembered, anyway.*

"Well," Fred was saying, "which basket did you use?"

"I apparently forgot to take a market basket," she answered quickly, "so I selected a box."

"What was in the box?"

"It had held, according to the legend outside, evaporated milk…"

Together they rose, noted the time, two a.m., and walked downstairs to the kitchen table. Atop the kitchen table was a fiber box, on the outside of which was splashed the name of a popular brand of evaporated milk. Inside the box a careful check indicated exactly the items Mary Hale had enumerated for Fred Hale on waking, just prior to two a.m.

MARY was an exquisite woman of twenty-five; in her nightgown she was exquisite plus, even when, as now, her cheeks were deathly pale.

"They weren't here when we went to bed," she said flatly.

"No."

"And I wasn't out of bed."

"No."

Even the sales slip, showing a total of five dollars and twelve cents, was tucked in among the mysterious items. Only, there was nothing mysterious about the items. They were real. The Hale family would eat everything here except the cat and dog food.

"The doors were all locked?" said Mary dully.

"All locked!"

"Fred, let's sell out! Let's go far, far away from here! Unless you think, as I'm beginning to, that I'm going mad."

"We can't run away," said Fred Hale. "Nobody ever runs away from the feared, successfully. Besides, my business is here..."

"But for *me*, Fred! You love me, don't you? I'm more important to you than your business?"

"Darling, you are all my life, everything I want, am, hope to have or be, but don't you see that we have to fight this thing out, right here where it started?"

"But none of it is possible, no matter what outlandish stuff one might believe in!"

"No, it isn't possible, but take a gander at that box of stuff from the A & P! That's real, baby, and if we find your calling card, this morning..."

"And when it began, the necklace was real," whispered Mary. "So were the three dozen stockings, the half dozen pairs of shoes that just fitted me. So were the dresses for each social occasion, the coats, jackets, ensembles..."

"For a total of eleven hundred forty-seven dollars, to date, and thirty-nine cents! And none of it came out of my pocketbook or bank account, or out of yours."

They were back in bed, with the alarm clock wound and set to waken them in time to drive the ten miles to the big store and hunt for the calling card, when Mary remembered something and just did manage to forbear gasping. Just before she wakened, perspiring in terror, George Bannett had said, almost casually:

"I'm coming to wherever you spend your days, and take you away! I'm coming sometime today! You might as well get set. Will you come with me, Mary?"

"I'll come, of course, George, you know that. I'll follow you to the ends of the earth!"

"If you knew where the ends are," he had said, smiling at her, "you wouldn't wonder nearly so much, what all this nocturnal prowling means. If people just knew how active they are, in what they call dreams, if they had the remotest notion of what *dreams are intended to hide*, a vast lot of time in human life would be conserved.

Well, it is conserved now, but the dreaming sleepers would *know* it!"

Of course she could never tell Fred any of that.

JUST before they slept they checked on all the other stuff that had weirdly materialized after one of Mary's "dreams"—rather the total that all her scavenging dreams added up to. They still bore the price tags. Mary had been afraid to wear them, lest someone from wherever she had got each item—*and George had paid for it!*—should recognize it and start yelling, "Thief! Thief!" She hadn't stolen anything, but surely she—and George Bannett—had broken and entered. But *had* they? While the strange facts of cash in cash registers had been reported to police, and eventually had got into the newspapers, so that a public avid for mysteries awaited each new, and brief report with eagerness, no "breaking and entering" report had been given to the police or the newspapers. It was presumed that the "prowler or prowlers" possessed keys. Mary Hale—and George—had returned at least three times to three scenes of their "crimes," while policemen stood guard at all locked entrances and exits, but no policeman, though each one had been tremendously chagrined, had seen anything unusual, or heard anybody, or *anything!*

The newspapers had built up quite a case of negligence against the local police in Lancaster and several neighboring cities:

"Madame Blavatsky could have explained it perhaps," said one imaginative reporter. "She knew how to make earth spirits, kobalds, leprechauns, gremlins, and pixies catch and carry for her; it looked like instantaneous transmission of material items; nothing else seems to explain the cash in the registers, exactly totaling missing goods, in some instances! In other instances it couldn't have been checked but may have been merely pay for goods taken mysteriously in the night."

WHEN the store opened, Mary Hale and her husband were the first inside. Mary led the way to the kennel ration section, looked swiftly around to make sure she wasn't observed—and came up with the calling card!

By the time Mary and Fred reached home again, Mary was fit to be tied. She didn't believe in gremlins. Or kobalds, or leprechauns.

Inside her own home, Mary had hysterics. No telling where it might have ended had not Fred spoken out at last:

"Darling, I might as well confess. It's been a gag, understand? I got all this stuff at the different places, and planted it. I hoped I'd never have to tell you, but I thought I was in love, for a little while, with a woman named Georgia Bannett. I thought if I pulled a bit of stuff on you, and sent you off your rocker, maybe I could get a divorce…"

Mary stared at Fred in horror, her mouth hanging open.

"But, *Fred,* I have always told you the details of my dreams just before we found the stuff I dreamed I bought! You *couldn't* have…

Then it struck her: *"Georgia* Bannett!"

Could she even ask a question about "Georgia" without telling something about "George!"

The doorbell chimed. Fred went to answer, returned almost at once with a queer expression on his face.

"A man to see you, Mary," he said. "It's the darndest coincidence…"

"Coincidence, Fred?" she heard herself asking.

"Yes. His name seems to be *George Bannett!"*

Fred trailed Mary as his wife, marching as if to the guillotine, went to the door, opened, looked out into the smiling face of—the man in her dreams, every last one of her dreams, her prowling dreams.

"George!" she managed.

"Bannett!" he snapped briskly, scarcely friendly at all. "Look, sister, this bill has been running long enough. Eleven hundred forty-seven dollars and thirty-nine cents. I never expected to have to spend so much money to get such a little way with any woman. I've come for either the money or the stuff!"

"Then you're not here for, that is, you didn't come to take…"

"The stuff? Yes, I did, if you don't pay up!"

"Mr. Bannett," said Mary, vast relief bubbling up in her, "is your wife's name *Georgia?"*

"Got no wife. That's my sister's name. She lives out in California. Not married, either. Why?"

"Never mind, and say, you can take back all that stuff, even today's vegetables and canned goods. Fred, if you'll just fetch it..."

"Never mind, Fred," said George Bannett, "my men'll get the things!"

NO SOONER had George Bannett spoken than every last one of the dream-propelled items piled themselves on the porch at his feet. Mary gasped. Fred Hale gasped, too.

George Bannett checked the items against his list, nodded.

"All of it seems to be here," he said. "Now, take it out to the car!"

Instantly the stuff was gone. George Bannett grinned.

"Gremlins today leprechauns yesterday, kobalds tomorrow!" he said, thumping the brim of his hat. "Want to go to my car and check?"

"Don't need to," said Fred. "There are garments on hangers in the tonneau now. There weren't any a second or two ago. No doors opened, no windows. How was it done?"

"I just told you. Well, so long."

"Before you go," said Fred, "what's the sense of all this? What were you trying to prove?"

"Why did you tell your wife you had thought yourself in love with Georgia Bannett, when she was out in California, and has been, for years?"

"Maybe," said Mary, looking queerly at Fred, *"he's* been dreaming true, too!"

"Dream?" said George. "Nobody dreams. Everybody thinks he does. What actually happens is this..."

George Bannett was gone, *in a flash*. The next instant he stuck his head out the window of his car, clear across the highway and yelled:

"I almost forgot, Mary! I really came for you. You coming?"

Instantly, as if there were no need to think about it, and just as she was, Mary started running toward George. She hadn't taken two steps before she found herself sitting beside him, quite comfortably, too. As the car started smoothly away she was aware of all the small voices, all around them, in the car, under it, on the roof, blending in what sounded like a single small, *very* small, voice, which said:

"If more people knew how much fun it is, a lot more would be going in for it!"

Mary Hale laughed, happily, and George Bannett grinned at her.

"There'll be no more *day*dreaming, Mary, understand?"

THE END

EMISSARY

By Charles E. Fritch

In the still of night, they came across the hills from places that still shimmered with a strange, unrelenting fire.
They were the monsters, the new mutations—but somehow they were old...old...

Night came to the valley as it always did, slowly, almost re-luctantly, with the pale glow of twilight lingering beyond the bristling mountain like some giant radioactive jewel half concealed. The light faded perceptibly and darkness crept forward on silent feet, while across the valley came the hushed frantic whispers and the hurried slamming of doors and the bolting of locks that came and echoed with every night. Doors stayed open briefly, though the night was warm, and the cabin lights blinked their neon eyes through the openings to stare sightlessly into darkness until, one by one, they winked out as the doors shut upon them like closing eyelids.

John Corlan stood at his doorway and stared into the deepening night, watching the lights dancing in the warm air like bewildered fireflies and then disappear, not to return. He peered intently into the gloom, trying to see what distant shapes moved stealthily among the tall trees, and was glad he saw no movement. The wind felt of his hair with cold fingers, and he shivered, holding the metal door tighter so he might slam it shut if need be. He stood there silently until all other lights had gone, and his own cabin light behind him cast a golden-rimmed shadow into the world of night.

"What's out there," he wondered, half-aloud, and he clenched his fists helplessly and blinked and strained his eyes to see what secret lay covered by darkness. The breeze swept murmuring through the bushes, and he trembled and wondered if it were only the night wind that chilled him. But he saw nothing except the gray shapes of trees swaying against the night sky.

He heard a movement behind him, a soft touch at his shoulder, and a quiet, feminine voice saying. "Close the door, John, please." Her voice was not tinged with fear, bearing only the element of practical necessity. It was as though she had said, "This is the way it is done and the way it will always be done. Though I am not afraid, we must be practical."

Practical! He almost laughed aloud at the thought. It was superstition, plain and simple, with no proof of the night-fear that had come to dominate their society.

"All right," he said, and he closed the door and the lock clicked, and he drew the bolt securely. "But a lot of good it'll do! We lock our doors and put bolts on them to make sure they don't get in by counterfeiting our thumbprints; we barricade ourselves in our tiny metal worlds—but we don't keep them out, not really. They scratch and claw and they howl and even if they don't we imagine they do, and we pretend we don't hear them even while we lie shivering in the dark like frightened children. They may as well be in here!"

"John—"

"I mean it, Eve. What is out there? We don't really even know that. Why do we have to lock and bolt our doors when night comes? This is the twenty-first century, not the Middle Ages! What is there to fear out there besides the night and the darkness?"

She shrugged. "The tales—"

"Superstition," he scoffed. "Mutations from the Third War! Monsters! Yet no one has ever seen any of these creatures. I'm sick of all this cowardice. We don't even know what we're hiding ourselves from. The only things out there are animals and the products of our imagination." He looked at the door. "I've got a good mind to—"

"No, please, for my sake." Her small arms went around him as though she was holding him from some terrible precipice, and he knew she couldn't have offered a stronger argument.

"Don't worry about that," he said, shrugging helplessly, his tone ashamed. "I'm just as much a coward as the others."

She looked up at him, lovely yet intensely practical. "It's something we have to face, like having to wash and eat and sleep. I hate it as much as you, but I don't want you out there tackling monsters single-handed. Some people have tried it—"

She didn't elaborate on the thought, but she didn't have to. He held her close, feeling her heartbeat belie her outward calmness.

"Why do I have to be like this," he wondered to himself. "Why can't I be content like the others?"

He thought of his friend Frank Seyton, who had been curious too, dissatisfied with breathing the stale-seeming fresh air of the metal cabin, with feeling its walls closing you in like a trapped animal each night.

"I'm going out there, John," he had said one night. "I'm going to find out what's really there."

The next morning his cabin door was open, and both he and his wife Vicky had disappeared.

"But what *is* out there," John Corlan wondered furiously. "What!" He clenched his fists savagely and did not know.

The evening passed, as it always did. They ate pills and concentrates and sat quietly in cloud-foam chairs sipping familiar drinks and listening to music seeping like gentle mist from the walls. As though from a distance noises came, almost inaudibly, as though someone were at the door, or at one of the windowless walls. But the soundproofing helped dim the noise and the music played its tune.

Eve looked up at the noise but said nothing, pretending not to hear.

They sat listening to the music, not hearing it, staring at the metal walls that could sprout pictures which moved and danced at a person's whim but which were now silent and gray.

After awhile, she said quietly, "You're going out, aren't you?"

"Why do you say that? No, of course I'm not going out."

"You're thinking about it."

"I always think about it."

"Please don't."

"I'll tell you before I do," he promised.

But he wondered if he *would* go out. He could scoff all he wanted and rant and rave over being cooped up, and he could blame the night noises on animals—but the mutation theory, however unpleasant, had a generation's insistence that it was true.

The Third War, with its germs and its radioactivity that made few places on Earth livable, might also produce strange creatures that lived by night away from those who would persecute it by day. Night was its friend, a concealer of strangeness, a natural ally to produce fear in the normals.

In the still of night, they could come across the hills and forests that sheltered the valley, from places that still shimmered and glowed with a strange unrelenting fire. It certainly was not impossible. There was even one theory, he recalled, about the mutants' bodily structures disintegrating under normal sunlight, but the scientist who ventured the opinion did so without insisting upon a physical examination of one of the creatures.

He allowed a trace of a smile to curve his lips. It was almost funny. And it would be funnier still if—if—

He let the thought play through his mind, as he had let it many times before. He completed it, as if there were nothing out there, nothing really to be afraid of. The greatest fear was fear itself, fear of the unknown. They had built it up during the past generation and now everyone believed it. Tell it to a kid often enough and he'll hold it as gospel when he's a man. The noises they heard were animals and nothing more.

But what of Frank Seyton, and Vicky, and the others who had disappeared?

He didn't know, and he wondered if he ever would, or just go on living the way he had, helpless and shut in at night. He could take a gun out there with him, just in case, a weapon that could knock into eternity anyone or anything that came near him uninvited. With a gun he would be safe as long as he stayed on guard. Why not? He could be an emissary to the world of the night, break down the unnecessary barriers put up between them and the darkness. The thought was exhilarating.

Restlessly, he played the controls on the chair arm beside him, and a three-dimensional world of celluloid sprang to life with the walls confronting them. Magically, the world reconstructed itself and together he and Eve traveled across the canyons of time to the world that was; to the Europe of years ago, with its historic landmarks and monuments intact; to once-virile Africa, before uranium was discovered there; to Eastern United States, where tall towers of steel now existed only on film. They marveled at the wonders that had once been the world and forgot temporarily what lay beyond their door in the real world.

"It must have been nice then," she said.

"Yes," he agreed.

Then, you could go out in the dark walking into the crystal air, watching the stars trace patterns across the night sky. There were no wars then, no flights to save humanity, no fears of creatures that didn't exist.

"Yes," he repeated. "It must have been *very* nice."

After awhile, they allowed the beds to blossom from the walls like weird mechanical flowers, and they turned out the lights and undressed in the pale glow of luminescence that came as though from nowhere. The music murmured tunelessly as they lay silent in bed, listening for the real and imagined noises from the outside.

When he could hear her sleeping, John Corlan stealthily slipped from the bed, dressed, found his flame pistol, and stood in the darkness contemplating the move that might be his last. He hesitated, remembering himself saying, "I'll tell you before I do."

"I'm going out," he said quietly.

In the semi-darkness his wife stirred but did not waken. Satisfied, he went to the door, slipped the bolt, placed his thumb in the slot and heard the soft answering click. He swung open the door...

Darkness, velvety smooth and unbroken. A cool wind that greeted him with eager arms. As he stared into the night, the moon came from behind clouds and swept the land with a pale hand that covered the trees as though with snow.

He stepped forward, clutching the pistol tightly in his hand, feeling his heartbeat quicken perceptibly.

"There's nothing to be afraid of," he told himself. "Nothing to be afraid of. Nothing to be afraid of."

The door clicked shut behind him, and he stopped and for a moment felt sudden panic, a helpless sense of being alone, cut off, in a strange world. It swept over him in a swift tide, and fervently he looked around him. He remembered the gun in his hand and looked in the darkness for something to shoot at.

Trees rustled, whispering secretly, and he fought off the urge to fire into them. "Getting jumpy," he told himself. "There is nothing out there."

Something moved at the edge of the forest.

He cried out in sudden terror and whirled to press his thumb into the lock. Whirled—and stopped.

"John," a voice said quietly behind him. "John Corlan."

He froze with cold, unreasoning fear, and his heart beat an insane tempo. Slowly, he turned, slowly as though he were on a pivot, unable to resist. The flame pistol was still in his hand, but his fingers felt numb and he knew he could not shoot.

"I knew you'd come out sooner or later," the voice said. "I've been waiting for you."

The man stood smiling at him in the moonlight not ten feet away, his face chalky and unreal.

John Corlan gasped. "Frank Seyton. But that's not possible. You're—"

"Dead?" Seyton furnished. "Far from it; in fact, I'm more alive than I've ever been. You have a lot to learn, John, about this world of ours. You see, there aren't really any monsters out here, just as we suspected there weren't. Only us. There's nothing to be afraid of, nothing at all."

"Nothing—at all?" He felt like laughing and crying in relief all at once. "But why didn't you come back?"

"Who would believe me?" Seyton wanted to know. "They prefer to believe tales of goblins and ghosts to reality. And I couldn't return to the life of being caged in like an animal." He looked upward. "Not after being out in the night, with the wind and the sky and the forests and all nature before me. Look at the stars, John. Do you realize how long it's been since we've really looked at them?"

John Corlan tore his gaze from the man and stared at the patchwork sky. "Some people have never seen them at all," he remembered. "I hardly blame you for not coming back."

"I knew you'd see it my way," Frank said approvingly. "Of course I couldn't stay here without Vicky, so I went back and got her. I imagine our disappearance caused quite a stir."

"It sure did; they figured the monsters ate you up," John Corlan laughed. It felt good to laugh again, to know that all your fears were foolish. At the thought he became suddenly self-conscious and pocketed the flame pistol. "I wasn't taking any chances," he explained, somewhat ashamed.

There was a movement near the forest edge and Vicky glided toward them, smiling. "I'm glad you finally came out, John. Where's Eve?"

He motioned to the silent cabin. "She may be a little harder to convince," he warned.

"You can do it," she said.

She drifted toward him and put her arms about his neck. Surprised, he started to resist, but her perfume came over him and he relaxed.

"Welcome to the monsters," she said, kissing him.

Her touch was electric. His head whirled and his heart beat an unaccustomed tempo, and he felt suddenly as though he were poised at a great precipice, ready to fall. The air went rushing past in a sudden whir. The air flamed with invisible fire.

Then there was silence and the moonlight and the three of them standing in the night looking at each other. Frank stood smiling, and somehow it seemed like the most natural thing in the world that this was the way it should be. All at once, the night seemed friendly again.

After that, he met the others. Some he knew, persons who had disappeared and been given up for dead; others he did not know, who had come from beyond the mountains seeking such a valley—but all were as human as he was. They met in a glade that smelled of strange perfumes and cast dancing shadows across white smiling faces. The glade murmured with the sound of their voices, and for the first time in a long while, he felt content.

He said finally, "I'll have to go back after Eve."

Frank Seyton nodded. "Bring her here, John. The more we have on our side, the better for all of us," he suggested.

Minutes later, John Corlan was pressing his thumb into the lock and swinging the door open. He closed it with the customary click and waited for his eyes to become accustomed to the dimness. It was strange to be in the narrow room after being in the open.

Suddenly the lights flared, and he blinked and held his hand to shield his eyes from the glare.

"Hey, take it easy," he said good-naturedly. "You want to—"

He stopped, stunned, for Eve was in the center of the room, wide awake, the pistol in her hand pointing directly at him.

"Watch where you're pointing that thing," he warned.

"Stay where you are," she said.

He frowned. "Say, what is this?"

"How do I know you're not one of them," she said, trembling a little. "One of the mutants in disguise. Maybe they killed John and sent you in his place."

"This is silly," he scoffed. "There aren't any mutations or monsters or anything else out there. Just people as real as I am. Eve, it's wonderful. Frank's out there, and Vicky, and others. I was right. There's nothing out there to fear. Nothing at all."

"Nothing?" The gun wavered a fraction and suddenly she became aware of the weapon and lowered it. "But—"

"They want me to bring you out there, convince you there's nothing to fear."

She hesitated, and then said firmly, "All right. I'll go out with you. Tomorrow."

"What? Look, being practical is one thing, but really—"

"Tomorrow," she repeated mechanically. "Tomorrow morning when the sun is high and bright and warm in the sky. That's when I'll go out."

He grew suddenly pale. "But you can't!"

"Why not?"

"I don't know why not, but you just can't, that's all. It's not allowed."

She stared at him. "Not allowed?"

"Well, what I mean is—well, somehow I don't care to see the daytime anymore. It's been rotten and dirty and it's destroyed the world, and it'll probably destroy this settlement if we give it time.

You've never been out in the night, Eve; you don't know what it's like, when the forest is alive and the stars are out. Have you ever really taken a long look at the stars—?"

"Get out," she said quietly.

"What? But—"

"Get out," she repeated, but the words choked a little this time and she brandished the pistol for emphasis.

"Now see here—" He stepped forward, but a lance of fire darted past him, and a sudden animal fear grasped him. "Eve—" the word caught in his throat.

He could see tears welling in her eyes, reflecting like bright diamonds in the harsh lighting. "Get out," she cried, "get out, get out."

A finger of flame pointed past him as she clutched the pistol in a frantic grip, and hastily he stumbled backward, his thoughts jumbled and desperate. Automatically, he groped for the lock, but his mind was unable to comprehend what was taking place. His glands took over and shouted: run, run, run. Then the door was wide and he was out in the night, and the door clicked and there was darkness again. The bolt was drawn into place, and he could hear her sobbing muffled through the door.

Frank and Vicky were beside him.

"Don't worry," Frank said consolingly, "at least you're free; you're one of us now. You'll like it beyond the mountains."

John Corlan shook his head bewilderedly. The dark cool night seemed good after the bright enclosure of the cabin, with its walls of gray metal on all sides surrounding him like a cage.

"I don't understand," he said slowly. "When I was in there with her, I wanted to kiss her. I didn't want to make her angry. I just wanted to kiss her. I felt as though, somehow, that would help make everything all right. The way you kissed me, on the neck—"

"It's all right," Vicky said, leading him from the cabin and the muffled sounds of crying from within. "We'll get her eventually."

"Yes," he said vaguely. "Yes, I suppose we will."

Carefully, he massaged his throat, wondering briefly at the flake of red that powdered his fingertip. Then he forgot about it as the night, cool and serene, enveloped them. It felt good to be out again.

But he couldn't help but wonder what it would be like, not to see the sun.

THE END

MIDGETS AND MIGHTY MEN

By Lee Francis

One question haunted John Kindred: What mad mind had created the plague that was changing men into monsters?

IT WAS five-fifteen when I left the *Telegraph* city room and caught a yellow cab. The cabby tried to talk himself out of driving me out to Mount Mead Hospital.

"Listen Doc," he argued. "I gotta stay downtown. My motor's on the fritz. Might not get us out…"

"I'm not Doc," I said, "and I know some of the answers. You want to stay downtown because you can make more money on short hauls during the rush hour. I'm a reporter and I'm going to Mount Mead. I'm going in your cab."

He snorted something I couldn't make out, jammed the gear shift into low and pulled swiftly out into traffic. I was grinning and he saw my unlovely face in the rearview mirror.

"Okay, wise guy. Have it your way," he said.

He missed a streetcar by a fraction too trivial to be calculated. He went through two red lights and thumbed his nose at a copper. You guessed it. The guy was plenty sore.

When I paid him off at Mount Mead, he hated like poison to give me any change for a five-spot. I waited until he dug out six-bits, a dime and a nickel. I pocketed the change without tipping him and went up the broad, sandstone steps to the hospital.

I wasn't in a very good mood myself.

The *Prophet*, otherwise known as Howland Briggs, City Editor of the Telegram, had sent me out for an interview with John Kindred. Kindred was a member of the staff at Mount Mead and author of the latest best-smeller, "The Balance Is Broken."

I didn't like the assignment. I'm very healthy myself, and barring accidents, hope to stay that way. The worst sickness I ever suffered was measles at the age of five. I'm short, not exactly good looking with a broken nose that set itself, and a mass of red hair that frightens small children until they scream for their mothers.

I went into the marble lobby and headed for the snub-nosed nurse at the switchboard.

"I want to see Doc Kindred," I told her.

She looked me over and reached a quick decision.

"Doctor Kindred is busy. He can't be disturbed."

"For how long?"

I didn't like her. She had dark eyes that flashed fire. I guess she figured me for one of Kindred's poor relatives.

"He's busy for the entire afternoon."

"Okay," I said. "If that's the way you want it."

She went back to her work and I wandered over to the elevators. I waited until one came down with a woman carrying her baby. She was followed by someone who looked like her husband, because he had that halo around his head that new fathers always get when their first offspring enters this cruel world.

I smiled at the nurse who ran the elevator.

"Take me up to Doctor Kindred's office."

She gave me the fishy stare.

"Doctor Kindred is on the fifth floor. I run past it. No visitors on five."

She was a stiffly starched little thing, but I saw the humane look in her brown eyes.

"Look," I said, "I'm going to the fifth, on this elevator. You going along?"

She decided she was. When I got out on the fifth floor, she went back down in a hurry. Probably decided that her name was mud, from then on.

I WALKED along the hall. It was wide and long. There were a lot of impressive looking walnut doors with names printed across them in gold gilt. I found one that read:

Dr. John F. Kindred

I knocked.

"Who is it?"

The voice sounded so tired that I felt sorry for its owner.

"Me," I said, and went in.

An old gentleman was looking at me over the desk, from behind silver rimmed specs. He must have been well over sixty. His hands, visible against the dark covers of a book, were long-fingered and fragile.

He spoke again, with just the ghost of a smile on his lips.

"And, who is *me?*"

I shook my head.

"I'm the great unknown," I said. "I'm the guy who writes the headlines for the world to read."

It was a cheap sounding thing for a man to say, but it was the truth and that's the stuff I deal in.

"Oh!" he said. He put the book down and scratched his chin. I was to remember that habit. That single long finger without any blood to color it, tracing a furrow down the left side of his chin.

"I suppose the *Telegram* wants something to print about my book?"

My eyelids went up just a fraction.

"Telegram?"

He smiled again.

"I know you," he said. "I've seen you around."

Kindred was nobody's fool, I decided. I drew out my billfold and gave him my card. "To prove that I'm not an imposter or an autograph hound. I don't suppose they bother you much, up here."

That smile, soft, almost gentle. "You managed to beard the lion in his den," he admitted. "What is it you want to know?"

I wasn't sure. The *Prophet* had asked for a feature yarn on Kindred and his book. I had read some of it the night before. "The Balance Is Broken" was a screwball thing that only a doctor could fully understand. Something about the balance of size being broken. How midgets and giants were starting to appear in great numbers. How it might affect the world. Personally I hadn't seen any giants lately, and the only midget I know, sells papers on the corner of Ninth and Grove Streets.

"Give me some hokum about the book," I said. "How you came to write it—what you eat for breakfast—how you keep from turning into a midget or a giant."

I'll admit I wasn't showing much respect for the old gent, but I don't go much for pill peddlers.

More blood than I thought his heart could pump suddenly colored his cheeks.

"You don't believe the facts I've set forth in my book?"

I guess I grinned a little at that.

"Look, Doc," I said. "Just between you and I, what you sell the public is your own business."

THAT didn't go over so hot with him. I thought he was going to toss me out. Not that he'd have to try very hard. I was changing my mind about him even as I talked. If he'd said "scram," I'd have faded out of his life. He was on the level and I knew I'd opened my mouth too wide.

"If I proved that the book has a solid foundation on truth, would you help me? Would you champion my cause?"

He had me there. Something about Kindred made me *want* to help him.

"Look," I said. "I'm a dope. I'm a thirty-dollar model marked down to twenty-two-fifty. I don't believe in anything. On the other hand, I'm a sucker for guys who are on the level. I came here for a gag story. Now the story has me gagged. If you can convince me, and I can convince the *Prophet*. I'll sell your stuff. The *Telegraph* stands behind me on most everything I tackle."

He nodded thoughtfully.

"Who is the *Prophet?*"

I grinned.

"Just a moniker for Howland Briggs, the best editor this side of Hades."

He kept right on thinking, and his finger crept up and scratched at that chin once more.

"I read some of your stories on the Williamson Case," he admitted. "You're a fellow trying to cover up a soft heart with big words. I'm going to show you something that will shake you from the ground up. After that, I'm going to let you leave here without a word. Use your own judgment."

That business about me being a softy at heart really hit the bull's-eye. Dad always used to say that I had a steel coated finish over a baby-blue heart. Kindred was hitting pretty close to the belt.

He took a small key out of his desk and arose.

"Let me warn you that you can't publish a word of what you see, at least, not yet. The public isn't prepared to withstand the shock. People would seek comfort in disbelief. They'd call you a liar, and brand us both as fools."

He went to the door, turned and continued:

"Later, perhaps the world will be ready to accept the truth. When they are, God grant it, we will be ready to help them."

I was beginning to get excited about the thing. Why Kindred first chose me to bear the cross, I don't know. Somehow, though, I had decided that this wasn't phony. It was the real thing and I wished heartily that I had read more of Kindred's book.

I followed him down the hall. There was a big steel door on one side, without any lettering on it. He opened it. There were wide stairs leading up toward the sixth floor.

"The elevators no longer run to the sixth," he said. "Those few doctors who are allowed up here, possess keys that they swear not to let out of their possession. Our secret cannot be betrayed."

My heart started beating in three-quarter time. I smelled medicine. I followed him up to a small balcony. He produced the key again and opened the door to a long, wide ward.

I took three steps into the ward and stopped short.

I opened my mouth and it stayed open for a long time before I thought about closing it. Kindred was watching me and I was watching the horrible collection of freaks on the hospital beds.

"Take hold of your nerves, man," Kindred cautioned. "Walk the full length of the ward with me. Look all you want to. They are harmless. Don't talk. They are sensitive to sound. It's very quiet up here."

IT WAS. The sounds of the street were gone. White curtains masked every window, so that light could come in, but you couldn't see out. The beds were white. The floor was spotless. It was as clean as—Heaven.

It wasn't the silence or the color scheme that bothered me. I seemed to float along, without knowing that my feet were carrying me. I felt suspended in space—and frightened.

The man in the first bed was quite young—about thirty. His body wasn't bloated. It was just big all over. He wore a hospital gown and I'll swear before a jury that he was eight feet tall. His legs extended beyond the foot of the bed, propped up on some cushions on a chair. He stared at me and he smiled sleepily, vacantly. I had never seen a man so huge. Yet, I knew it wasn't healthy. He appeared very weak. He could hardly move.

The next bed contained a woman, maybe forty years old. She was in pain. Her features, her build, were normal. She was normal, that is, in proportion. Actually, she wasn't over thirty-five inches long.

"THE BALANCE IS BROKEN."

I'll say it was. I started to get an entirely new conception of Kindred's book. I wanted to apologize to him. I couldn't say anything. I kept walking, kept seeing in each new bed, a less or more serious change in a human body. These people had not always been dwarfs and giants. They had been normal. There were over a hundred of them in the ward. A hundred souls suffering both from pain, and from the terrible mental change that must have taken place within them.

Near the far-end of the ward, we met a nurse. She was a lovely girl, I thought, as I stared at her for the first time. She had deep brown eyes protected by long lashes. Her complexion was creamy. Her very red lips opened slightly as she stood before me.

Kindred gave her a tired smile.

"I'd like you to meet my daughter Joan."

I took her hand. I wondered how she had the nerve to face this mess. It didn't amaze me to find that she was Kindred's daughter. This was exactly the kind of work she would want to be doing, if she was like her Dad.

I said, "I'm very glad to meet you. Your father has succeeded in jarring me out of a nasty little rut I was in."

"I'm glad," she said simply. In those two words she put warmth and real understanding. "We've been fighting alone for so long. Perhaps you can help."

A sudden roar of pain came from the far end of the ward. Joan Kindred hurried away. I wanted to follow her. The sound of that cry frightened me. It was angry—unnatural.

I watched her as she went to the bed of the giant at the end of the line of beds. I saw her take the hypo from its case and jab his arm. When Kindred finally took me out, she was sitting beside the bed stroking the man's forehead. He was moaning like a sick child. I would have liked her to stroke my forehead. It might relieve the headache I had just then.

HOWLAND BRIGGS, the *Prophet,* isn't very sympathetic with screwball reporters. However, I don't approach him with new or startling plans unless I know something of what I'm talking about. I sat down on the corner of his desk, swinging one leg. After a while he looked up from under his eye shade. Howland has gray-green eyes that look right through you. His chin is sharp, and his face, having already served him for fifty years, shows a lot of age and worry lines.

"Well?" he said shortly. "If you got it, write it."

I grinned.

"I got it," I said. "But I can't write it—not yet anyhow."

He was busy again, checking copy for the Five Star Edition.

"Bosh," he said.

"Let's go down to the bar."

"Haven't time."

This was an old line with us. He knew just what I was going to say next. I said it.

"I got a headline, but I can't let them set it."

He responded as I knew he would.

"Guess I *am* thirsty."

He got up, stretched his lanky six feet and removed the eye shade. I followed him down the hall to the elevator. Followed, because my five-foot nine inches can't keep up with Howland on the straightaway.

We didn't say much until the third beer was half gone.

"Well?" he said. "Spill it."

"The beer?" I asked.

He frowned.

"The story."

I told him all about what happened to me out at Mount Mead.

"Kindred tells about this change taking place, in his book," I explained. "He tells it as something that may happen. Actually, it *is* happening. Certain glands are drying up, Kindred tells me. There has to be a cure. There's a cure for everything, somewhere, if you look far enough. Trouble is, Kindred is working alone."

The *Prophet* thought for a long time. Then he cussed quietly.

"Unless you've been drinking more than I think you have, we've got the biggest story the Telegram ever handled."

"And can't use it," I added.

He swore again.

"So you promised in the name of the paper that you wouldn't release the story. I suppose you think you did exactly the right thing?"

He sounded so damned high and mighty that he made me sore.

"I did," I snapped, "and you're not running a line of what I told you, not while I'm still breathing."

The *Prophet* grinned. It was sour and lopsided.

"You know me better than that," he said. "Tell Kindred that we'll publish exactly what he wants us to. Tell him I said that the *Telegraph* will donate as much money as he needs to carry on his work. He's to give us the first break when the story comes to a head. Does that suit you?"

It did. Briggs wasn't fooling. He didn't own the paper, but he handled it with a rich man's dough, and he had the key to the cash box. I felt a little sentimental for a minute.

"The first symptoms of the disease, or whatever it is, show up in a high fever and heavy beating of the heart. The people who have these symptoms usually rush to their doctor right away. Mount Mead has warned doctors to rush these cases to the special ward. So far, they've kept it quiet."

He had forgotten the beer.

"Kindred wants me to scout around," I said.

The *Prophet* kept on nodding.

"I got some ideas," I said. "How about releasing me for a week or two, for a little snooping?"

The *Prophet* grinned at me.

"You solve a murder case or two and right away, you're a mental giant."

I was sober, though. This wasn't any joke.

"Well," he said, "it's the craziest thing I ever heard of. I know Kindred and I know Mount Mead. Everyone out there is dependable. If you can work with Kindred, go ahead. Report in at the end of the week. Call me if anything comes up."

He got up and walked out of the bar. I sat there for a long time, trying to think of a place to start. The more I thought, the more I figured I was Little Red Riding Hood, lost in the big dark woods. I had about as much chance tracking down that disease as Jonah had getting out of a whale—if there ever had been a whale.

THE intern with a hair growing from a mole on his chin, put the bag down on my desk.

"Doctor Kindred told me to turn this file over to you," he said. "It contains all the material you asked for."

I thanked him and he left. I had a two-by-four office on the fifth floor of the hospital. It wasn't quite up to par with the other offices. I suspected it might have served once as a linen closet. I didn't have my name on the door. I didn't want it there.

I opened the case and took out a dozen sheets of paper. They were covered with names and addresses. That was all, except that this list covered every malformed creature who suffered on the floor above. It was the list of those people stricken by the strange malady.

I was working on a little idea of my own. I didn't dare tell Kindred what I was thinking about. I asked for the list and got it.

For five minutes I studied the group of names. On the second page, my thoughts were abruptly punctuated by the most horrible scream I had ever heard in my life. It came from somewhere on the floor above, and it started low, covered all the notes to the top of the scale and faded into a low, terrible growl.

If you combined Leo, the Lion, and the wail of a fire siren, you'd hit it pretty close. I scattered the list on the floor, getting to the door. Kindred was ahead of me, running toward the door that led to the next floor. I caught up with him as he unlocked the door. We went up on the double. I don't know what I expected to see.

But it wasn't the slim bladed surgeon's knife sticking upright in the chest of the giant on the first bed.

JOAN KINDRED was there when we arrived. Tears streamed from her eyes. The girl had courage. She didn't even care if a murderer had been there a few minutes before. She was sobbing because life had at last been drained from the man on the bed.

We all started talking at once. Kindred removed the knife, and I cautioned him to use a sheet in doing it. I didn't want to lose the prints. The other patients were excited in a drugged, sleepy sort of way.

"Who the devil had a chance to get in and out of here?"

Kindred seemed for the first time to awaken to reality.

"My God—someone—from outside."

Joan's voice quavered as she spoke. "Honestly," she said, "I don't know how anyone could have escaped before I came. I was in the laboratory at the far end of the ward. I heard him cry out. It didn't take over fifty seconds to reach the ward."

"I saw—only the knife."

"No one came down the stairs," Kindred said.

I was remembering the little balcony at the top of the stairs. I opened the door and went out there. The balcony overlooked the garden, six floors below. I tried one of the windows. It was the French type, pushing open easily. Joan and her father came and stood behind me. We looked down through six sections of steel fire escape.

I kneeled and studied the spotless white paint on the sill of the window. There was a tiny, black smootch. The same mark synthetic rubber makes on a clean floor.

"That's where your murderer escaped," I said. "He's had time to get out the back gate. He's done a neat job, with a weapon that you can only trace back to one of the hospital operating rooms. If my guess is correct, there will be no prints on the knife. You can't hang a man because he left a black smootch on the window sill. That, however, is the only clue. You can't can the police, or stir up a fuss. If you do, the whole story will be out about this secret ward. The murderer did some very nice figuring. He knows all the answers."

Kindred made a hopeless gesture with his hands.

"You're right," he admitted. "For the present, the body will have to be placed quietly in the morgue. Nothing can be said beyond the walls of Mount Mead. There is no other way."

I shook my head. I was getting stubborn about the whole deal.

"The murderer didn't figure on me," I said.

DOWNSTAIRS, in the linen closet I called my office. I went carefully over that list of names. The man with the knife in his chest was Carl Finch—1138 Fletcher Drive, City.

That was my first stop.

For reasons of my own, I didn't ask Kindred many questions about his patients. I'd rather find out for myself. To begin with, John Kindred was a doctor and research man. I, on my Sundays off, was a more or less a lousy private sleuth. I didn't ask the same kind of questions that Kindred did, and I didn't seek the same answers. I wanted to find out everything I could about the late Carl Finch.

1138 Fletcher Drive was a pretty decent sort of place. Super modern, it was made of stucco with a lot of glass block windows. I decided on a direct approach, rang the bell and a maid in a black skirt and white apron opened the door. She was young, sleepy looking, with a too red mouth and eyes that told you one thing while her voice told you another.

"I'd like to speak to Mrs. Finch," I said.

She smiled. "There isn't any Mrs. Finch," she said.

I had bungled that one badly. It hadn't occurred to me that Carl Finch might not have been the marrying type.

"Oh?" I said. "Well, I'm from Mount Mead Hospital. I wanted to contact some of Mr. Finch's relatives."

At the mention of Mount Mead, her eyes opened wide. Her lids fluttered. She grasped my arm with tense fingers.

"Carl—Mr. Finch? He's all right?"

I stepped inside, so that she had to retreat ahead of me.

"He's dead," I said.

I thought she was going to pull a faint. She tottered back on her heels, then got control of herself and stood her ground.

"I'm—I'm sorry," she murmured. "I said there isn't any Mrs. Finch. She was killed last week. An automobile struck her when she was crossing the street. Outside of her, there are no more relatives. No one cared if he lived or died."

Death strikes twice, I thought.

This girl was taking Finch's death pretty hard. I wondered why.

"How come you're still working here—alone? You still on the payroll?"

Her face turned a nice pink.

"That's none of your business. I'm staying here until Mr. Finch's estate is taken care of. He left orders to keep the house cleaned up until he came home."

"He didn't know that his wife was dead?"

She shook her head.

"Then how could he give you all these instructions?"

WE WERE standing in the hall. An open staircase climbed upward to the second floor. She had hold of the stair rail and her knuckles were white because she held it so tightly. She was frightened and she was gradually catching herself in her own trap. I wasn't sure what the trap was, but I was sure that this babe wasn't on the level.

"It ain't any business of yours," she said at last. "You get out of here right now. How do I know Mr. Finch is dead? Maybe you're just waiting for a chance to hit me and rob the house."

I drew a card from my pocket and she looked at it. Her eyes narrowed.

"I don't want no trouble with a reporter."

"And *I'm* not looking for trouble," I said. "Maybe we better sit down and talk things over—carefully."

She sighed.

"Come on."

Rosa May Bronson, that's the name she gave me, had been employed by the Finch's for six months. Mr. Finch had been stricken with a high fever a month ago, and they had rushed him to Mount Mead Hospital. They hadn't seen him since. Mrs. Finch was away every night, one night she didn't come home. The next morning the police came and said she was at the morgue. She had been killed by a hit and run driver on Walsh Blvd. That was seven days ago.

Mr. Finch's lawyer called. He told her that there were no other relatives, according to the information he, the lawyer, had. That Mr. Finch could not be notified of his wife's death, for the present. He advised the maid to stay in the Finch home and keep it in order until Carl Finch could be interviewed.

"And that's all of it," Rosa May ended. She was sobbing into a handkerchief. "Now Mr. Finch is dead, and I'm just waiting—but who for—*what* for?"

She sat opposite me, and her dress crept up to expose some pretty, well shaped knees. The knees were pretty evident, but she seemed not to notice. She regarded me with grave, tearful eyes.

"What would *you* do? I don't have anyone to depend on."

It was a badly worn old line, but not bad when coupled with her eyes and slim figure. Rosa May Bronson had enough attributes to get her by in this cruel world.

"I'd look for a new sugar daddy," I said, and stood up. "It's getting pretty stuffy in here."

She swore at me softly.

"You ain't got any heart."

"Finch had one big enough for both of us," I said. "He kept you around for a long time. Probably he left some cash for you in his will. Faithful servant and all that."

She was on her feet, eyes bright with eagerness.

"You think he might?"

Then the eyes clouded and I stood there grinning at her.

"Why—you—dirty…"

"Okay," I said. "You asked for it."

I went out into the hall. She followed me. Just as I reached the door, I thought I heard footsteps upstairs. I hesitated, looking back at the girl. She heard the sound also. I was sure that she did. Yet, she wasn't frightened by the sound. She was frightened of me.

"Got company?" I asked.

"Snob," she snapped. "That's the cat. He's—noisy."

"Yeh," I said. "Yeh, he sure is."

I went out.

A WEEK consists of seven days, which manage to tangle themselves together terribly when there's work to be done. By the time the next day of rest came around, I'd covered every name and address on Doctor Kindred's list—and learned just two things.

First—every man and woman on the list had come from somewhere in the neighborhood of 1138 Fletcher Drive. Second—there were half a dozen new patients coming into Mount Mead each day now, and the hospital couldn't keep its gruesome secret much longer.

On Sunday afternoon, I sat in Kindred's office with Kindred and Joan. I had a lot of admiration for Joan. I knew how tired she was, and yet how cool and lovely she managed to remain through it all. I wondered why I couldn't have been tall and handsome.

We had been talking about the rapid increases in the cases.

"I can't understand it," Kindred said. "The disease doesn't seem to be a type that would carry from one person to another. When the fever breaks, there are no open sores or infection. Just—that horrible—change of size."

I saw Joan shudder.

"That serum you use isn't a cure, is it?" I asked.

He shook his head. "No! It isn't really very successful. It dopes the patient and makes him rest. However, it also takes away his strength. If we didn't control those—those giants, no telling how much trouble they might make. So far, that's all I've been able to do."

"Maybe you ought to call in more experts," I suggested.

He looked startled.

"Did you have the impression that I was working alone?"

Joan broke in.

"Dad's secretive only because he doesn't want the public to know. There are a hundred men of science and medicine, throughout the country, working with us."

I felt like a chump.

"You—haven't traced down anything important yet?"

Joan was addressing me. Every time she spoke to me, it made the blood rush into my face. She had a way of catching me off guard and making me into a befuddled halfwit. I just sat and perspired when she was around.

"Could the disease be man-made?" I asked Kindred suddenly. "Could it be injected into a man or woman, by someone deliberately trying to cause this horrible trouble?"

Kindred looked stunned. Joan shot a disappointed glance in my direction.

"It's possible," Kindred said slowly.

"Surely you don't believe a human being would be capable of such a crime?"

Joan had interrupted us.

"Haven't you been reading dime novel stories? Perhaps imagining a few of your own?"

I felt damned foolish talking the way I was, but I'm stubborn and I've got a one track mind.

"Maybe I'm batty," I admitted to them both. "Don't pay any attention to me," I was thinking of the knife in Carl Finch's back. I was thinking of how Mrs. Finch died a few days before her husband was murdered.

"The murder has me puzzled," Kindred said, as though he had been reading my mind.

"Yes," I said absently. "Maybe Rosa May knows more than she's telling. Maybe the cat *wasn't* a cat."

"*What?*"

I came out of the trance. I stood up. They were both staring at me with amazement.

"Bats in my belfry," I explained. "I'll see you both tomorrow. Need some rest."

I left Mount Mead.

"PAPPY" REESE has had charge of the *Telegraph* morgue for more years than I've been alive. There are two kinds of morgues. One of them is for filing dead bodies on ice. The other is used for filing news stories, pics, and stuff handy to a going newspaper. I prefer the second kind. Ours is hidden at the back of the building, where filing cabinets tower over your head and Pappy Reese rules the roost.

I went in to see Pappy. He came out of the darkness, peering at me with watery eyes behind dusty specs. He didn't have many teeth.

"Hello, Wonder Boy," he said.

I made a pass at him.

"Pappy, ever hear of a guy called Carl Finch?"

I could almost hear the wheels on Pappy's head start whirring. They might have been a little rusty, but Pappy usually hits the jackpot on the sixty-four-dollar question.

"Carl Finch," he said, and repeated it over and over. "Now, let me think."

He scratched his grey head and shuffled away down the lines of cabinets. Over his shoulder, he said:

"There *was* a Finch. His name wasn't Carl. Kicked out of Mount Mead Hospital back in twenty-nine. Illegal practice."

He stopped and opened a file, having reached his alphabetical destination.

"Couldn't be the right one, though," I said. "This Finch didn't h…"

I stopped short. I had been about to say that Carl Finch didn't have any relatives. How did I know that? I had taken Rosa May's word for it. Now, wasn't I an intelligent moron?

I waited while Pappy Reese brought out a heavy manila envelope. On it he had written:

"File—Richard Finch Versus City Medical Board."

He placed the envelope on the table and spilled out some clippings. There was a news pic, a couple of front page articles, and some smaller stories, evidently written as Finch faded from public life. I read them all over quickly. Richard Finch had made a nice chunk of cash on the side, to the disgust of the upright city officials (the story said). He had been kicked out of the medical profession. Had lost his license. Finish—for Richard Finch.

Not much. Nothing to connect him with the murdered Carl. I looked at the pic once more and nearly shouted.

There was Doctor Richard Finch leaving the courtroom during his trial. At his side a woman walked, her beautiful face cruel with anger. It was Rosa May Bronson, Carl Finch's maid.

Only the line under the pic said she wasn't Rosa May Bronson at all, but, "Mrs. Richard Finch, who stood by her husband faithfully throughout the trial."

That did it.

I visited Shelton Brothers, the lawyers who represented Carl Finch. They didn't talk much, but they guessed it wasn't any secret that the Finch estate had been quietly settled, leaving the home and fifty thousand dollars to Mr. and Mrs. Richard Finch who now resided in their brother's home.

So—now I knew that Richard and Rosa were husband and wife. I also knew that I was the prize sap of the century. It had taken me a week to dig up information that Pappy Reese could have supplied within twenty minutes after Carl Finch died. Well, I guess that's how it goes.

AT TEN-THIRTY that night, Joan Kindred phoned my apartment. If I'm any judge of women's voices, she was scared stiff.

"I must see you right away," she said. "Father's running a high fever. He's out of his head. Come as soon as you can."

I got her address for I hadn't been at the Kindred home before. Then I said goodbye, caught a cab and told the driver to drive like hell. He didn't spare the horsepower and we pulled up before a modest English bungalow on Parma Street, just ten minutes later.

Joan met me at the door.

"Doctor Joad is already here," she told me. Her eyes were deep set and dark with lack of sleep. She led me in. I tried to remember Doctor Joad. He was a white haired, decent kind of chap who had been working for some time, with Kindred. Joan led me upstairs without another word. Kindred, lying in his bed, looked very bad. He kept murmuring something over and over.

None of us could understand.

"He's been talking like that for some time," Joad said. "I'm afraid he's contracted his own disease. Been working with it too long."

I didn't like that. Joan sat down. Her eyes kept shifting from one of us to the other.

"Doctor Joad knows nothing of your work on this—this disease," she said. "I think it time he learns what we know."

Joad looked at me with watery, puzzled eyes.

"I don't think I understand."

Joan spoke directly to me.

"You said some very odd things to Dad and I, remember?"

I nodded, not trusting myself to speak.

She arose and went to the window. As she walked, she spoke mechanically, "Father retired at eight tonight. At nine-thirty I thought I heard sounds on the porch roof above the library. I blamed it on bad nerves. Everything was quiet after that. When I came in to say good-night, he was in a coma. The window was open. *He never sleeps with it open.* I remembered what you said."

Her breath was coming hard. She was badly frightened. I caught up with her as she pulled the curtain aside.

"I—haven't touched anything," she said in a low voice.

On the edge of the sill, just a foot above the porch roof, was a clear, sharp black mark on the white paint. I dug some of it off with my nail. It smelled like composition rubber.

"I guess the police should know about this," she said.

WHEN I saw Kindred the next day, it had happened. His facial expression was pinched and tired. He was awake, staring at me with frightened eyes. His entire body had grown much smaller. Doctor John Kindred had changed overnight into a...midget. I talked with him for some time and his mind was clear.

"Joad knows all about it," he explained. "I explained that there is no cure thus far. He can prevent me suffering any great pain."

I watched him shudder.

Giants and midgets, I thought. Giants and midgets.

"You didn't notify the police?"

He shook his head.

"Joan wanted to. I asked her to wait. There's a chance that we may catch *him*. Perhaps we can force him to give us a cure. If the police handle it, he'll have time to escape. Everyone will die."

I nodded.

"Give me a few days," I said. I took a deep breath. "Did you ever know a man named Richard Finch?"

He shook his head.

"Only Carl Finch, the man who was murdered. Never heard of him until he entered the hospital."

Wrong number, I thought. Try again.

"Have you ever heard of a disease even remotely like this before?"

"Never," he admitted. "Last night I slept soundly. I wasn't aware that anyone entered the room. The needle must have done a swift job. I didn't awaken while he was here."

"The—the man—or woman, *did* use a needle?"

"Joad found the mark on my arm. It's so tiny you'd be apt to miss it. No pain where it entered. No swelling."

Anyhow, I thought, I've got something to work on now. I tried to say something that would cheer him up. I said I'd call him in the evening, and let him know what I'd accomplished.

He took my hand.

"You're all right," he said. Tears gleamed in his eyes. "The thing had me fooled. You were the one who realized that it wasn't a disease at all, but the result of the work of some fiend, God speed."

Downstairs, I met Joan. She looked fresh and more at ease this morning. She took both my hands in hers and smiled up at me.

"I don't think I ever told you what a grand person I think you are."

I'm afraid the color of my face spoke volumes.

"It—isn't much," I blurted out. "I'm doing what I can."

She was standing too darned close to me. I felt funny all over.

"You're sticking by Dad and I when I don't know who else we could ask for help. I—appreciate it more than—than I can express."

She leaned forward on tip-toe and kissed me softly on the cheek. I felt as though the fever had hit *me*.

I tried to say something, and only stammered a lot of meaningless words.

"I—that is—thanks—I'll try..."

Then I made a run for it. I felt like a damned fool. Why didn't I sweep her into my arms and cover her lips with kisses? Why didn't I whisper sweet, sentimental words in her ear? Bunk, I thought. You're just a guy who loves a girl. You'll never make material for a love story.

I wandered three blocks in a mental haze. I swore solemnly that I wouldn't wash my face for a month. No—not until Joan kissed it again. Then I realized I had to get my feet down on the ground and start out to justify her faith in me. I felt like St. George starting out to slay the Dragon.

It occurred to me twenty minutes later, as I paid off the cab driver a block from 1138 Fletcher Drive, that I'd be damned lucky if I escaped being slain myself. Probably by something a lot less romantic than a dragon.

FOOLS rush in where Angels fear to tread. I knocked on the door. This time, Rosa May Bronson, or Finch, came to the door without the maid's uniform. She was dressed for the street, in a light sport coat and a small, brown felt hat. Her face colored with anger when she saw me.

"Well, if it isn't Wonder Boy," she said.

She caught me with my guard down. A few years ago, I managed to blunder through a couple of pretty decent murder mysteries, and was promptly labeled Wonder Boy for the stories I turned in on them. I had been quite proud, being just a punk then. Now the title tasted plenty sour.

The point was, Rosa May Finch had been doing a little snooping herself. She knew who I was.

"Okay," I said. "So you know me. Don't you invite your friends in?"

She started to push me ahead of her, out the door. I side-stepped, pushed my foot into the door and waited.

"Don't be so cold and unfriendly, Rosa May," I said. "After all, you made a pretty good impression on me the other day. I had to come back and look some more."

Her cheeks were flushed.

"Listen, smart guy," she snapped. "You're out of your class. Better run for home before something happens to you."

"*Someone like Richard Finch?*" I asked.

That shook her. She stopped pushing me. Her arms dropped at her sides. Her face turned pale.

"How—did—you…?"

I grinned, pushing the door open wider.

"Wonder boy," I said. "Mastermind, Mrs. Rosa May Finch. Now—do we talk?"

She didn't answer. She had lost all interest in going out. She let me go in, and I followed her to the library. I sat down, crossed my legs and reached for a cigarette.

"Take off your coat, kid," I said. "We're going to make talk."

She removed her coat slowly, as though undecided just what to do. I had been listening carefully ever since I came in. Listening for that cat that made footsteps like a man. I didn't hear a sound.

"Wait here," she said. There was fear in her eyes. Not fear of me. I knew that by the way her eyes shifted around the room. She went to the hall. I heard the key turn in the front door. Then she came back. She sat on the divan and said:

"It's warmer—here near the fire."

I was as close to the fireplace as she was. We both knew it. I smiled.

"I'm on fire now," I said. "The very presence of you in the room does something…"

"Shut up."

She didn't feel in the mood for my kidding.

"Okay," I said. "I've got questions. Questions like—where is Richard?"

That rocked her a little. She was still pale, furtive.

"My husband died—eight years ago."

I nodded.

"Sure," I said. "Buried without record. Not a line of type about his death. No, Rosa—try another. That's not good."

She stood up and took three faltering steps toward me. She collapsed to the floor, close enough so that her hand rested on my knee. Her arms crept around my waist.

She started to sob, and she wasn't acting. I'll swear that Rosa May Finch was deathly frightened.

"Oh God—Oh My God! What have I done to deserve this? I played straight with him!"

FOR a full minute she let herself go. I watched her shoulders rise and fall in agony. Her cheek, resting against my knee, was wet with tears. I don't sympathize much with bums, but I was feeling damned sorry for her. She wasn't pulling this on me. It was the real thing.

I lifted her head in my hands. I was so startled that I clamped the palm of my hand against her forehead. It was burning with fever.

"Good Lord," I stammered. "You...you...?"

She nodded, tears streaming down her face.

"He isn't dead. I wish he was."

She leaned back, still on her knees, her head lowered, staring at my feet.

"He's a beast. A damned, dirty beast. He's doing something that no human being has a right to do. He's trying..."

She stopped abruptly.

"Talk," I said sharply. "He's the one who sent those people to Mount Mead, isn't he? He's giving injections."

She nodded drunkenly.

"We fought this morning. I was tired of it—frightened. I wanted to run away. He tied me to the table and put some of that awful stuff into me."

She broke down, not crying—not speaking. Her body rocked back and forth in misery. She had a bad case of chills. I helped her to the divan and she stared up at me.

"Giant or midget," she whispered. "I'm to be one or the other, Wonder-boy. I'm..."

She fainted.

I went to the phone, a cream colored dial affair on the desk. I picked up the phone and started to dial.

"Put it down, wonder-boy."

The voice was a man's, intensely cruel. I put the phone back in the cradle—slowly. I turned around even more slowly. The man in the door held a shining black automatic. It was a heavy caliber, pointed at my chest.

The man was Richard Finch. I knew him at once, though I had seen only that one pic of him, taken several years back. I started at his feet and worked upward with my eyes. Shining patent leather shoes, dark, carefully pressed trousers, and blue-black coat. His face was thin, with deep-set greenish eyes, a hawk-like nose and a straight white lipped gash of mouth.

"Sit down, wonder-boy," he said. He practically purred the order. I was beginning to loathe that *wonder-boy* stuff. I sat down because I didn't want to tackle that gun.

He crossed the floor swiftly, walking without a sound. He sat on the edge of the divan, touching his wife's forehead with light fingers, never taking his eyes from me.

"Coming nicely, isn't she?" he asked. "Or wouldn't you know anything about the serum?"

I shook my head.

He smiled. It wasn't much. The straight lips didn't curve. They parted, showing white, wide teeth.

"I'll have to show you," he said. "Perhaps we can even arrange for a demonstration."

I DIDN'T have anything to offer to the conversation.

"I think we can safely leave Rosa May here," Finch said. His fingers traced a line across her forehead. "Suppose we retire to the laboratory? It should prove most interesting to you."

I walked out into the hall. He didn't prod me with the gun. He stayed a short distance behind me.

"Upstairs," he said.

I went up slowly, dragging it out. The second floor was split in half by a long hall. Three doors opened on one side. Only one door on the other. I stopped and looked at him questioningly. He motioned toward the single door.

I went in. I was startled because I expected to see a cross between the morgue and Frankenstein's mansion. I got an eyeful of clean, white laboratory. It was brightly lighted by one entire wall of glass-blocks. It was filled with tables and test tubes.

At the far end of the room was a long table, with four straps that looked as though they might hold a man down regardless of how much he fought to free himself.

Finch pushed me toward the table. I didn't argue. The longer he carried that gun, the surer I was that he planned to use it.

"I'll have to strap you to the table," he said.

I said, "Why?"

Finch smiled.

"You're going to die within the next hour anyhow. I'd like to tell you a little about myself first. If, during that time, you decided that death was too unpleasant to face without a struggle, I might be hurt in the scuffle."

"Very neat explanation," I admitted. "Can't see how I could hardly refuse to do as you want me to."

He grinned again, waving the gun slightly.

"Hardly."

I was close to the table now. I could almost feel his breath on the back of my neck. I whirled around, jerking aside to get out of line with that gun. At the same time, I snapped my left shoulder upward and connected with his chin. That threw him for an instant. I heard his teeth snap together. He had his mind concentrated on that gun. He pulled the trigger and the bullet smashed past me into the wall.

He stepped back two paces and started to lift the gun again. I knocked it out of his hand. He stood unarmed, frightened without the weapon, the fear showing in his narrowed eyes.

"You're tough," I said, "as long as you've got lead to sling. Now start slinging something else."

I let him have it with my right fist. I hit him so hard and with so much hate behind it that the blow hurt my knuckles. He went down and the wind hissed out of him. I strapped him to the table.

After a while he opened his eyes. I guess I failed to realize just how cool a cookie I had on my hands. He smiled a little crookedly. His lip was cut wide open and I guess that smile must have hurt.

"We seem to have changed places," he said. "Well, it can make little difference."

I had been doing a lot of wondering about Richard Finch. Rosa May was still downstairs, I thought, under the influence of the strange drug he had given her. When she recovered, she'd be like those people at Mount Mead. Richard Finch was responsible for all that.

Why had Finch done this? He could make no personal gain. How could I trap him into telling me why? How could I make him affect a cure? That last question was all important.

"Just how much difference *does* it make—your being in my place?"

He looked at me a little dreamily.

"The job is done," he said. "In twenty-four hours the city will writhe in pain. Its people will suffer even as I have suffered for these terrible years."

SO THAT was it. The guy was sore because once, a long time ago, the city had taken away his privilege of practicing medicine. I was beginning to understand more about what had been happening. Until now, I had blamed it all on a deep, desperate plan to undermine the morale of the people. Now I could see that it was even worse than that. It had all happened because one crazed man was getting his revenge. That meant I was dealing with a crackpot. It meant that I had to think fast and allow for him to try almost anything.

"You can go a little deeper into that explanation," I said. "Just how can you cause more trouble than you already have? You're tied down securely for the duration."

He chuckled.

"You're thinking of the serum, and the injection needles. You're wondering how I can hurt people unless I'm free to give the injections?"

I nodded. I thought I'd better keep quiet. I could learn in only one way. I could listen.

He laughed again, and it wasn't like any laugh I'd ever heard before. In spite of the straps, he was stretched out, relaxed like a cat.

"The needle was quite primitive," he confessed. "You see, I have often wondered about people. You'll find that a little man, living with his larger friends, considers himself a misfit. He'll fight at the drop of a hat. You should know."

I felt my face getting red.

"Sure," I admitted. "Sure, the little guy is afraid he's looked down upon. He might get overlooked when the hero medals are passed out. He's on guard and ready to fight for his rights."

He nodded.

"And the giants of the earth?"

I could see the point.

"He likes to push people around a little, just to show he can do it."

Doctor Richard Finch nodded. He was enjoying himself a lot.

"I saw that a long time ago. Once I committed a crime. If I had had money and a good lawyer, I could have escaped punishment. I had neither. I was robbed of everything. I lost everything in life that I ever wanted."

He took a deep breath. In spite of his bravado, I knew he didn't like the idea of being strapped to that table. He had planned it a little differently.

He went on talking.

"I'm a patient man, but I planned a revenge. Experimenting with the glands that control the growth of humans, I hit upon the serum. I haven't been able to control it. I don't know, at the time it's placed in the blood stream, how it will react.

"Some people grow—some shrink. I don't want to know how to control it. If I did, it would become an instrument to do good. As it is, the serum serves my purpose."

I nodded.

"It produces misfits," I said. "If you can produce them by the thousands, you'll turn them against each other. They'll make this a damned unpleasant place to live. Good, Doctor Finch, very good. But you overlooked just one thing. You can't use the serum any longer. You're tightly trussed up and you're going to stay that way."

He shook his head slowly from side to side.

"I don't *have* to use it. It's already hard at work. It will remain at work, you can't get the truth from me, I won't tell you how it works, and you're powerless to harm me until you find out."

HE HAD me there. I figured it wouldn't be simple. The serum wouldn't be a thing that you could put into the city water supply, for instance. That was corn, and Richard Finch *wasn't* corny. Not by a damned sight. Sweat started to ooze from my forehead. My hands were clammy. I wanted to wrap my fingers around his neck, but I couldn't—not yet.

I said, "Okay, Finch. You know as well as I do that Doctor Kindred has been stricken by your disease. He's the only man who knows about it except me."

I didn't mention Joan Kindred. I didn't want to mix her up in this mess.

"I can't turn you over to the police because they haven't the imagination to believe a story like the one I'd have to tell. While I wait for you, you lay there and do some thinking. What you've got on your mind isn't very healthy. You might decide to help me."

He didn't even blink.

"I doubt it," he said. "I'd rather die than spoil the progress I've made. I told you that I was a patient man. More patient, I imagine, than you can afford to be under the present conditions."

He had me. I went out and turned the key in the door. I went downstairs and into the library.

I wish I hadn't.

Rosa May Finch was still there, sitting on the divan. She was pointing a little automatic pistol, aimed at my head. It wasn't the gun that made me turn white. It was Rosa May herself.

She wasn't bloated or misshapen in any way. She was, if anything, even prettier than she had been. Her dress couldn't grow as she had grown, and shreds of it clung about her body.

Rosa May Finch had changed all right. I'll swear that if she had stood up, she'd have touched the ceiling. The serum had worked. She looked like an Amazon, but maybe the biggest Amazon that had ever lived.

"Up with your hands," she said.

I had no idea of doing anything else.

"What did you do with my husband?"

I nodded over my shoulder.

"Upstairs," I said, and wished at once that I hadn't said it.

A smile came over her huge face.

"Come over here, Wonder-boy," she said. I went. She placed the pistol carefully at her side.

"You know," she said with a half smile, "I don't dislike this idea at all. I've seen Richard do some terrible things with that serum, but this time he made a mistake."

I agreed with her, silently.

She leaned over. She had to, to reach my mouth. She kissed me—hard. She put her hand behind my head, and crushed my face against hers. She mashed me up against her until I wondered if I'd ever walk again. Then she pushed me away. It wasn't any fun, being pushed around by a giantress who didn't know her own strength.

"I've always liked you a lot," she said. "It's no thrill to kiss you now. When *I* wanted to play, you *didn't.*"

Boy, I'd play now. I'd let her use me for any little game she wanted to invent, if by doing so, I could just get out of her reach.

"We're going up to see Richard now," she said. She stood up and pushed me along with the muzzle of her gun. Every time she pushed it into my back, I tried not to fall down.

When she saw Richard tied to the table, she laughed loudly. It wasn't a pleasant laugh. I won't try to describe the expression on Finch's face when saw her. He just shrank into himself. His face was ghastly. He muttered just one word.

"*Rosa?*"

She walked over and poked a finger into his ribs. It hurt him.

"What's the matter, Rich?" she asked. "You used to like to be tickled."

He said nothing.

SHE brought the palm of her hand down against his face. It came away red with blood. Finch gasped and tried to get free. His cheek was open and bleeding. Her nails had cut a gash from his cheek-bone down to the corner of his mouth.

She seemed to forget me. She was interested only in hurting the man on the table. I had been doing some fast thinking. I couldn't let her kill him. I'd never find the secret of the serum, and how he planned to use it.

"Take it easy," I cautioned Rosa May. "Keep him alive. You don't know your own strength."

She pivoted, facing me.

"Shut up," she snapped. "He's been pushing me around for a long time. I've had to hide up here like a prisoner. I never got any decent breaks. He made me submit to a shot of that serum because he hoped to make a midget out of me. Then he could have made me suffer even more."

She took a deep breath. Her bosom was rising and falling swiftly. In a way, Rosa May Finch was pretty nice. Her huge body was perfectly proportioned. Barefooted, she stood there like a Goddess. The whole world lay at her feet, waiting for her to tread on it.

I said, "Okay, kill him then. Once he's dead, you can't make him suffer any more. Why not give him a dose of his own medicine? If he turns giant, you can shoot him before it's too late. If he reacts, in the other direction, it would be nice to have a midget around to kick now and then. Think it over."

There was a light in her eyes that was terrible. She smiled. It was a smile that I hope never to see again. This was the biggest bluff I had ever tried to pull. One or the other of them was going to see through it sooner or later. I hoped it wouldn't be before I had accomplished my purpose.

"You get good ideas," Rosa May said.

I heard Finch gasp in horror.

"No, Rosa, you can't do it. Not to me."

She forgot all about me then. She slapped him again.

"Oh, I can't—can't I?"

She strode across the room, knocking stuff off the tables as she moved. There was a locked cabinet against the far wall. Rosa May knew her way around.

She ripped the padlock off. Half of the door came with it. She found a hypodermic needle. There were dozens of them, filled with a green liquid. She put her first and second fingers on either side of the tube, her thumb on the plunger.

Finch started to writhe around on the table, fighting away from her. He called to me a couple of times, but I pretended not to hear him. It was hard to watch it happen. Hard, even when I knew he had done the job himself a hundred times.

I kept thinking of that surgeon's knife sticking into Carl Finch's body, and it made everything easier.

Rosa May ripped half of his shirt off, found the thick vein in his upper-arm and sent the needle home. She drained the tube and tossed it on the floor.

"Now we'll wait," she said savagely. "You'd better start shrinking, Rich. I'll blow your head off if you grow any larger."

The room got very quiet. Ten minutes passed. Rosa May didn't look at me. I was glad. I sat in a chair near the door. Fifteen minutes. The stuff reacted fast. Probably because of Finch's fear. His eyes became bright with fever. His face was flushed and red. Perspiration poured down, his face. What was left of his shirt became soaked with sweat.

Rosa May continued to stare at him.

After an hour, Richard Finch started to shrink.

That's the only word for it. I saw his face become smaller. I heard Rosa May sigh. Now she would have her fun. She wasn't to be robbed of her pleasure.

As Finch grew smaller, she tightened the straps that held him. Two hot, insufferable hours passed and the change was completed.

FINCH'S eyes were like animal's eyes. They were clear and understanding. He wasn't over three feet tall. His clothing hung loosely around him; his feet had slipped from his shoes.

I stood up and edged closer. I still had my gun hidden in my arm holster. I just wasn't ready to use it.

"So, we've got him where we want him, have we, Rosa?"

She looked at me and scowled, as though she just remembered that I was there. "Shut up."

I said, "I'm not shutting up any more. I didn't know where the serum was, Rosa. Now I do. I couldn't give a shot to your husband until I knew where it was. You've done that for me. Now your part of the job is done. Rest easy and keep your mouth shut. When I get done with Finch, we'll know how to cure you— and the others. Richard is going to talk, *aren't you Richard?*"

He swore at me. He reminded me of a monkey. An ugly, very bad tempered monkey.

Rosa May came after me slowly.

"You cheap little trickster," she said. "I *like* being this way. When I was normal, I got kicked around. Now *nobody* can hurt me. Not even you, understand?"

She made a grab for me and I slipped the gun but from under my coat.

"Look out, Rosa, I still carry a sting."

She didn't stop, and I had to shoot her on the hand. I didn't have the heart to make it worse. She let out a howl of surprise and pain and tried to knock me down. I shot again, through her shoulder. She went down on her knees, sobbing with pain.

"I'm sorry," I said. "I hated to hurt you. You're not a bad kid, but your size has gone to your head."

"You stinking little…"

She lunged toward me and I got out of the way. There were tears in her eyes. Blood gushed from her shoulder. She needed care right away.

"Listen," I said, standing a safe distance away, "I'm a funny guy. I didn't want to hurt you. I kept that gun out of sight because I wanted to learn some things that I'd never have learned if I'd used the gun too soon. If you try to get me, I'll drill you through the heart. I'll do that because you're not very damned important, compared with what's at stake. Now play ball, and cut out that rough stuff."

She took one long, pitiful look at me and started to cry again. She buried her head in her hands.

"You're a crumb," she said. "A miserable little crumb. I tried to be nice to you and you wouldn't let me. You'd kill me, just like Rich would. I can't trust either of you."

I PUSHED the gun into my coat pocket where it would be handy. I found Finch's shirt (the part she'd torn off him) and wrapped it around her shoulder. There was a first-aid kit on one of the benches. She sat quietly, staring at me with puzzled eyes, while I bandaged her shoulder. It wasn't a bad wound. It hurt her pretty badly but she didn't cry again.

Then I left her alone and went over to Finch.

"How would you like to die?" I asked as calmly as I could. I wasn't, clowning. I had an act to go through and I knew I had to do it.

He wasn't as cocky now.

"You can't hurt me," he said, but he knew I could. "I've done what I started out to do. I expect to die. The sooner you pump lead into me, the better. You'll never find the cure you're looking for."

I grinned.

"Then there *is* one?"

He hadn't meant to give it away. His mouth snapped closed.

"I'm not going to kill you," I said slowly. I acted as though I was thinking of something pretty nasty to do to him. "I've got a better plan."

"I'm not interested," he snarled.

"You will be. I'm going to take you down to police headquarters. I'm going to buy a little boy's suit with short pants and parade you up and down every street in town. I'll tell the cops some damned fool story about you being a vagrant and breaking into my house. The charge won't stick, but by the time they start to realize that you're a midget, your picture will be on every damned front page in the country. You're quite a freak, Finch."

He was jumping around on the table all right now. He was taking a new interest in life.

"You wouldn't..."

I laughed.

"I might even dig up that picture taken of you when you were thrown out of the medical profession. Sort of a *then* and *now* comparison. The paper would eat up that stuff."

His voice came, very low and hoarse. I heard Rosa laugh. Just a little laugh—half triumphant—half frightened.

"I—couldn't stand that stuff. I've suffered enough."

"Some people think you should suffer more," I said bitterly. "I'm one of them."

"Please," Finch begged, "you're—taking advantage."

Funny about that guy. He was a crook and a murderer—worse, yet he still had his own sort of pride. It was breaking him, just as I hoped it would.

"And *you* weren't taking advantage of those poor damned souls at Mount Mead? You won't take advantage of thousands more? Tell me, Finch, where is the antitoxin that will cure this thing? Tell me, and I'll give you a fighting chance."

There was a gleam of hope in his eyes.

"What—chance?"

"I'll return you to normal size," I said. "I'll give you an hour start and I'll come after you."

He shuddered.

"You're—a—killer."

I shrugged.

"Just a wonder-boy," I said, "Just a little guy, like the ones you talk about, who's gonna drill you before this is over with."

Finch shuddered.

The afternoon sun was hot on the glass-block wall. Rosa was silent, waiting. I had no idea where I could get that antitoxin. I was still powerless.

"All right," Finch said in a tired voice. "I can't face the public—like this."

"I know," I said. "Where's the antitoxin?"

"Let me up, and I'll get it."

"That's not even smart." I grinned. "I'll get it. Rosa will stay here and watch you."

He swore.

"There's a tank in the basement. Fifteen gallons. I mixed up a lot when I was experimenting with animals."

I turned to Rosa May.

"Watch him while I'm gone," I said. Her lips parted. Her eyes were wide, almost—yes, I guess, almost *devoted.*

"You trust me—after what happened?"

"Why not?" I asked.

I FOUND my way into the foul cellar. There was a smell of death down there. Shrunken cat bodies—dead rats. A skeleton of a dog. The tank was of clean, light metal. Full of heavy liquid. I went upstairs with it. Rosa May hadn't moved. She watched me when I went to the table and opened the tank.

"There are clean hypos in the cabinet," Finch said. "For God's sake, make sure you get a clean one."

He was still stalling. I knew it, but I couldn't figure out why. I knew how to cure the cases that existed. I still didn't know how Finch had distributed the serum so that it would affect the entire city.

I found a hypo, filled it with the amber fluid and shot the stuff into Finch's arm.

"You're the first victim," I said. "If it works on you, it will be safe for the others."

"Quick," his voice came in sudden gasps. "Loosen the straps. It will react swiftly. My arms and legs may be broken if..."

I loosened the arms. As swiftly as a cat, his right arm was free. He twisted half around, and yanked the gun from my pocket. I pivoted and hit him beside the head. Then, while I expected him to shoot any second, I backed away.

"Sap," I said. I didn't mean Finch.

He laughed.

"Don't worry—too much," he said. "I'm not going to shoot you. I've a better plan."

I waited.

"'If I shot you, I'd be found sooner or later, and suffer for it. If I don't shoot you, and remain alive myself, you'll hound me until I have to give up."

His lips curled until his teeth were bared in a snarl.

"You have the antitoxin. You can cure Rosa and the others, but you'll never duplicate that antitoxin. If you do it will take years of research. Meanwhile, thousands of people will be stricken. They'll fight and die and behave like the animals they'll be. The thing will spread until there is no one left to control or cure it. You see, wonder-boy, I already have my revenge, and you're *not* going to parade me in the streets as a freak."

He was breathing hard. His body was responding to the antitoxin, growing, swelling.

"You were almost clever enough," he said. "You can't make me suffer any more. I'm just a bit too smart for you."

He turned the gun on himself and pulled the trigger. I sprang forward, ripping the weapon from his already limp hand. Rosa May started to cry again.

"That won't do any good."

I turned on her, shouting. She stopped crying and just looked at me.

I stood near the table, looking down at the limp body of Richard Finch. This was the corpse of the only man who could have helped me save the horror that was to come. I felt sick to my stomach for being such a dope.

I found the needle and went to Rosa.

"You're no good to me this way," I said. "I'll make a normal woman out of you, unless you want to commit suicide like he did. I'm so tired I don't care much if you do."

I meant it. I was all washed up. I gave her the shot and sat down with my back to her, staring at the corpse on the table. It was trying to open a safe without knowing the combination. The corpse had a lot of knowledge locked in its dead brain. Carelessly, I had brought the whole thing on myself.

ROSA MAY FINCH was badly shaken. She sat at my side in the coupe. She had a new dress on, and the bandage on her shoulder was well hidden. The can of antitoxin was on the seat between us. I drove directly to Mount Mead. I met Joan Kindred on the sixth floor. Her eyes questioned Rosa May's presence. I introduced them.

"Joan—meet Rosa May Bronson." I had a reason for using that name.

The name she had given me first.

"Rosa May was Carl Finch's maid," I told Joan.

"The man who was murdered?"

I didn't tell her that he was murdered by his brother, because he knew too much.

I just nodded.

"I came to see your father."

I felt strange with Joan's eyes on me like that. She wasn't satisfied with the way I was acting. Neither was I.

She wanted to see me alone. Neither of us had forgotten that kiss. I guess I'd never forget.

"Dad's resting well," Joan said. "He's in a private room."

"Good," I had the can of antitoxin under my arm. Rosa May had her arm through mine. She held on tightly. "Let's see him right away."

I had to act coolly toward Joan.

It had to be that way. This was the last part of the last act. After this—curtains. Curtains so far as I was concerned, for the only girl I had ever loved.

Joan led us down the hall. She paused at the door, opened it and let Rosa May and me go in. She took my hand before I got away from her and said:

"I—I worried when you were gone."

I pushed past her.

"I get by okay," I said.

She didn't answer. She kept staring at me as I approached her father's bed. I could *feel* the dismay, the wonder, locked inside her. I was hurting the girl as deeply as she could be hurt—and doing it deliberately.

Rosa May stood near the door, her eyes travelling occasionally toward Joan, then back to me again. Doctor Joad came in and I put the can in his hands.

"There's the antitoxin I called you about," I said. "An injection of that will cure your patient—and the others. In a few days other cases will be coming in. You'll run out of antitoxin. You'll be unable to cope with them."

I stopped talking, looked down at Kindred and smiled.

"Your troubles are over, Doctor," I told him. "But listen closely. I told you who was responsible for this. Before he died, he injected the stuff into rats and cats by the score. It will take some time for it to react. The animals that were given the serum will not change in size. They were given small doses until they could take the full amount without a size change.

"These same animals will spread the disease with their teeth and claws. Every person scratched will get the disease. In a few weeks, every animal in the city will be a carrier."

I paused, heard Joan sigh. Doctor Joad was busy with the needle. He was giving Kindred an injection.

Joad said in a matter-of-fact voice, "The disease will not spread. Every animal will be gassed, if I have to do the job myself. You've done more than your share. We'll take care of it from here on."

"Thanks," I said. "I'm—a little tired. I'd rather not answer any questions. I don't think it would do any good. The man who is responsible, is dead. Once the disease is wiped out, it will never happen again."

Joan started to walk toward me. There was a bewildered smile on her face.

"I think we owe you more than you'll ever know."

THAT wasn't what she was thinking. She was pleading with me to be alone with her. She was cutting me right across the heart-deep.

I looked at Rosa May. She was smiling. It wasn't a sarcastic smile. She was sincere enough. She wanted me to leave, and I had to leave because she wanted it.

"I hope you'll excuse us," I said. There was a hell of a lump in my throat.

Joan turned and left the room. She looked very straight and determined. Doctor Kindred looked up at me. There was confidence in his voice.

"You'll be around to see us—soon?"

"I'll be around," I said.

We went out with them staring at our backs. I felt sick all the way down to my shoes. On the elevator, the little nurse who had first taken me up to the fifth floor handed me a note. I took it and winked at her.

"Thanks, baby," I said. "You don't have to write me notes. I can see the love in your eyes."

She froze up like a fish, but her eyes were twinkling.

In the coupe, Rosa May and I drove away from Mount Mead. After a while, Rosa May looked at me.

"You're in love with Joan Kindred, aren't you?"

I didn't say anything.

"She loves you. You know you hurt her pretty bad?"

"I made a deal with you," I said. "I won't walk out on you."

It's a hell of a deal, I kept thinking. A hell of a deal, but it's saved a lot of lives.

"It was lucky I knew about Richard's work," she said after a while. "He told me what he planned to do, but he didn't think that I'd ever dare tell you."

I couldn't resist making a crack at that.

"You set the price pretty damned high."

She laughed. It was a pleasant laugh and she wasn't trying to hurt me.

"I made you promise that you'd take care of me, and me alone. Made you promise that I'd get the breaks, and own a share in you—for keeps. Is my love too shabby for you? Was the deal a bad one?"

I shook my head.

"I'm not the sentimental type," I said. "You told me something I had to know. I promised in return to fix things so you wouldn't worry any more. That I'd stick around and play the game the way you wanted it. Is that fair enough?"

"No," she said. "Pull over to the curb."

I pulled over and stopped. It was part of the price. It was also the first time I'd taken orders from a woman.

She put her arms around my neck and made me kiss her. Her lips were hot and starved. She did a good job of making me forget almost everything else.

I must have put the note in my pocket carelessly. When we came out of the clinch, the note had fallen to the floor. It was partly open and I could see Joan Kindred's handwriting. I pushed it over with my foot so it was hidden from Rosa.

I tried to drive slowly and read at the same time.

"I know something is wrong," Joan said. *"I feel it inside. I'm not going to follow you or try to bring you back. You're not fooling me. I know, after that kiss, that you love me. You'll come back—sometime. I'll wait."*

That's all I read. I brushed my hand across my eyes.

"What's the matter?" Rosa May asked. "You got something in your eye?"

"Yes," I said. "A cinder."

"You aren't going to break your promise? I told you enough to save all of them. You're going to keep your word?"

"I'm keeping my word," I said savagely. "Stop crabbing. We been together just two hours now and you talk like we been married ten years."

"I'm sorry," She leaned against me. "I'm scared. You're the first guy ever treated me decently. You're the first guy I ever really loved. I been kicked around so much, I'm afraid of getting kicked some more. You know how I feel, don't you?"

She was warm and snug against me. She put her head on my shoulder and kissed my neck.

"I know," I said. "I'm not sore. Just a damned cinder in my eye. It hurts—pretty bad."

I didn't tell her that she was the cinder. I wanted to feel noble because I had saved the population of a whole city.

All I could think of was Joan—and what she'd said about me coming back. How could I? I'd never broken my word before. Could I this time? I knew suddenly there was always a first time for everything…

THE END

If you've enjoyed this book, you will not want to miss these terrific titles...

ARMCHAIR SCI-FI & HORROR DOUBLE NOVELS, $12.95 each

D-131 **COSMIC KILL** by Robert Silverberg
BEYOND THE END OF SPACE by John W. Campbell

D-132 **THE DARK OTHER** by Stanley Weinbaum)
WITCH OF THE DEMON SEAS by Poul Anderson

D-133 **PLANET OF THE SMALL MEN** by Murray Leinster
MASTERS OF SPACE by E. E. "Doc" Smith & E. Everett Evans

D-134 **BEFORE THE ASTEROIDS** by Harl Vincent
SIXTH GLACIER, THE by Marius

D-135 **AFTER WORLD'S END** by Jack Williamson
THE FLOATING ROBOT by David Wright O'Brien

D-136 **NINE WORLDS WEST** by Paul W. Fairman
FRONTIERS BEYOND THE SUN by Rog Phillips

D-137 **THE COSMIC KINGS** by Edmond Hamilton
LONE STAR PLANET by H. Beam Piper & John J. McGuire

D-138 **BEYOND THE DARKNESS** by S. J. Byrne
THE FIRELESS AGE by David H. Keller, M. D.

D-139 **FLAME JEWEL OF THE ANCIENTS** by Edwin L. Graber
THE PIRATE PLANET by Charles W. Diffin

D-140 **ADDRESS: CENTAURI** by F. L. Wallace
IF THESE BE GODS by Algis Budrys

ARMCHAIR SCIENCE FICTION & HORROR CLASSICS, $12.95 each

C-58 **THE WITCHING NIGHT**
by Leslie Waller

C-59 **SEARCH THE SKY**
by Frederick Pohl and C. M. Kornbluth

C-60 **INTRIGUE ON THE UPPER LEVEL**
by Thomas Temple Hoyne

ARMCHAIR SCI-FI & HORROR GEMS SERIES, $12.95 each

G-15 **SCIENCE FICTION GEMS, Vol. Eight**
Keith Laumer and others

G-16 **HORROR GEMS, Vol. Eight**
Algernon Blackwood and others

If you've enjoyed this book, you will not want to miss these terrific titles...